THE HIGHLANDER &
THE QUEEN'S SACRIFICE

The Queen's Highlanders
Book 1

Heather McCollum

ARE YOU SIGNED UP FOR DRAGONBLADE'S BLOG?

You'll get the latest news and information on exclusive giveaways, exclusive excerpts, coming releases, sales, free books, cover reveals and more.

Check out our complete list of authors, too!

No spam, no junk. That's a promise!

Sign Up Here

www.dragonbladepublishing.com

Dearest Reader;

Thank you for your support of a small press. At Dragonblade Publishing, we strive to bring you the highest quality Historical Romance from some of the best authors in the business. Without your support, there is no 'us', so we sincerely hope you adore these stories and find some new favorite authors along the way.

Happy Reading!

CEO, Dragonblade Publishing

Dedication

For Jenny, my dragonfly sister.

We met as grad students in the lab decades ago, had our babies together, and became best friends. You are brilliant, kind, and fun, and I know you would keep me safe if someone attempted to poison my dresses!

Scots-Gaelic and Old English Words

àlainn – lovely

blaigeard – bastard

cac – shite

daingead – damnit

dolt (old English) – stupid fellow

falbh – go

God's teeth (old English) – common curse

magairlean – ballocks

mattucashlass – double edged dagger

mo chreach – my rage (common curse)

popish – 16th century derogatory reference to Roman Catholic

sgian dubh – 6 inch, black handled, single-edged dagger

tolla-thon – arsehole

yaldson (old English) – son of a prostitute

Kerr,

Put your sword away and use that clever tongue of yours, brother. We are depending upon you to accomplish your mission and return to unite our clans. My heart is in your hands. May God guide you and keep you safe while you remain tucked in the bosom of our enemy.

My devotion,
Your dearest sister, Rhona Gordon

CHAPTER ONE

"By the pricking of my thumbs,
Something wicked this way comes."
William Shakespeare, *Macbeth*

Whitehall Palace, London, England
February 1571

"I HAVE A letter and gift from Mary Stuart, the queen of Scotland, for her cousin, Her Majesty, Queen Elizabeth," Kerr Gordon said from his seat on his tall black horse. Rain dripped from his woolen tam, which hardly protected him from the soaking tempest God had cast as an added obstacle to his mission.

Even in the darkness Kerr could see the man's sneer. "Leave it here," he said.

"I have strict orders to lay the gift in your queen's hands and to read her the letter myself."

A man behind the first English guard chuckled. "The popish Scot can read. Imagine that."

Kerr's hand itched for his sword, but skewering Englishmen before Whitehall Palace would not afford him admittance to England's mighty Queen Elizabeth.

"You will have to get past Lord Walsingham to gain access to Her Majesty," the first guard said. "Best of luck." He laughed but waved Kerr through the gate. "You can pay a lad to care for your mount at the stables," he said, pointing off to the left. "When Walsingham or Lord Burghley turn you away, you can sleep with your mount for the night and be off in the morn."

Kerr tapped his horse, Caspian, and plodded through the increasing mud, the cold rain tapping like flung pebbles against his cape. *Bloody awful night.* Kerr had never visited court in England and only twice in Scotland, preferring the lush and open moors. But he knew a soaked, dirty Scotsman would be denied entry into Elizabeth's presence. Perhaps he could find a tavern or public bath to wash in. First though, he needed to find them shelter.

The stable doors were closed for the night. Kerr dismounted, his boots squishing into the noxious mud, and pushed against one side, working the latch. It was locked from the inside.

"Daingead," he muttered. There was no turning around, and he was not sleeping in the downpour. Leaving Caspian draped with a woolen blanket, Kerr walked around the barn to the fenced paddocks and climbed into one.

"Cac," he cursed as he sunk into the muck that smelled like horse dung. If he didn't need Queen Mary's letter of support in his quest, he would never have taken on this onerous task.

Trudging across the paddock, Kerr pushed through the un-barred gate and into the stall. A large white horse raised its head from its hay feeder to eye him suspiciously. But it wasn't the horse that made Kerr pause.

"I think we have a bit of time to play before I slit your throat." The man's voice was rough with malicious confidence. Rain beat hard on the slate roof, and Kerr strained to hear.

He moved around the side of the white horse, a hand on its side and his other pulling the deadly-sharp *mattucashlass* from its scabbard strapped to his leg.

"You think you be so clever, girl," the villain said, "with your studies of powders and poisons. The dandy who hired me warned me about you."

Kerr looked over the stall door toward the glow of a single

lantern at the far end. The man stood before a courtly-dressed woman who was tied and gagged, helpless to the brute who brandished a dagger before her. His other hand stroked his erect jack from his unlaced breeches. Rape and murder then.

That was all Kerr needed to see to condemn the man, but without knowing who he was, Kerr shouldn't kill him. *Aye, I should.* But this was England, and Kerr was a Highlander. If he were thrown in the gaol, there would be no support from Queen Mary for the Gordons. *Ye must end this feud.* His sister's words beat in Kerr's heart.

Kerr shed his water-logged cape and tam and climbed over the gate, landing with a thud in the middle of the stable aisle. The bastard whipped around, his blade held before him as he scrambled to pull his breeches closed.

"Who are you?" the man yelled.

"Someone who can slice your head from your shoulders in one stroke." Kerr slid his sword free.

The man motioned toward the woman who fought against the gag between her teeth. He lost the grip on his breeches, and they fell around his ankles. "She's no one of import and a traitor anyway." His words came out in a rush as he crouched to yank his breeches up. "And I can share. Truly, you can even have her all to yourself."

"I am not someone who rapes and kills lasses, ye foking bastard." Kerr snapped the *mattucashlass* through the air, hitting the man's thigh.

The fiend squealed, dropping to the floorboards. "Mercy," the man called as Kerr strode past him to his helpless prisoner.

Curls cascaded around the woman's shoulders, her eyes wide with long lashes. She wore rich clothes in the English style, her full skirts tied close to her legs with a rope so that she looked like a trussed-up goose. A mumble came with force from around a silk scarf, and her wide eyes narrowed as her gaze moved between the whimpering man and Kerr. Kerr stepped before her, noticing a slight floral scent mixed with rain.

"Hold still," he said and raised his hands behind her head to find the knot. The woman stared up at him as his fingers tugged at the silk tied tightly in the soft curls of her hair. She sucked in hard through her nose and let out a gust of breath when the gag dropped away.

"You lying bastard," she yelled. "I am *not* a traitor." She glared over Kerr's shoulder at the man on the barn floor. "Who do you work for?" She jerked her arms against her bonds as if she wished to beat him soundly.

"Wait," Kerr said, capturing her bound hands in one of his. She stilled, but from the fierce expression on her face, it was taking all her will not to rush at the fallen man to seek revenge. Kerr cut the rope around her wrists with one of his *sgian dubh's*, and she pushed at him to get out of her way, nearly tripping. "I need to free your legs, lass," he said, bending toward the rope wrapped around her voluminous skirts.

"Watch out!" she yelled.

Crouched, Kerr spun on his heels, his fist shooting upward to clip the ruffian under the jaw. The bastard's feet left the ground with the force of the impact, sending him sprawling backward, and his blade skidded across the hay-strewn dirt floor, his trews once more around his ankles.

"Oh no," the woman yelled, staring at the prostrate man. "Did you kill him?" she asked.

Kerr opened his mouth and closed it, his brow furrowing. She looked and sounded upset by the thought.

"God's teeth!" She scowled at Kerr. "Cut me free."

MARGARET DARBY, BETTER known as Maggie, kicked at her layers of petticoats the moment the mountainous man cut the rope around her legs. Skirts in hand, she hurried to the fallen man, crouching down next to him. She pressed her fingers against his neck.

Thump. Thump. "Alive," she whispered. Her head dropped forward, her shoulders rounding in relief. "Thank God," she said.

"Pardon, lass," her rescuer said, and she turned to take in the man who could have ruined everything. He wore the costume of the Scottish Highlander, a woolen wrap of plaid design around his narrow hips, the end of it reaching up to cross one stout shoulder to fall diagonally across his chest. His leather boots were laced up the fronts of his legs, where she could see several more daggers lashed. His tunic lay wet and molded to his muscles, the bleached linen stark against the tan skin of his neck and face. Maggie hadn't seen any Highlanders before. Did they all look as rugged, fierce, and full of masculine strength?

"Ye are angered that I harmed him?" he asked.

Mesmerized by the flash of white teeth in his perfect mouth, it took a moment for Maggie to comprehend his question. But then she frowned. "I am angered that you almost killed him." She turned back to the traitor. "And I was well in control of the situation." She slapped the ruffian's bristled cheeks lightly, trying to rouse him. "God's teeth. Wake up."

"Are ye two...?" The man hesitated, and she peered back at him, noticing how his clipped hair hit around his strong jawline. "Lovers?" he asked.

Maggie blinked, the word sinking in, making her frown turn to disgust. Her eyes widened. "Lovers? You jest. This..." she glanced back at the man who was stupid enough to think she'd meet him unprepared. "This creature? You think we are lovers when he had me tied up while threatening me with a knife?"

The Highlander shrugged his massive shoulders. "Some lasses like to be tied up."

Her mouth dropped open as she stared at the man's strong form and lush mouth. Did he pleasure ladies who like to be tied up? "By this man?" She slowly shook her head. "Have you seen his teeth?"

The Highlander looked down at the prostrate man, his

mouth open to expose his blackened, broken teeth. "Bad teeth don't hinder a man's jack."

Maggie straightened in a huff. "They certainly hinder any type of attention from me or any other woman who refuses to roll around with unwashed, crude swine." They stared at one another in the glow of the lantern she'd brought with her.

"I will escort ye inside to safety," he said, glancing down the aisle toward the gates that led into the dark bailey. "We can report him to the guards." The Highlander stepped closer to her.

"I would know your name," she said and frowned at the breathlessness in her voice. She cleared her throat, tipping her chin a bit higher like she'd seen her friend, Cordelia, do many times.

The man was handsomely made and was obviously more rugged than any man she'd seen before. Even rain-damp he looked commanding and powerful, not at all like the overly decorated men at court.

"I am Kerr Gordon, sent to speak with Queen Elizabeth of England."

"Cur, as in mad dog?" she asked. "What mother would name her babe after a mad dog?"

He frowned. "'Tis spelled K.E.R.R. A Scottish name."

"Well K.E.R.R," she spelled out, "I am Maggie Darby, well Margaret, I should say. Mistress to Queen Elizabeth and her protector."

"Ye protect Queen Elizabeth?" he asked, his voice even despite the question in it.

Maggie frowned at him. "My father inspected King Henry's clothing, Queen Mary had a Spanish lady inspect her garments, but then my brother inspected King Edward's clothing, and I inspect Queen Elizabeth's clothing for poisons and anything that could cause harm. So yes, I protect the queen's body."

"People send her poisoned gowns?" Kerr asked, following Maggie down the swept stable aisle.

"Catherine de Medici of France has poisoned people with

perfumed gloves, and there are whispers of enemies lacing gowns as well. Lord Burghley is convinced our queen is in jeopardy of one. Therefore, I try on all gowns, gloves, hats, basically anything that touches Her Majesty's skin." Their boots thudded on the hard packed ground, barely heard over the rain, as they walked down the aisle between the horse stalls. "And that man," she said, glancing over her shoulder, "was hired by someone to stop me."

"Because ye found something?" Kerr asked.

She hesitated. "Well… no. But I received a note telling me to meet someone here tonight who would give me information about an upcoming plot."

"The black-tooth man who tied ye up."

"No. The script was finely wrought, cultured, regal. I am certain the author hired this ruffian to do away with me." She looked back down the dark aisle where the man lay unmoving.

"After he raped ye," Kerr said, anger making his burbling brogue sharp with lethality.

They stopped before the stable doors, which she saw the brute had barred. "He would not have gotten far."

Kerr stopped, his body turning toward her. His hands landed gently on her shoulders. "Do ye not know the depravity of men, lass? That bastard had his jack out and ready. He would have taken out his lust on ye before slitting your throat." The Highlander looked back as if he were going to charge down the aisle to finish killing him. His handsome features took on the darkness of death.

Kerr Gordon seemed truly concerned for her. No one at court had ever asked her to be wary. To them, she was another disposable attendant in the queen's service. Elizabeth's sacrificial lamb.

Maggie stood there, breathing in the smell of rain and fresh hay, studying the man who cared enough about her, a stranger, to aid her and then warn her to take care. She swallowed against the tightening of her chest, shaking off the familiar heartache.

"Like I said, he would not have gotten far." She reached

down her petticoat and knocked against the iron and leather cage underneath. The dulled thump made the Highlander look down, and she shifted. "I am wearing a chastity belt."

His brow furrowed. "They are but legend that fathers use to scare their daughters."

She chuckled. "One was sent to the queen when rumors were circulating about her and Lord Robert Dudley being too intimate. 'Twas a jest. The queen scoffed and sent it away to me, her wardrobe keeper. It is made of iron and leather, and I have the key back in my chambers." She smiled broadly and exhaled long. "The scoundrel would have been quite put out when he lifted my petticoat to find me locked up tight."

The Highlander stared at her for a long moment. "He would have still cut your throat."

"He would have had to untie my legs to spread them before realizing my maidenhood was protected, and I can do quite a lot with my feet." She pointed to the ground, and his gaze followed as she drew the hem of her gown back, showing a pointed blade sticking out of the tip of one short, leather boot.

"Someone sent your queen a dagger-tipped boot?" he asked, his face open in bewilderment.

Maggie's smile filled with pride, and she shook her head. "My father and I fashioned the spring-loaded blade, from a castoff pair of the queen's boots. There is a lethal dose of poison secured in the point. If I had stabbed him with the tip, the poison would have exploded out of it. He would have fallen, leaving me to escape." Her smile slipped away. "*After* he had told me who sent him. Since you interrupted, the man will endure torture to pull the name from him."

The Highlander stood at the stable doors, unmoving as he assessed her. Maggie was tall like her queen and wore raised heels, but she still had to look up at the towering man before her. He studied her intently, his face giving nothing away. Did he disapprove of her? *I care not.* Lord Walsingham, the master of the queen's security, approved of her methods, well most of them.

"Are you planning to frown at me all night, or can we go inform the guards before the villain wakes?" she asked.

Kerr slid the heavy bar across to fall with a thud on the packed ground where rainwater was starting to leak under. "Ye feel bad for the man for having to endure torture, yet ye had planned to kill him with poison?"

"Torture would be far worse," she said. "Have you seen what they do in the Tower of London to those thought to be traitors?"

"Nay. Have ye?"

"No, but I've heard about it from Lord Johnathan Whitt. He has told us about the rack and hot poker." They strode out into the rain, which was slowing. Pulling her cloak up over her hair, she watched him walk over to a loosely tethered horse. "And the beatings will knock a man unconscious. 'Tis barbaric," she said, shaking her head.

Kerr ran his hand down the horse and checked his knot. "I will return," he said as if the horse could understand him.

They crossed the bailey toward the gates, the cold winter breeze sending a chill along her skin. "Have you ever tied a woman up…" Maggie looked at the Highlander. "To pleasure her?"

"I do not talk about—"

"I mean how is that enticing in any way?" she continued. "The woman would not be able to touch you." She stopped and looked up at him, her curiosity emboldened by the darkness. "Or is it done so that she takes all the pleasure? The ties removing her worry that she should be reciprocating?"

"I do not talk about tupping," he said.

"I am merely curious," she said. "I strive to understand everything I encounter that I do not. It was the way I was raised."

"To ask personal questions about tupping?"

She snorted softly. "To understand the world and everyone in it so I can distinguish threats."

"If a man ties ye up without ye asking him to, he is a threat."

She shook her head. "I don't ever intend to ask one to tie me up." He hadn't answered her questions, but then they were of a personal nature. Would she ever let the Highlander tie her up? Ask him to? So he could pleasure her? The thoughts bubbled through her like bubbles in a beaker over a flame.

"Ye are like no lass I've ever met," Kerr said. "Are all Englishwomen like ye?"

Thank goodness the brawny Highlander could not see the flush she felt filling her cheeks. Not from the talk about being intimate and his odd notions of courtship, but that she was indeed considered unlike other ladies.

"No," she said. "I am said to be... different." She couldn't count the number of times she'd been called foolishly reckless, the queen's jester, or too odd to be so close to royalty.

She turned her face to the damp, foggy night. "I am much more resourceful and cleverer than most." She had to be to stay alive in such a position. It was her duty as a Darby. "Like my father and brother before me."

"Are they still alive?" he asked.

"Of course," she said, annoyance lacing the words. "My father helped me load the poison in the boot tip." She flapped a hand toward the gate. "They live comfortably near the Thames."

They trudged in silence, Maggie holding her skirts to keep them out of the mud. She minded where the point of her boot fell. It would not do to unintentionally poison someone.

"Ho there," Kerr called to the guards at the gate, and they turned, pulling their short swords when they saw them.

"'Tis Mistress Darby," Maggie called out. She hurried forward. "Master Henry. Giles," she said. "There is a traitor unconscious on the floor of the stables."

They looked from her to Kerr. "What are you doing with the Scot?" Giles asked, frowning.

"He... happened upon me."

"Are ye aware," Kerr said, standing before them, "that there are villains about who tie lasses up and threaten to rape them and slit their throats?" Even rain-damp and without raising a sword, the Highlander was menacing. Broad and tall, he looked strong enough to knock both guards to the ground.

"Are you well, Maggie?" Henry asked. He tried to come forward, but Kerr didn't move, and Henry didn't look like he wanted to get any closer to him.

"Thank you, Henry. I am, but I will be even better once the villain is in the Tower being questioned as to who is plotting to poison the queen." That threw the two guards into motion. Giles yelled to another guard up top, and then he and Henry trotted toward the barn.

"I will escort ye inside the palace after I secure my horse," Kerr called to her as he followed the guards. "Wait near the door there," he said.

"I am not leaving until I know that brute is in chains." She trudged back. Even though Kerr had knocked the man out, she was truly responsible for catching the traitor. And her skirts were already ruined, the water spots probably not coming out of the silk, so there was no need to hide from the rain further. She had hundreds of dresses from Elizabeth's pile of cast-offs. Rich gowns and accessories were the only advantage to being Elizabeth's apparel examiner and wardrobe keeper.

Maggie kept up with the Highlander but had the feeling he was walking slower than his normal gait when she saw him glance back several times. The two guards were already inside the stable and down the aisle as she and Kerr entered, and she threw off her hood.

"This yaldson down here?" Giles called, bending over the man as Henry crouched next to him, his lantern illuminating the back of the stables.

"Praise God he didn't rouse and escape," Maggie said, releasing her breath. "Yes," she called. "Unless you see another fellow laid out unconscious down that way."

"You said he was alive to be taken to the Tower for questioning," Henry said.

She frowned at Kerr and hurried down the aisle. "Has he

died?"

Henry pushed back on his heels. "I would say so."

Maggie stopped short beside the man they had left unconscious, and her hand pressed against her lips. "Holy Jesu," she whispered and felt her world tilt as she looked down at the man who had lured her to the stables. Her hand went out, steadying herself on the Highlander's strong arm.

"He's about as dead as they come," Giles said, and all four of them stared at the man whose head had been sliced nearly off, bright red blood covering the ground under him.

CHAPTER TWO

"Praise your children openly, reprove them secretly."
William Cecil, 1st Baron Burghley, Queen Elizabeth I's
Advisor

KERR STOOD WITH Maggie Darby before the regal William Cecil, Lord Burghley, Queen Elizabeth's trusted Secretary of State. The man looked down his long nose, made to seem even longer with the extension of his white beard. Despite the late hour, the man wore his velvet garments, neck ruff, and silk hose.

"You are telling me…" Lord Burghley said, "that you alone, Mistress Darby, met with the murdered ruffian in the stables?"

"Yes, milord. He was working for someone at court, someone of high rank from what he insinuated and from the script of the note given to me." She pointed to the crumpled, water-stained note Cecil now held. "Since I left him alive to summon the guards, I believe the veiled traitor followed me to the stables and killed the man he hired when we left him."

Did Maggie realize that if Kerr hadn't intervened, she would have had a second attacker to stab with the tip of her shoe? Was there enough poison in it to kill two assassins? Apparently, there were more dangers at court than having Elizabeth order his execution for being from a Catholic clan supporting her cousin, Mary Stuart.

"Lord Burghley," Maggie continued in earnest, "we should be looking for someone with blood on themselves. With so much in the stables, at least a drop or two should mar the man's breeches, hose, or shoes." Her gaze moved to the guards behind Cecil as if inspecting them for the incriminating blood.

Cecil cleared his throat to gain her attention. "Alone. You went alone to meet with a paid assassin and possibly a high-ranking traitor?"

She took a moment to glance down at her skirt before meeting his gaze. "I did not know from the note who would show, but yes." As if reading the rebuke coming, Maggie tipped her chin a little higher. "To discover the name of a possible traitor within the queen's court who might send ratsbane or some other poisonous powder to Her Majesty. A fan could deliver ratsbane right up her nose. Or powdered hemlock could enter the queen's body through the wound on her ankle." Maggie clasped her hands as if she suddenly realized she was flipping them about.

Despite her soggy dress and damp, disheveled hair, she stood tall, meeting the statesman's tired gaze. "'Tis my sacred duty to discover traitors who threaten our queen."

Cecil swore beneath his breath, rubbing a hand down his bearded chin. "Your father will find his grave with the risks you take." His sharp gaze turned to Kerr. "And who the bloody hell are you?"

Kerr held out the folded sheaf that introduced him, and the man took it, breaking Mary Stuart's seal. He walked to one of the lit sconces lining the hall where Maggie had led him inside Whitehall.

When William Cecil raised his eyes back to him, Kerr bowed his head briefly. "I am Kerr Gordon of the northern Gordons of Auchindoun Castle in Banffshire."

Cecil frowned. "A Catholic Highlander loyal to Mary Stuart. And you have come to Whitehall to present a gift and letter from Mary to Her Majesty, Queen Elizabeth." That was what the letter of introduction said, but from the minister's assessing look, he was intelligent enough to know there was more to Kerr's story.

"Aye. And I came upon Mistress Darby needing assistance in

your stables."

"I needed none," Maggie murmured, but her tone did not sound as confident as before. "And we really should be inspecting people's clothing for blood."

Cecil ignored her, his sharp gaze remaining on Kerr. "The Gordons have been loyal to Mary's mother, Mary de Guise, and have attempted to help Mary Stuart while she remains on English soil at Sheffield Castle near Leeds. Are the Gordons involved in a plot to free Mary and put her on the throne of England?"

Maggie's eyes opened wide as she turned to Kerr.

Kerr liked the directness and obvious intelligence of William Cecil, especially after being warned about the constant lies and hedging at court. "Nay," Kerr said, meeting the man's gaze, "although I would be foolhardy to admit such whilst standing here in the center of England, in a palace housing Her Majesty's guards."

"Then why did Mary Stuart send you, Master Gordon?" Cecil asked.

"As ye are aware, the Scottish queen is most displeased with her confinement. She sends me with a letter of entreaty to read to your queen and a gift for me to present on her behalf."

Elizabeth's advisor stared at him in silence. Cecil needed more information if he was going to let Kerr anywhere near his queen. "In return for my service," Kerr said, "to brave what she calls this pit of vipers and risk my freedom and head in coming here, she will influence Clan Hay to accept my sister as a wife for the son of the chief, thus ending a feud between our clans."

"Influence how?"

"Letters to their chief, George Hay, who supports her over the Protestant regents dictating her son, James. The skirmishes between our clans have become bloody, and Queen Mary has agreed to intercede to put an end to it." Kerr spoke the words, trying to keep his brother's broken body out of his mind, the smell of old blood mixed with dirt as they carried him off the battlefield.

But as Cecil stared at him, Kerr let down his guard enough so grains of truth could slip through his practiced request. "I have a sister who fancies a Hay. Mary supports their union to quell the violence. With a word from her, George Hay will allow it." Kerr held Cecil's gaze so he would see the truth in his words. "Not everything, milord, is about Catholics trying to regain power."

"And yet, Mary Stuart is powerful enough to ally feuding clans." Cecil let out an exhale that sounded very much like a sigh. He looked to the guard who stood behind him. "See Master Gordon is given a bed." He looked back at Kerr. "There is no mass said at Whitehall."

"'Tis a good thing I didn't bother to bring my prayer beads and golden idols," Kerr answered.

Maggie made a little sound, a cross between a hiccough and a chuckle, and held her hand over her mouth. "Pardon," she murmured.

Cecil turned and walked away, his heels clicking on the stone floor. His words carried in the silent hall. "A time for your presentation to Her Majesty will be scheduled if the queen wishes to hear the letter, otherwise you may leave it and the gift."

"I must speak it," Kerr said, and cleared his throat, "with great emotion to have Mary's assistance." She had ordered him to practice reading it before her as if he were an actor on a stage, only agreeing to help his sister's cause after she was satisfied with his delivery.

Cecil stopped, glancing back at Kerr. "A servant will inform you of the queen's decision." He continued to walk away, his velvet cape swinging with his gait.

"This way," the guard said, his nose tipped higher as if Kerr smelled bad.

"I would see Mistress Darby safely locked in her room."

"That is not needed," Maggie said as they walked down the corridor, turning in the maze lined by wood paneling, portraits, and statuary on pedestals.

"Someone just tried to kill ye, lass, and whoever sent him is obviously deadly and still loose."

She flipped her hand and shook her head briefly but had nothing to refute. "It is this way." As they walked along the corridor, rapid footsteps came from behind, making all three of them halt.

"There you are, Master Edward," the man said to the guard leading them. "Lord Burghley has redirected me to put Master Gordon in the vacant room next to Mistress Darby since the servant rooms are full at the moment." He looked at Kerr. "Since the Highlander has already saved her once tonight, it would be helpful to have him nearby."

"I could have saved myself," Maggie murmured.

The wiry man had dark hair and one of those curling mustaches that Englishmen liked to wax so it curled on the ends.

"Bloody lucky," the guard, Edward, murmured. He turned on his heel and marched away with annoyance. So far, Kerr wasn't making any friends at court.

The second guard led them along the corridor. "The room looks out on the gardens. Quite nice actually. Luck is with you, Highlander. Perhaps that means your letter and gift to the great Queen Elizabeth will be received." The man smiled encouragingly, making him look like a simple-minded dolt in his uniform that seemed too big. What type of palace guards did the security advisor employ? Kerr had been warned about Francis Walsingham, Elizabeth's spymaster. That the man was keen and suspicious of everyone.

Maggie took the lead while the guard prattled on about the beauty of the rooms they passed as if giving a tour. Kerr followed silently, his leather satchel over one shoulder, his sword strapped to his other side. It was a wonder Cecil hadn't ordered him to surrender his weapons. Between guards like this man and the ease in which Kerr had gained access to Whitehall Palace, it was a wonder the English queen was still alive.

They walked through a grand hall where a throne sat against one wall, draped with cloth of gold. A candlelit corridor split off from it, lined with paintings and statues to create an impressive showing of wealth and status. Even the finest halls of Edinburgh Castle did not compare to this display of affluence.

Long minutes later, they climbed a set of stairs. Kerr couldn't help but notice the sway of Maggie's hips. The full skirts hid most of her below the waist, but it couldn't hide her gait. Did all women look so alluring while climbing stairs? He hadn't noticed any before.

Maggie looked back at him. "Is she as beautiful and bewitching as they say?" she asked.

"Who?" he asked.

"Mary Stuart," she said, her brow furrowing as if she was annoyed that he was unable to follow the path of her thoughts.

Mary Stuart was beautiful, but her rapid switches between hysterics and smiles made it difficult to gauge how to deal with her. "Some say she is," he answered.

Maggie turned forward again, and he came to walk beside her while the spry guard led them down the hallway. "What say you?"

"She is comely and richly dressed, but like a bird held captive, she pales and sickens."

"Have you been bewitched by her?" Maggie asked.

Kerr walked along, knowing full well that whatever he said would be relayed to Cecil and perhaps Queen Elizabeth. "I respect her position and royal lineage, but I have never been bewitched by anyone, including Mary. I am exempt from such feelings."

"So you have never loved?" Maggie asked.

"I love my sister. She and my father are all I have left in my immediate family. Her happiness is my happiness, and she wishes to marry a Hay."

Maggie turned her face to him. Even in the dimness of the hall, he could see her smile. "That is a different kind of love, Highlander, but it is strong enough to send you into a viper's den."

"Ye speak like ye are well versed in the emotion," he said,

casting a glance at the guard who, no doubt, listened to their words.

Maggie shrugged. "There is a lot of talk about courtly love here at Whitehall. Some, who agree with the queen, believe that love only makes one do foolish things like giving away one's power."

This was a well-known reason that Elizabeth gave for not choosing a husband.

They stopped at a door. "This is my chamber."

"And your chamber is right beyond," the guard proclaimed, again with that overly confident smile. "The key is in the lock and the bedding is fresh, quite comfortable for you, Master Gordon." He stood still. Was he waiting for a shilling? Did Elizabeth and her counselors depend on visitors to pay their servants?

Kerr fished out a coin from his satchel and held it before the man. "Thank ye."

The guard's eyes widened slightly, but he took the coin, nodding. With a broad smile that looked like he might be laughing at Kerr, he strode away, leaving Maggie in a dark corridor alone with a near stranger. Aye, it was no wonder she'd almost been killed in the stables without anyone seeming overly concerned.

The key clicked as Maggie turned the iron lock of her door and pushed it open.

"I will inspect it first," Kerr said, stepping around her into the dark room.

"I am completely capable," she murmured.

Someone had started a fire in her hearth, which gave a glow, illuminating gowns hanging about the room on hooks. The walls were nearly covered with the hanging fabric ensembles. A long table ran almost the length of the far wall, stopping short of the hearth where glass vials and crocks sat in organized rows, a large book splayed open with quills and ink. The air held a tangy scent of herbs and potions that mixed with the flower smell Kerr had noted on the lass.

Maggie's bed was fairly large and surrounded by velvet curtains suspended from four posters. She had two windows that must look out over the privy gardens that were said to be rich, vast, and quite green when not gripped in winter's fist.

Kerr walked the perimeter of the room, past two filled bookcases, moving around the gowns and lined rows of shoes in every design imaginable. Illumination increased as Maggie lit several lamps from the hearth fire, setting them strategically about before dropping to her knees to check under the bed. "No one here," she said, rising. "Although…" Her word trailed off as she walked over to another table that was bare, glancing under and around it. "The gloves." She straightened. "They are gone. The ones I was testing."

"How many?" He walked over, his footfalls muted by the thick rug on the polished wood floor.

"Six pairs of leather and jeweled gloves. They were from various countries, sent with ambassadors. Quite expensive."

Maggie frowned as she turned in a slow, tight circle, staring at the floors. "Although not as expensive as the gowns, some of which are worth a year's wages to the common man."

"Carrying a gown out of here and down a corridor could have been noticed," Kerr said, still hunting around the room for a culprit, "whereas gloves would not."

Maggie strode to one corner of the room, taking inventory of the queen's wares by moving them about in a methodical inspection. She moved from item to item in a clockwise direction. Kerr joined, shifting through the pieces of expensive-feeling fabrics, although he didn't exactly know what he was looking for.

She ducked to look under the table at ornate boxes, lifting lids and then reaching high on her toes to check the shelves where various pieces of jewelry, fans, and more boxes sat. Even in her damp, heavy dress she flitted about like a sparrow without knocking anything out of place.

"Has anyone ever broken into your room before?"

She stopped, looking at him with pinched brows. Maggie had

the most unique almond-shaped eyes and full, lush lips. Pale freckles lay scattered across the canvas of her smooth skin. "No," she answered. "Curious that it occurred when I was expected to be dead in the barn." She looked at the door. "And someone had a key because I felt the tumblers move when I turned mine."

"A servant?" he asked.

"Or anyone who has a servant, which basically means anyone at Whitehall."

"Why lock the door at all?" Kerr said and watched her continue her inspection. She swiped solid pieces like fan handles with one finger, looking to spy anything that may have come off of them.

She huffed. "I will have to check every piece of clothing again." Her hands perched on the hips of her muddied gown.

"Ye put everything on before the queen does?"

"Yes," she said, turning to look at him as if inspecting him too. "But I check everything first so that I do not succumb to poison myself." She pointed at her long table with the crocks and vials. "I have no intention of sacrificing myself because of laziness and negligence. I test everything before I don it. I wear it for several hours and describe any strange sensations or reactions on my body." She pointed to her book.

"What type of sensations does that iron contraption under your skirts give ye?" he asked.

Maggie frowned at him, although he caught the slightest lift to the corner of her lush mouth. "Chafing, heaviness, and annoyance will be noted. Effectiveness is yet to be evidenced."

"Bloody hell," Kerr swore. "I should hope ye do not have another opportunity to test it."

She placed her hands on her abdomen as if adjusting the contraption. Did she wear nothing between herself and the leather? He swallowed, changing his glance to the hanging costumes. "So ye test them before the queen wears them."

She gave a quick nod. "Then in the morning when her ladies come to request a costume, they pick a gown I tested for Her

Majesty to wear that day. I quickly put it on to double check, and then they take it to her."

She walked along the row of gowns hanging from pegs nailed to a sturdy bar, and pulled off a lavish gown of burgundy, laying it across her bed. "Since I do not know which particular gown she will choose, I must be confident about any of them." She huffed. "I will guess which costumes she might request and examine them tonight." She plucked at her own wet skirts. "After I bathe and change into something dry."

"Before ye rust," he said, nodding to her hips shrouded in iron.

She snorted softly. "That will be the first to come off."

Maggie brought a lamp closer to the burgundy dress, bending over it, her fingers touching and turning the jewels around the neckline that would rub first her own and then the queen's skin.

"I will leave ye then," Kerr said, "but ye must bar the door. In case the one who hired the slain man tries to finish his task."

"I'll drag that before it," she said, nodding to the large trunk flanking the table.

"I will be sleeping in the room next door," he reminded her. "Scream or pound if ye need assistance."

"Thank you for your concern, Master K.E.R.R.," she said, spelling his name out with a smile.

The heavy trunk scraped along the wooden floor as Kerr tugged it closer to the door. "I will stand in the corridor until I hear ye turn the lock and move the trunk over. Good eve."

"Good eve," Maggie said without coming over. She turned immediately back to the dress, opening the stomacher and front ties.

"Maggie," he said.

"Mmm hmm?"

"The door, lass. I have a need to shut my eyes and cannot leave ye without knowing ye are secure."

She frowned but traipsed over, lifting the key from a hook where it rested. "Good eve, Highlander." She shut the door and turned the key. The scrape of the trunk followed, and he turned toward his own door.

Thump. Heavy iron hit the floor behind her locked door.

He paused, listening closely, and swore he heard Maggie give an exaggerated sigh. Her chastity belt? He grinned for the first time since stepping foot in England.

CHAPTER THREE

"There, on the pendant boughs her coronet weeds
Clamb'ring to hang, an envious sliver broke.
When down her weedy trophies and herself
Fell in the weeping brook. Her clothes spread wide,
And mermaid-like awhile, they bore her up.
Which time she chanted snatches of old tunes,
As one incapable of her own distress,
Or like a creature native and endued unto
that element. But long it could not be
Till that her garments, heavy with their drink,
Pulled the poor wretch from her melodious lay
To muddy death."
William Shakespeare – *Hamlet, Ophelia's death*

"I ASSURE YOU, she will find this burgundy gown without fault," Maggie said to Lady Marjorie Radcliff, a lady to the queen's bedchamber. "I've worn the garment since dawn without even a tickle of sensation." Maggie stood in her white, lace-edge smock as Lady Radcliff and another lady, Lettice Knollys, carried the costume together out the door.

"'Tis good that the queen rarely wears gloves," Lettice said.

Maggie shook her head. "At least six pairs were stolen last night, ones I had finished testing."

"There are dangers everywhere," Marjorie said softly, her dark cow-eyes sad as if she saw too much of it in her service to the queen.

"I will be here today, re-examining all the costumes," Maggie said. "Nothing bad will befall Her Majesty, at least not from her garments. I swear it."

Marjorie smiled. "We are grateful for your service, Mistress Darby."

Maggie let the gratitude fill her chest. This was what the Darbys did to protect the realm. Even her mother had donned the gowns of Catherine Parr for the short while she was at court before King Henry died.

Maggie closed the door behind the ladies. Twirling in her smock, she let her gaze fall over the various dresses, trying to guess which Elizabeth might request for the St. Valentine's festival the next day. She spotted white ostrich feathers on the bed. "God's teeth," she whispered and scooped up the forgotten fan. Even though it was winter, Elizabeth used her fan daily to show her various moods: irritation, flirtation, fury, sorrow, contemplation. The fan spoke a silent language.

Fan in hand, Maggie yanked open her door. "Ladies…" The rest of her call fell silently back down her throat. She swallowed, her eyes wide as she stood before the large form of Kerr Gordon in his Highland dress. His piercing gaze dropped, and Maggie held the full fan before her unbound breasts that were visible through the thin material of her smock.

Like a storm coming in from the sea, Kerr's face hardened. "Ye should not open your door in your smock," he said, his voice gruff with reprimand.

Irritation helped her rein in her flying heart. "And ye shouldn't be visiting a lass so early in the morn," she said, imitating his brogue, although she failed entirely at capturing the burbling sound that brought to mind open moors, unfettered wind, and snowcapped mountain peaks.

The man looked fresh, his short beard trimmed, and his hair

still damp as if he'd been up at dawn washing. His tunic was clean and his kilt dry and neatly wrapped around his narrow hips in a pleated drape. How exactly did he manage that wrap?

He followed her gaze by looking down at his loins, and she felt her cheeks heat. "I have never seen the Highland costume up close before," she said in excuse and met his eyes with a tip of her chin. "I would like to see you put it on."

His eyebrow rose. "Ye wish to see me get dressed?"

"Yes," she said, but then her cheeks grew warm as she realized that his loins were probably bare beneath. "I mean to say... I wish to know how it is fashioned without falling down." She shook her head, ignoring her blush. "What can I help you with, Master Gordon?"

The slight grin hovering over his mouth slipped away. "While I await the queen's summons, I will help ye discover your intruder and the traitor behind the villain last eve," he said. "I will also affix a sturdy bar on the inside of your door."

It was then that Maggie realized Kerr held a length of thick wood and a hammer. "Oh," she said. How had she missed that? *Because I was focused on his loins.*

She moved aside, letting him into the room, closing the door. "One second." She hurried behind a changing screen where she shoved her arms into the sleeves of a thicker robe. Her day costume required a maid's help to don, so the robe would have to do since there was no way under heaven that she would ask Kerr Gordon to help cinch her stays.

Maggie raked her wavy, tousled hair with her fingers, pulling its length over one shoulder before emerging. "Don't touch anything," she said when she saw him inspecting her vials and beakers on the table.

"Ye are quite learned with chemical substances, then?" he asked, turning to her.

She felt her heart speed up at his casual perusal of her undress. "I have studied them my whole life. It is a tradition within the Darby family and my employment."

"To put yourself in harm's way?"

She studied him. "Don't you do the same for Mary Stuart?" She watched his rugged face for some clue as to what immediate answer ran through his mind, but like a tasteless poison, he gave no indication.

"I protect my clan and my sister. And Mary Stuart will help me do so."

Maggie opened her mouth, questions multiplying by the second.

Rap. Rap. Rap. "Maggie? We are here to help you dress."

Cordelia and Lucy! "God's teeth," Maggie said. "Hide," she whispered to Kerr, while flapping her hands.

For a moment he just stood there as if he didn't know the meaning of the word. She jabbed a finger toward the suspended poles that held gowns draped along a thick cord on the other side of the room. "I cannot be found with a man in my room while in this state," she said, her words tumbling over each other as she held out the skirt of her robe and smock. Queen Elizabeth demanded chastity and propriety amongst her ladies. Even though Maggie wasn't one of the queen's immediate ladies, she was expected to behave as one.

Rap. Rap. "Maggie? Are you in there?"

Maggie flew over to Kerr. "I... I am indisposed. One moment," she called toward the door as she shoved at his shoulder to make him turn. It was like shoving a mountain. Thick muscle formed his frame into one belonging to one of the Greek gods that she'd studied in her father's book of legends. Throw the Highlander in the white drape of the Greeks and he'd look able to throw lightning bolts down from the heavens.

"Please," she whispered. "'Tis Lucy and Cordelia, but if they say a word that I had you in my room, I could be dismissed." The thought of such shame, having to ask her father to take her in after the disgrace, made her stomach roil. Her friends wouldn't tell anyone on purpose, but something as scandalous as this could slip.

Kerr moved then, letting her push him toward the clothes. "Not a grunt, growl, or word," she whispered.

"I don't grunt," he said.

"Shhhh," she said, her eyes wide and teeth clenched. She turned, running for the door. Glancing back, she saw him duck his large frame behind the thicker evening costumes in the corner. Lord help her. She was hiding a mountain behind silk.

⇶⇷

KERR WATCHED MAGGIE'S shoulders rise and fall as she stood before the door as if she tried to calm herself. She opened the door and two lasses walked right in, one after the other. "Were you pissing or something?" the first asked, laughing lightly. She wore a blue dress, her hair a light gold color.

"Lucy," Maggie said as a rebuke. Maggie gestured toward her table. "I was mixing a dilution."

"You have so much in that head of yours," the other said, "no wonder you do not try to attract a suitor." So Maggie was not enamored of anyone?

"Come now," Lucy said, motioning her over to where a bum roll waited with a fresh smock.

The other woman wore a green gown and had red hair like the queen was said to have. "I have plans to meet Lord Whitt in the privy gardens this morn, so I have no time to stand about waiting for your poisons to dissolve."

Lucy snorted. "Perhaps, sister, you should borrow that chastity contraption. Jonathan Whitt is said to have a randy jack."

"Hold your tongue," the sister snapped and then smiled. "Although it is powerful."

"Cordelia," Lucy said in exaggerated shock. She snatched one of Maggie's pillows off the end of her bed and threw it at her sister, but the woman caught it. "Disgraceful," Lucy said but smiled.

"You and Maggie know nothing of the sport of love," Cordelia said, tipping her nose higher. "We are at court where the rules are different. It is not expected that I be completely ignorant of carnal delight."

"The queen is a virgin," Lucy said. "She might release you if she discovers your trysts, and then you will have to live with Mother."

Cordelia gave a dramatic shudder. "The horrors." And Lucy laughed.

Maggie stood watching them, an uneasy smile on her face, while sending furtive glances toward his hiding place. Hell, the lass would give herself away.

Maggie pulled a gown that was draped over a chest. "I will wear this blue ensemble."

"With no gloves," Cordelia said, looking about the room.

"I heard all six pairs were stolen," Lucy said, shaking her head. "If Mother hears there are thefts at court, she might demand the two of us come home." The words came like a pout. "Even without Father there, she will think it is safer. Especially if she hears you are having trysts, Cordy."

"Then don't spread rumors," Cordelia said and crossed her arms. "'Tis right odd that they didn't steal some of the jewels you have hanging about in here. All the court is abuzz about it. Lord Burghley has been locked up with the queen and Lord Walsingham all morning."

It was very odd that jewels hadn't been lifted. Kerr had thought about it all last night until he did not hear Maggie moving about anymore.

"Off with your smock, then," Cordelia said, pulling the robe from Maggie. Lucy bent to catch the hem, lifting it. Kerr's brows went up, and he closed his eyes.

"This one is clean," Maggie said. "I donned it this morn."

"Oh but this smock is so lovely in silk," Lucy said, going to the one she'd laid on her bed. "It slides across the skin."

Kerr suddenly imagined white silk sliding along Maggie's

naked stomach and squeezed his eyes shut. *Ye damn randy fool.*

"I will wear it for the evening meal," Maggie said.

"A hammer?" Lucy said. "What are you doing with this in your bed?"

Kerr's eyes snapped open to see the woman holding the hammer he'd brought to fix the door.

"I... I had anticipated difficulty in removing the chastity belt that was given to the queen as a jest."

Both ladies stared at her. "You mean to say you put that contraption on?" Cordelia asked, turning to look at the bench where it sat.

"And how would a hammer help take it off?" Lucy asked.

Cordelia looked back to the tool. "Are you sure you didn't bring the tool in for another reason? To use... in your bed." The woman smiled mischievously. "It has such a long, thick handle."

"Cordy!" Lucy yelled, dropping it with a bang on the floor.

Maggie, a set of stays and bum roll tied over her smock, held her blushing cheeks in her hands. "You two are worse than the lords after their pints." She pointed to the door where she must have spotted the heavy bar. "I am actually having a bar installed across my door so no one can break in again when I'm here."

"Pleasuring yourself with a hammer?" Cordy asked, and she and her sister doubled over in laughter while Maggie shook her head, muttering.

"I am sorry, Maggie, for my sister's scandalous mind. Come sit." Lucy beckoned Maggie over to a chair where she braided her thick hair, tying it up in a bun. Cordelia brought over a woman's decorated hood that matched the gown, and Lucy set it over Maggie's head.

"Mother wishes for us to visit this Saturday," Cordelia said. "And you are to come too, Maggie."

"She thinks so highly of you sacrificing yourself for the safety of the queen," Lucy said.

The word *sacrificing* grated on Kerr's nerves.

The two ladies left with promises to see Maggie later. As the door shut, she leaned her forehead against the door, and he emerged.

"They have no reason to think anyone was in here with ye," he said.

She turned, leaning against the door as if it was holding her up. "Thank goodness they think me beyond reproof."

"Except when ye have a hammer with ye."

"God's teeth, they are incorrigible," she said, but her blush remained.

Kerr walked toward her. "So, ye do not often have men hiding amongst the petticoats in your bedchamber?"

Her lips parted, and he watched her breathing push her exposed breasts above the tightly laced bodice. "Never."

"Then I am honored," he said and stopped. He lowered before her, but she didn't back up. His hand slid under the edge of her petticoat, the fabric skimming his hand, and picked up the hammer.

"Oh," she whispered and stepped back as he straightened.

"I will fix the bar before we leave."

"Thank you," she said and whisked away to the bed to straighten the sheets and move the silk smock.

Kerr went to the door. "Hopefully Elizabeth's housekeepers won't mind a little added security," he said.

"Lord Burghley is always concerned for my safety and would approve any added protection to my person just like he watched out for my brother with the young King Edward."

"He trusts ye."

"'Tis my family legacy to provide this roll to the rulers of our great country."

He glanced at her long table of jars and glass phials. "So ye have said."

"Oh."

He held the first bracket against the solid wood frame and plucked one of the nails he'd set between his teeth, hammering it into the wood, followed by the second one. "But ye are clever enough to save yourself through study and experiments," he said, looking back at Maggie who watched him.

Maggie's perfect nose wrinkled. "Despite the queen's name for me, I do not intend to die in her service."

Name for her? Kerr had heard that the English queen gave nicknames to those close to her, people she trusted. Lord Burghley was her Spirit. Lord Robert Dudley was her Gypsy because of his dark eyes and hair like the adventurous Romany people, and Lord Francis Walsingham was her Spymaster.

"What does the queen call ye?"

Her nose tipped up slightly. "I am her Sacrificial Lamb."

MAGGIE WALKED SWIFTLY to keep alongside Kerr's stride as they entered the garden. He hadn't said anything when she admitted her nickname, but the look on his face could be best described as belligerent. He'd finished the brackets and tried the bar in silence. It seemed quite sturdy, and she would sleep better knowing no one could come inside.

Her breath puffed out in frozen clouds as they walked together, her slippers crunching along the path in the privy gardens that wound beside Whitehall Palace. "In the summer, this would all be flanked in green," she said to break the silence. "The flowers give one a reprieve from the unpleasant smell of court when it gets hot."

With the winter cloaking everything, most of the bushes were twiggy hedges, except for the holly bushes. The trees stretched overhead in various places. Their winter-bare limbs, meant to give shade in the summer, resembled knobby fingers reaching out overhead as they walked beneath.

As the silence stretched, broken by Kerr's heavy footsteps and the periodic tweet of a few sparrows, Maggie glanced across at his strong profile. Kerr Gordon was a warrior from the bottom of his leather boots to the top of his dark hair. There was even a scar along his jaw, and she wondered if someone had tried to cut off his head.

She cleared her throat. "Thank you for installing the bar across my door," she said. He did not reply but continued to survey the path and surrounding area before them. "Do not feel obligated to guard me as I walk the grounds. I am surely safe here in broad daylight." She saw Cordelia sitting on a stone bench with Lord Whitt. Cordelia saw her, and her eyes widened at the sight of Kerr.

"Ye should not think of yourself as a sacrifice," Kerr said, his words surly.

Maggie looked away from Cordelia. "Her Majesty does not mean anything macabre by the name. But no, I do not think of myself that way." Was the name causing him to be so quiet?

She smiled to herself at the thought. "That is why I take great pains to check all her gowns and accessories with a diligent process of swiping and testing. My father taught my brother and me the ways of poisons to keep us safe."

"Did he also teach ye to wear a chastity belt and poison tipped shoes?" Kerr asked, finally turning his face toward her.

Her heart gave a rapid strum. "Not the chastity belt, but the shoes." She leaned in a bit. "The Spaniards speak of poison tipped shoes, so I told him we should devise some."

He met her gaze, but he did not look merry. "What else do assassins use?"

"The French like to poison gloves and stockings with ratsbane powder. The Portuguese send the China drink, which only the bravest of tasters tries."

"How about the Catholics?"

"No one at court counts themselves as Catholic, so it is difficult to guess their methods. And since they are spread out across the world, it is better to guess lethal tactics based on location."

"There are no Catholics at court?" he asked.

Maggie shook her head. "Even if the queen is tolerant, her

council is not." They continued down the path, a chirping of birds above making Maggie tip her head up to look. "Every Catholic is thought to want your Mary on the throne of England."

"She is not *my* Mary," Kerr said. They paused before a low limb blocking the path. "My father and brother…" He paused. "My father is a practicing Catholic, my sister too but not as strictly. I worship as is expected at Auchindoun."

"And your brother?" she asked.

"He practices nothing now that he is dead."

Despite the evenness of his tone, Maggie laid her hand on her arm. "I have a brother. His name is William, and despite him teasing me whenever we are together, I would mourn greatly if he died. I am sorry, Kerr."

"Thank ye." Kerr bent below a limb, and they continued to the back edge of the gardens.

"But you still have your sister," she said.

He said nothing, the silence between them like a physical tether: Maggie waiting and Kerr deciding if he could trust her enough to tell her anything more. They stopped where a copse of trees marked the end of the royal property.

"Rhona has a gentle countenance, and I wish her to have happiness in this very unhappy world, even if our father does not seem to care."

"And she loves a Hay, your enemy?"

"Aye. Percy Hay, the son of the chief, George Hay, who is my father's lifelong enemy. Mary Stuart will endorse the union if I deliver her letter and gift to Elizabeth." He turned his intense gaze on her. "So she is not *my* Mary, but my sister is *my* Rhona."

Maggie clutched her fist before her heart and swallowed hard. "Rhona is lucky indeed to have you." What would her life be like if she lived away from court? Lived with her family again. Would William grow to care for her like Kerr cared for his sister?

She turned, following Kerr's narrowed gaze, to see three of the spaniels in the distance. The small dogs leaped and tugged at something near the base of a tree. It was hard to see what poor animal they must be after. The sharp teeth of a dark brown dog sunk into a pale hand buried in the ground. Maggie's had risen to her mouth with her gasp.

CHAPTER FOUR

"No more tears now; I will think about revenge."
Mary Stuart, Queen of Scots

MAGGIE'S HAND WENT to her stomach at the gruesome sight of three dogs digging away at the loose dirt, trying to rip up a long, slender arm. Kerr was already halfway over to it before Maggie's mind untangled enough so she could follow.

Kerr reached the tree. "Go on," he said, shooing the dogs away and bent down to have a closer look at the pale appendage.

Maggie reached the area but stood far back as he grabbed it. "It is a woman?" she asked, holding her scented pomander to her nose.

Instead of digging farther to unearth more of the body, Kerr pulled the white arm up from the dirt. "Good Lord," she said, gasping and jumping back. He turned. "What…?" she murmured, coming closer.

It was not the limb of an unfortunate woman at all but a long, dirty lady's glove. The fingers were puffed full of the wool Maggie had stuffed inside to collect any possible poison. "It is one of the stolen gloves." She pointed to another bit of white sticking up from the cold ground. "More of them perhaps."

The dogs, who belonged to some of the court ladies, continued to dodge around them as Kerr pushed away the loose soil. A crow cawed in the hedgerows, and the small unruly pack ran off toward it. Kerr continued to tug and dig around the freshly made shallow grave of gloves. "I am sure these are the ones I was inspecting for the queen," Maggie said.

She counted quickly. "All of them are here." She met Kerr's questioning eyes. "Why would someone risk stealing from the queen only to bury them in the back garden?"

"Perhaps there was evidence on them of poison," Kerr said, watching the dogs run toward the far end of the gardens where two other ladies walked arm in arm.

Maggie's eyes widened. How horrible it would be for one of the sweet pups to be poisoned. She shook her head. "Good Lord," she whispered, sending up a quick prayer on behalf of the pups.

The spaniels leaped around the skirts of the laughing ladies. "They seem unaffected," Kerr said.

"Let us hope that continues." She pulled the gloves from Kerr, shaking them free of as much dirt as she could. "I will have to test them again to know for certain, but they are too dirty to be given to Her Majesty."

"Maggie?" Cordelia called from farther down the path. She hurried up to them, Lord Whitt at her side. "Who is your friend and, God's teeth, what are you doing?"

Lord Whitt frowned at Kerr. "'Tis unseemly to be tucked away in the garden with a..." His gaze dropped to Kerr's dress. "A Scot."

"A man," Cordelia said at the same time. She dropped Lord Whitt's arm to come forward. Even though Lucy and Cordelia volunteered to help Maggie dress, they were still considered ladies at Elizabeth's court. Their widowed mother was Baroness Cranfield, who lived in London in a lovely home where Maggie had visited. The aging lady, a devout Catholic, was not invited to court, but she had sent her daughters in hopes they would find rich husbands while walking the gardens of Whitehall, rich husbands like Jonathan Whitt.

"Lady Cordelia Cranfield, Lord Johnathan Whitt, this is Master Kerr Gordon from Scotland," Maggie said, making the formal introductions. She frowned at the way Cordelia stared at Kerr like he was a piece of pork pie she wished to sample.

Kerr nodded, keeping his own frown to match Lord Whitt's.

"Gordon?" Lord Whitt said and sniffed. "A Catholic Clan who hopes to see Mary Stuart on England's throne. I am surprised Lord Walsingham and Lord Burghley let you onto the palace grounds."

Kerr stood with his legs braced, and Maggie could envision him pulling his long sword on a battlefield. "I do not meddle in the affairs of royals," he said. "I am merely here to deliver a message to your queen."

"And walk amongst the gardens with one of her attendants?" Lord Whitt said. His narrowed gaze shifted back to Cordelia. The man was jealous that Cordy had wanted to follow the brawny Highlander. They certainly didn't need Lord Whitt's interference into what was being unearthed, literally, as a possible new plot against the queen. Rumors would spread, and Elizabeth would become unbearably fearful of every little thing.

Maggie stepped closer to Kerr, coiling her arm around his. Her heart flipped a bit at the strength in the limb, the corded muscle of his forearm under her bare hand. "I asked Master Gordon to escort me about while he is here," she said, her gaze going to Cordy. No doubt Maggie would be thoroughly interrogated by Cordy and Lucy when they got her alone, but Maggie didn't want trouble for Kerr because of some petty jealousy on Lord Whitt's part.

"I am quite partial to Master Gordon's attention, because he saved me from a ruffian who trapped me in the queen's stables last eve."

Cordelia finally took her eyes off Kerr, her lips parting in shock. "Maggie? You didn't say. Just about the stolen gloves." Her eyes dropped to the dingy gloves she was holding.

"I was well enough… due to my…" she cleared her throat as it was hard to admit that she might have actually been in dire circumstances. "Due to my rescuer, Master Gordon."

"And you found the gloves?" Cordy asked. "In the gardens?"

Maggie glanced back at the tree. "Yes, mysteriously buried by that tree. Did either of you see anyone near it?"

Johnathan strode past them to look around the base, kicking at the disturbed dirt as if they might have missed a clue. Maggie tamped the annoyance down. As if she'd miss a clue when she spent every day looking for them. "We saw nothing over here until Lady Cordelia spotted the two of you," Johnathan said, his narrowed eyes shifting to Kerr.

Maggie looked between Johnathan and Kerr, feeling the tension mount. There were unspoken accusations in the courtier's gaze. "Master Gordon was rescuing me last night," Maggie said. "He had only just arrived at the palace when my room was broached," Maggie said, "so no need to squint your eyes at him, Lord Whitt," Maggie said, making the man's face redden and his frown increase. "There was no time for him to enter the palace and steal them. The guards from last night can attest to the time of his arrival."

Kerr stood like a mountain, waiting for the opportunity to erupt. "And I have no need for ladies' gloves." His hand went to the hilt of his sword, which he withdrew a few inches. "They interfere with my grip," he said, his voice deep and riveting with his northern accent. Maggie certainly wasn't immune to its lure, and from the looks of it, neither was Cordy. And perhaps neither was Johnathan, who stared at Kerr like he'd never seen a creature like him before.

Kerr's arm tightened, and he tugged Maggie forward. "I will see ye back to your laboratory," he said. Cordy and Johnathan watched them as Kerr pulled her back onto the path.

"I should report this to Lord Walsingham," Maggie said. "This seems more complicated than simple thievery."

"And ye are still at risk, especially now that ye've been seen with the missing gloves." Kerr sounded upset by the idea of her jeopardy. The thought warmed Maggie. She'd never been protected before. When it came to keeping alive, it was all up to her and her knowledge.

As they rounded a high shrub, they nearly ran into a man. "Ho now!" the man called out, and they stopped short before the impeccably dressed Thomas Howard, the Fourth Duke of Norfolk.

A short ruff fell under his strong chin, and his doublet of black velvet matched his flat, brimmed cap topped with a white feather. The man spared no coin in dressing royally. Some whispered that he sought the crown, but Elizabeth had made it plain that if she were to marry, it would not be with someone she considered common or beneath her. 'Twas why the Prince of Anjou seemed more likely a candidate than most.

Maggie curtseyed as best she could with her arm held. "Lord Norfolk, pardon us in our haste."

Norfolk looked Kerr up and down, his frown growing. "Who is this now?"

"I am Kerr Gordon."

"Gordon?" Norfolk said, his brows raised high. "A Catholic Clan who supports Mary Stuart's return to the throne."

"My only mission here is to deliver a letter and gift to Queen Elizabeth from Mary Stuart," Kerr said. "Queen Mary only trusts certain clans to carry out her requests."

"Most interesting," Norfolk said. "Watch your step here, Gordon. Those supporting Mary are likely to lose their heads." Without waiting for a reply, he stepped around them, his short cape swinging as he continued to stride into the maze of winter shrubs.

Kerr walked Maggie to the palace side door, holding it for her and following her inside. They walked back along the familiar corridors of Whitehall Palace. He didn't need any instruction, as if he'd memorized the layout already, which was quite a skill to have. Every time the queen went on progress, Maggie would have to relearn all the corridors. But Elizabeth couldn't go anywhere without her Sacrificial Lamb.

They stopped before Maggie's door where Kerr raised his finger up high to touch a leaf sticking out of the closed door. "No one has entered," he said.

Maggie stared up at it. "You haven't even tried the lock."

"I placed the leaf in the crack when I closed it. It would be dislodged if someone opened the door."

"What if they saw it float down and replaced it?" she asked, turning the key in the lock.

"'Twould be at a slightly different height since they wouldn't have noticed from where it fell," he said, his lips turning up slightly at the corners as if he approved of her questioning. "But I will inspect the rows of gowns for hiding assassins to be certain."

He walked first into the room, his short sword out. Maggie closed the door behind them. "Cordelia will likely come to see me as soon as she relinquishes Lord Whitt."

Kerr stalked about the room. "Does anything seem amiss?"

Maggie checked her beakers and the two gowns she planned to recheck that day. "No."

Finally convinced she was alone, Kerr re-sheathed his short sword. He inhaled fully and let it out, looking to her. "Would ye like for me to assist ye in here today?"

Yes. "Oh no," she answered instead. Lord, she'd end up dropping her glass vials with the brawny man watching her.

He nodded. "Then I will check on Caspian."

"Your horse?"

"Aye. We have been traveling for several weeks and he deserves a thorough rub down."

"You... rub your horse?"

Kerr smiled. "Aye."

She swallowed, feeling a little thrill as they spoke. "You must have strong hands then."

He held them up before him. "Practicing daily with my sword does that."

"Certainly," Maggie said, smiling. "Perhaps... I mean you are welcome to practice in the garden or on the jousting field, I am sure."

He nodded and went to the door. "I will be in my chamber,"

Maggie said, mentally shaking off the strange pull she felt toward the Highlander. "I have too much work to do to be anywhere else." She turned then to the table and carefully unrolled the mass of dingy earth-tainted gloves. *Dirt. No white powder.* She would check for ratsbane anyway.

"Maggie," Kerr said.

"Yes?" she answered.

He said nothing until she turned to meet his gaze, and her thoughts evaporated like sugar granules in hot water. Dressed in his Highland garb, a frown in place under piercing dark gray eyes, he looked like a warrior ready for an attack. "Trust no one who comes to your door."

She took in a small breath, her heart having picked up the rapid beat of a bird's wings. "Only you?"

His mouth relaxed some. "Ye can decide that on your own, lass."

→》》》《《《←

PIT OF VIPERS? Kerr wasn't certain of that, yet, but the English court definitely wallowed in intrigue. One only needed to glance in the corners of the opulent halls to see clandestine meetings between whispering men, if not someone relieving themselves in a potted plant. 'Twas true that his family home of Auchindoun Castle was draftier and not edged with gold, but at least his sister forbade anyone from urinating in the corners. No wonder all the inhabitants of Elizabeth's court wore little perfumed trinkets to hold to their noses. How did Maggie stand it? The foul odors made him miss the wide-open moors of Scotland.

Had Maggie ever smelled the sweetness of Scotland?

Kerr once again forced his thoughts from the bonny *sassenach* like he'd been doing all day yesterday and today. He'd spent another fruitless night trying to find Lord Burghley again to no avail. He'd roamed the court, meeting any noble who didn't sneer at his foreign dress. No one outright condemned him for his family's loyalties to the Stuart de-throned queen, but whispers followed in his wake.

Rhona, his sister, had schooled him in court etiquette, but he wasn't going to smile all the time like a simpleton. He needed someone willing to introduce him to the English queen. He could always hope Lord Burghley would do so, but would the advisor broach the subject of a letter from Mary in such a way that Elizabeth would listen? If Kerr could not read the letter as Mary dictated, she would not send word to George Hay, supporting Rhona's marriage to the man she said she could not live without. And the union would quell the feud between the Hays and Gordons, preventing many deaths in the raids that had raged between the two clans throughout Kerr's life.

Kerr watched out one of the large windows along the hall where he'd left a Lord Winthrop and his wife who had said they would love to visit his "savage" country to take in the fresh air. But the man had then said he had no wish to be skewered, and the wife said she'd no wish to be raped. Because, unlike their pristine England, that is what every Scotsman had on his mind.

"Daingead," he muttered and wiped his palm across the warped glass as he followed the familiar gait of the woman in a gray cloak walking out into the bailey. Where was Maggie Darby going? Alone? Did she not remember that someone tried to kill her two nights ago?

Kerr turned on his heel, nearly bowling over a small gaggle of dandies, their necks in ruffs, making their heads seem to sit on lace serving platters.

"Ho now, watch where you are going, Scot."

"He shoved me."

"'Tis an act of war," another man said, and they all laughed lightly and straightened the plumage that he'd inadvertently ruffled.

Kerr strode out of the hall, down the stairs and out through the double doors, his boots churning up gravel in the bailey as he spied around the bailey. *There.* She walked out of the gate into the flowing crowd of Londoners. She cast a furtive glance behind her, and Kerr slid around the edge of the gate. She scanned the area and surged into the crowd. Kerr followed.

"Leaving already?" said the guard, Giles.

"Nay," was all Kerr said, hurrying past the onerous Englishman.

Maggie moved quickly, her slight build helping her pick her way through the mass of colorful people. Even with a hood over her golden red hair, Maggie was striking in her uniqueness and surprising in her actions. Surprising and risky. Even with the gray cloak, anyone could see she was dressed as a wealthy lady, one unaccompanied by any form of protection. Was she relying on her chastity belt and poison tipped boot?

"Och but, lass, what are ye up to?" he murmured, following.

Maggie continued up the slanted street, dodging hawkers, carts, and stray children. Her gracefulness gave her an advantage, but Kerr was fast, in a straight-path sort of way. People tended to veer away from him, so he was able to follow, keeping her in his sights. She clutched a small bundle before her.

She hadn't told him she was leaving Whitehall today. *I have no right to dictate her freedom.* But having saved her once, he felt... What did he feel toward the bonny, risk-taking *sassenach*? Protective? *Aye.* Like he did with Rhona? *No.* Whatever protectiveness Kerr was feeling for Maggie Darby was nothing like he had for his younger sister.

Maggie rounded a row of town houses near the Thames, traipsing toward the last one on the end. Well-cared-for walls of lime-washed daub and wattle showed between dark timbers. A chimney sat prominently on one side. It was a rich house compared to many in London with intact glass windowpanes and a swept front step.

Kerr watched Maggie knock and then enter, closing the door behind herself. What was she doing here, out of the palace? He looked around himself. There didn't seem to be danger lurking, but he didn't like the idea of Maggie being on her own. Could she have received another summons from the traitor, thinking she could outsmart a proven murderer? She'd made a report of the gloves to Walsingham, but the lord hadn't assigned any guards to protect her, just more around Elizabeth.

The last thought spurred Kerr to stride over to the door. No screams or angry voices came from within, so he raised his knuckles, his other hand sitting in familiar fashion on his short sword strapped to his side. *Rap. Rap.*

The door swung open immediately to reveal a tall young man, suspicion in his frown. Beyond him stood Maggie, her face open in surprise, but what drew Kerr's sword was the sight of Maggie half undressed. Her richly jeweled sleeves were untied and off her slender arms. Outer and inner petticoats pooled around her feet, she stood in her smock with her bejeweled outer bodice half unlaced. "Kerr?" she said. "What are you doing here?"

Kerr didn't have time to answer before an elderly man drew his attention with a long matchlock gun. The distinct smell of the firelit cord showed that the man wasn't bluffing. "Highlander," the old man said, his eyes narrowed as he spied through the gun's sight. "Take off your clothes. All of them. Now."

CHAPTER FIVE

"If by chance I talk a little wild, forgive me;
I had it from my father."
William Shakespeare – *Henry VIII*

G OOD LORD. MAGGIE stared in horror. "Kerr, do what he says. He is not lying." She looked to her brother, William Darby. "You need to get rid of that musket."

"Off with your clothes before you take another step into my house," Reginald Darby said. "I will not have the likes of you or anyone bringing the sweating sickness into my home."

"Father," Maggie said. "This is Kerr Gordon, and he will remove his clothes. Lower the matchlock." When no one moved, she sighed. "Kerr, take off your clothes. This is my father and brother, and my father… Well, he needs to ensure that we bring no sickness with us into the house."

Kerr never took his gaze from her father as he slowly unbuck-led the thick leather belt that held his kilt in place. Maggie finished unlacing the front bodice, scooped up the rich clothing and slid behind the screen William had set up when she'd entered. She heard the heavy belt and pleated wool hit the wooden floor. She paused.

I shouldn't, she thought. *I really shouldn't*, but she did. Maggie peeked out from the edge of the screen to see Kerr standing there before her brother and father. He pulled his tunic off over his head, and her breath caught.

Kerr stood straight and powerful. Most men, plucked of the plumage of their clothing probably looked less formidable, even weak. But not Kerr Gordon. He stood with his legs braced in a battle stance, shoulders broad, as was his muscular chest sprinkled with fine hair. Rows of muscle sat like waves on his torso down to narrow hips and...

Maggie's cheeks burned as she beheld his heavy jack, and she drew back behind the screen. She knew enough from listening to Cordelia, that the male member grew hard and upright when aroused for mating. Even though Kerr's jack was hanging low, there was no doubt it was powerful like the rest of him.

Taking a few even breaths, Maggie continued to pull her clothes off and threw the clean smock and dressing robe on that William kept handy for her periodic visits home.

As she tied the front closure of the robe, Maggie yelled out from behind the screen. "Father, Master Gordon is visiting Queen Elizabeth and is helping me with my investigation. I cannot emphasize enough that you should not shoot him."

"Here," she heard William say. "You can wear some of my clothes, but Father won't allow outside clothes or boots inside the house."

Maggie peeked out. Once again struck by the brawny, muscular frame of the Highlander, Maggie remained behind the screen until she saw him pull her brother's tunic over his head. It fell to his thighs, covering him. She stepped out as he pulled on a pair of breeches that were a bit too short for him, tying them with rope around his waist.

Kerr's gaze moved over her, touching every inch as if inspecting her for damage. To Maggie, it felt like a caress, and her cheeks warmed. No one had ever looked at her like that before.

"Ye mean to say, that every time ye come home, ye must strip all your clothes off?" he asked.

"Yes," Maggie said. Her hands flipped as she spoke. "My father is Reginald Darby. He worked for many years, decades actually, for King Henry, doing the same job I do for Queen Elizabeth." Maggie's breath came easier as her father lowered his matchlock, although he didn't blow out the match that would ignite the explosion. She really must get William to take the firearm out of the house. Her father's fear of illness, combined with his boredom, was making him act insane at times.

William took the musket, blowing out the match light. "And I was the clothing inspector for young King Edward." He set it next to the flame-filled hearth.

"Father," Maggie said. "We are clean now of any taint from the palace." She'd hidden away the costly gown under a blanket, and William carried Kerr's clothes and boots to a back room.

Her father's shoulders relaxed down a notch, but her brother returned to stand opposite Kerr, where they looked suspiciously at each other.

Maggie had always thought of William as large, tall, and well-fed. But next to the Highlander, her brother did not seem the brute with whom she'd always felt safe.

"Why did you follow my sister?" William asked. "It was obvious she was surprised when you knocked."

Kerr crossed his arms over his chest and looked at Maggie. "I thought perhaps ye had received another summons from the traitor at court and were lured away."

"What traitor at court?" William asked, turning to Maggie.

"Someone sent me a note to meet them in the queen's stables three eves ago. When I arrived, a local ruffian grabbed me. I was about to hear who had hired him to stop me and why when Kerr arrived."

"She was tied up and gagged with a man threatening to rape and kill her," Kerr said. "It was unlikely that he would have given ye any information before he attacked."

"I was wearing a chastity belt." Anger licked up through her, and she watched her father for signs of concern. Turning, Maggie walked close to Kerr, who stood without shoes.

"Which would not have protected your lovely throat."

"Hush," she said, using her gown to hide the stomp she gave to the top of Kerr's foot.

"Maybe he will talk some sense into ye about going out alone when there is a murderer still roaming Whitehall," he said, apparently unhurt by her own bare foot. "One who thought ye would be dead that night, so he freely broke into your bed chamber to steal those gloves."

Maggie opened her mouth to refute all of it, but Kerr was right. She'd been desperate to get home and hadn't thought anyone would notice. Most people didn't notice her once she covered her hair. They looked past her face with freckles across it.

"Murderer?" William asked, his eyes wide as he looked at her.

Maggie slid her foot off of Kerr's and crossed her arms over her chest.

"The ruffian's head was nearly sliced off at the collarbone," Kerr said, "while we were summoning the guards to the stables. And then Maggie's room at Whitehall was broken into while she was out."

"And that's why I'm here," Maggie said as if brushing off the rest of what Kerr had revealed. She brought her bundle of gloves over to the table near the hearth, which she was thankful was warm. The pension from her father's and brother's years of service kept them living in moderate comfort. Maggie too would continue the legacy, teaching whatever children she had to take over her position if it worked out with the future monarchs. Right now, it was whispered that Elizabeth would never marry and produce heirs. And if Maggie stayed in service, it was unlikely she would wed to have children either.

She unrolled the dirty gloves carefully. Her father unfolded his spectacles, settling them on the bridge of his nose. The aging Reginald Darby might be fearful of the clothes people wore in his presence, but his innate curiosity and brilliant mind overcame this fear when a puzzle was placed before him.

"Kerr and I found them buried in the privy gardens," Maggie said. "The spaniels that chewed on them are well." She glanced at

Kerr. "I checked again before I left the palace." She inhaled fully and turned back to look down. "There are a few tears from the dogs' teeth, but I see no other abrasions. I fear the dirt has disturbed any poisons that could be inside."

"Why poison them if they were going to be stolen?" Kerr asked.

All three Darbys looked at him. "In case they were found, which they were," her father said. "Traitors can be tricky." Reginald looked at Maggie. "Were they wrapped in something before burying them?"

She nodded. "That is why I brought them. The dogs tore away the linen." She pointed at the thin satchel that the gloves were buried in. "I did not detect anything, but because they were possibly wrapped to be found intact, I wanted a second opinion."

"They are too dirty now for the queen to request to wear them," William said.

"So Maggie does not need to put them on," Kerr said. "And risk herself."

William nodded. "'Tis a risk we take on for our monarch, but we are all trained to detect the worst."

"And the dogs are well," Maggie said, the words more for herself in case her father felt she should still wear the dirty gloves.

Reginald inspected each long glove, taking swabs of the insides to plunk down in his own vials. Maggie had done the same, but with an obvious traitor on the loose, one who had no issue with murder, she wanted to be certain.

Maggie retrieved two cups of daily ale and brought one to Kerr. "This may take an hour or more. William can give you back your clothes, and you can return to court."

Kerr met her eyes with the intensity of one on a mission. "I will leave here when ye do." She opened her mouth to protest, but Kerr continued. "'Tis my duty to keep ye alive to protect the queen."

At the table, Maggie's father nodded. "Yes. Maggie must protect the queen." He looked over his shoulder at her. "You must stay alive for as long as the queen."

"I will try, Father."

Kerr frowned, his gaze going back and forth between them. Maggie felt her cheeks grow warm again, and she took a long sip of her ale.

Maggie sat farther down the table on a bench. "Well if you insist on staying, you can at least have a seat and relax, and you might even get the benefit of having a warm bath."

"Oh yes," her father said while adding some solvent to the vials. "Everyone gets baths."

KERR CHECKED HIS pace to walk next to Maggie as they made their way through the shadowed streets. They had spent several hours at the Darby house. The family seemed to have higher than average resources, including a large bathing tub in the back room. Even though King Henry did not take advantage of bathing, he'd hated anyone else to have an odor and insisted on anyone wearing his clothes to remain impeccably clean. The habit took root in the elderly man along with his fear of tainted clothing. Kerr and Maggie were clean, sweet smelling, and properly dressed before leaving.

Maggie glanced over her shoulder toward her house. "He is still brilliant, my father," she said and stepped briskly around a puddle in the cobblestone road. "William says he has demency, that his brain is addled with age." She shrugged slightly, the gentle lift of her shoulders part of the way she communicated with her whole self.

"I suppose William would know since he lives with him while I am up at Whitehall," she said. "But Father is still a wonderful resource for me. His distrustful mind leaves no test undone."

"Aye," Kerr said. "'Tis fortunate ye have someone ye trust to double check your efforts."

"I do not bring everything to him, of course," she said. "Some of those gowns are thirty pounds and too rich to take from the palace, but since there is a mystery around these gloves, I thought I better."

"'Tis good he found no poison," Kerr said.

"Quite," she answered as they continued down the lane. "Although it doesn't shed any light as to why they were stolen and buried."

She paused at an old woman sitting by a post with a lantern above. Poorly dressed and gaunt, the woman looked like many Kerr had seen sitting about as if nowhere to shelter. Maggie paused by the woman, bending down to push a shilling into her hand.

The old woman smiled up at her. "Thank you, milady."

Maggie straightened and they continued. "Begging is illegal," she said, her voice soft. "The royal counsel thinks that if they don't allow it, it will go away." She sighed as if feeling the weight of the needy on her shoulders. "The penalties are brutal. Public flogging for those judged fit enough to work."

Maggie stopped several times to disperse her extra spending money that she did not leave with her father and brother. Kerr added to it, winning a smile from her.

Nearing the gates, Maggie patted the satchel her father had given her to hold the dirty gloves and ripped bag she'd found them in. "I will report all of my findings on the gloves to Lord Burghley," she said as if thinking out loud. "No poison and no explanation of why they were taken or abused." She let loose a big huff, clearly unhappy with the lack of information. "Luckily the queen does not like to wear gloves overly much, instead preferring everyone to see her long, straight fingers and rich rings."

When they entered the gates, the guards nodded to Maggie and didn't question Kerr's presence. They still made faces as if they would spout slander if not for Maggie's presence. He walked her back through the halls where they surprised one man pissing behind a potted tree, two lovers trysting behind heavy drapes, and Johnathan Whitt who was in a quiet conversation with Lord Norfolk. The two men halted when they spotted Kerr and Maggie, turning outward. They nodded, and Maggie curtseyed. Kerr stood watchful, his hands ready at his sides.

"Any clues regarding the recovered gloves?" Whitt asked.

"I am afraid not," Maggie said. "They are free of anything foul, except dirt."

Norfolk shook his head. "Dreadful. Lord Whitt told me about the crime. That someone could sneak into your chambers… Walsingham should do something more about security in the palace." He glanced at Kerr. "With so many foreigners about, there is bound to be crime."

Kerr kept his irritation in check, his words smooth. "Aye, when I forget my lady gloves, the first thing I attempt to do is break into a lady's room and pilfer a pair. Or six."

Maggie put a hand up to her mouth to stifle a laugh. Whitt sniffed indignantly, but Norfolk's mouth turned up in a smile. "Well then," Norfolk said, "hopefully Mistress Darby can find you a pair to wear to the Saint Valentine's festival tomorrow."

"Will the queen partake?" Kerr asked, looking between the two men. This could be his chance to speak with her. All he had to do was read the letter and give her the wrapped wooden box from Mary. Word would reach her that he'd accomplished the mission she had set him upon, and she would send the letter supporting the marriage between Rhona and Percy Hay.

Norfolk smiled. "Of course. She loves to dabble with all the handsome, intriguing courtiers. You might even win your audience with her."

Kerr cocked his head to the side, assessing Lord Norfolk. Lord Whitt obviously distrusted Kerr, whether for being Scots or being a Catholic Gordon. But Norfolk didn't seem to care. "Well then," Kerr said, "I will attempt to be as intriguing as possible."

Norfolk held his gaze. "See that you do."

"Good day Lord Whitt, Lord Norfolk," Maggie said, pulling

Kerr along as if she were concerned that their slight banter might turn toward darker talk or escalate.

They walked back to Maggie's room in silence, stopping before her door. "I will check your room," Kerr said.

"No need," Maggie said, smiling. She bent low and flicked a small twig that sat about a foot off the floor, caught in the door. "No one has disturbed my twig," she whispered and straightened.

Kerr felt his usual serious mouth soften into a grin. "Ye used my precaution."

Maggie smiled up at him with mischievous eyes, reminding him of a fabled wood nymph with her teasing grin. "Of course. It is clever and effective if it's almost undetectable. I will likely stick leaves and twigs in the crack of my doors now until the end of my days."

In the dimly lit corridor, the light blue of her eyes looked dark like sapphires. The softness of her lips turned up at the corners enough to show the edge of her white teeth. She was beautiful. She'd be even more so with the mountains of his homeland behind her and the fresh Highland breeze blowing through her long red-gold hair.

Her lips parted as she took in a slow breath, but then she turned away, jamming the iron key into the lock and turning it. "I have a multitude of gowns and accessories to recheck."

"I can help," Kerr said.

Maggie turned back in the open doorway. "Thank you, but…" She bit gently on her bottom lip. "I'm expecting Cordelia and Lucy to visit the moment they hear I'm back in the palace. They are trying to decide what to wear to the Saint Valentine's celebration."

Maggie slowly closed the door, leaving only her perfectly formed face in the crack. "And you can practice your speech from Mary Stuart. Tomorrow may be your only chance to deliver it." She slowly closed the door as he stared at her eyes until the oak separated them completely, leaving him in darkness.

Chapter Six

"To be a king and wear a crown is a thing more glorious to them that see it than it is pleasant to them that bear it."
Queen Elizabeth I of England

THE GREAT HALL of Whitehall Palace was flooded with the light from hundreds of candles. The one night's supply could keep his father's castle lit for a month or more. Such decadence was both praised by the European powers and despised by the poor of England. All it did was make Kerr ache to return to the rugged, open moors of his homeland.

Yet he stood amongst the richly plumed aristocratic men and opulently draped ladies in their voluminous petticoats. Some ladies had costumes with some sort of contraption beneath to make their skirts flare out two feet in every direction from their cinched waists. They could barely move about with such ridiculous, sprawling ensembles. He doubted that most of the doors could even accommodate them.

A long table sat at one end near the hearth, the glow from the flames shining off the polished shields, pikes, and swords hung over and around it. At home, Kerr knew exactly which swords hanging over their hearth were hewn for true defense and which were dull and ornamental. Even with Elizabeth's guards stationed at all the entrances and Walsingham moving about, surely some of the weapons gracing the walls next to rich tapestries and paintings were strategically placed to be grabbed if needed to defend their queen. Since Pope Pius had excommunicated Elizabeth the year before, security against Catholics, who'd been encouraged by Pius to kill the queen, had no doubt increased.

Did Pius realize how his decree had made life even more difficult for Mary Stuart, locked away and considered a plotting criminal by most? Did Pius care? Likely not. He wanted the "heretic queen" off the throne of England and Ireland and would stop at nothing to see it done.

Kerr stood away from the hearth closer to one of the archways where the hint of cool air could still be felt in the stuffy room. Between the candles, hearth, and press of perfumed bodies, refreshing air had been all but thwarted.

"I'm surprised Lord Burghley let you inside," said the guard by the arch where Kerr said. "I suppose you found a place to wash." He chuckled.

Kerr recognized the man as Henry, one of the guards by the gate the day he arrived. He didn't bother to look down at what he was wearing. He was clean from head to toe and wearing a bright kilt and bleached white tunic, his beard clipped and his hair hanging loose around his jaw.

"Congratulations on finding a bath yourself." Kerr stared out toward the man who had walked over to the opposite archway. "Good eve."

Kerr stepped away to get a better look at Elizabeth as Burghley escorted her into the room. The voices hushed in reverence and people bowed low as the English queen paused for dramatic effect, her sharp gaze scanning the room. It landed on Kerr, and he nodded slowly to her. She frowned slightly as if she expected him to grovel instead. She wore crimson and black velvet spread over one of the broad hip farthingales. The material was intricately stitched with birds in gold thread. Kerr had hidden behind it in Maggie's room the other morning. The gown must have been thoroughly checked and worn again by Maggie.

Maggie Darby. He'd spent most of the morning trying to see her, only to hear the chattering, laughing Cordelia and Lucy

56

sequestered in her room with her. Instead of seeking out a chance audience with the queen, Kerr had spent most of the day listening at the wall between them to make certain Maggie was safe. Was she still getting ready? Could she have succumbed to a chemical in the gown she was wearing tonight?

Kerr almost turned from the room to seek her out when she appeared behind the queen with her ladies. Where most of the queen's attendants were dressed in dark browns and grays, Maggie wore a blue gown with intricately stitched bands of tapestry on the bodice and the edge of her petticoat.

Maggie's gaze slid about the room. Did she search for the courtier she suspected of stealing the gloves? Her eyes stopped when they met Kerr's, and a gentle smile turned up the corners of her mouth. Kerr felt his own mouth relax and rubbed a hand over his mouth at the unfamiliar feeling.

"Continue," Queen Elizabeth intoned, and the musicians started up the lively tune that had given the room a festive feel before she entered. Lord Robert Dudley took Lord Burghley's place at the queen's arm. He escorted her to her throne-like seat at the back of the room where she could watch the dancing and partake in food that had most assuredly already been tasted for poison.

Maggie nodded to several ladies as she walked around the edge of the room, her blue gown flowing around a gentle swell at her hips, not like the platform that held the dresses out of many of the other ladies. Her hair was half up and tucked with pearls while a black velvet veil covered the golden curls going down her back. Curls that smelled of jasmine that her father worked into the soap he made. They had both returned with bars the other day.

Kerr frowned as Johnathan Whitt stepped before her, offering her a glass of wine and one of the gingerbread cakes that sat on platters around the room. Shaped into hearts and birds, the thin, crispy gingerbread represented the heat of love on St. Valentine's Day with its expensive spices to warm the tongue. Maggie took the wine but turned down the gingerbread, making Whitt frown when she moved on.

With slow progress, Maggie finally drew closer to Kerr. She picked up her own gingerbread from a tray and nibbled the edge, her gaze finding him again. Pretty white teeth, lusciously soft lips, a hidden warmth inside. Kerr shook his head slightly at the insanity of wishing he were a piece of gingerbread in Maggie Darby's fingers.

A deep voice beside Kerr sharpened his thoughts and tightened his stance. "I will introduce you to the queen." Lord Norfolk stood there, his gaze on the throne. "'Tis unlikely that Burghley or Walsingham will do so. Anything to do with Mary Stuart puts Elizabeth in a foul mood."

Kerr dragged his gaze from Maggie, whose smile had flattened as she watched Norfolk. "And ye would tempt her poor mood?"

The man, the ruff around his neck edged with gold leaf, shrugged. "She also likes a handsome man who banters with her, and I saw her watch you. Can you banter, Scotsman?"

Courtly love, and all the ridiculous flirtation required, irritated Kerr. He'd been warned about it by his sister. Poorly rhymed poetry and false words of love hid any sincere attraction. To Kerr, courtly love was another way of telling lies. "I banter with my sword," he said.

Norfolk chuckled. "Best use your tongue instead, else find yourself on the scaffold or at the very least exiled from her presence and palace." Norfolk took a few steps away. "Come, Scotsman."

Bloody hell. Maggie had almost reached him. She watched him over the rim of her glass, and he nodded to her and turned to follow the tall Norfolk in his green stockings and inflated short breeches.

The courtiers parted, allowing them to walk directly toward Elizabeth. Many of the attendees eyed him with open suspicion, turning to each other to whisper. Others looked at his costume and presence with mere curiosity. Lord Whitt stood talking with Maggie's friend, Cordelia Cranfield. Whitt murmured something through his thin lips, but she kept watching Kerr. He nodded to her as he passed, and she fanned her face with the splay of peacock feathers in her hand. Despite the musicians playing, the room had taken on a stillness as people watched.

Stopping several feet back, Norfolk bowed low, his flat, velvet cap nearly falling off. "Your Majesty," he said, his voice carrying. He stayed low, waiting. She said nothing, and the musicians quit as if some great drama was about to unfold.

Kerr bowed at his waist, his gaze on the crisscross ties of his leather boots. *One, two, three…* Rhona had schooled him in the bow, and told him to count the times his laces crossed one another to ensure he'd held the bow long enough to please a queen. He reached twelve and straightened. Had it been long enough? Elizabeth stared hard at him, her steely gaze taking in every detail he was willing to reveal. This was a woman with the courage of a king, much like Mary Stuart.

"Rise, Lord Norfolk, before your blood fills your head and makes you swoon," Elizabeth said still inspecting Kerr. "And introduce me to this handsome and defiant Scotsman."

"Your Majesty," Norfolk intoned. "This is Kerr Gordon from Auchindoun Castle in Banffshire, Scotland. He is the son of George Gordon, a Catholic."

Bloody hell. Not the best introduction.

"And where do your loyalties lie, Sir Gordon?" Elizabeth asked, her words clipped. "Do you seek me out to spill my blood on the altar of Pope Pius?"

"I doubt very much that I would have made it past your watchdogs if that were the case, Your Majesty," Kerr said.

She leaned forward in her high-backed chair. "To whom are you loyal then, Scotsman?"

Kerr met her hard stare. "I am loyal to my sister, a wholesome and strong woman who wishes to marry in order to prevent more bloodshed in my homeland."

Elizabeth set her large ostrich-feather fan in her lap and steepled her fingers to rest under her pointy chin. Her brows furrowed. "And why does that bring you to my court?"

Kerr inhaled and reached slowly into his layered cape that draped his shoulder. He produced the small, wrapped box Mary had given him to gift Elizabeth. "If I am permitted to give ye this and read this letter to ye, Mary Stuart will support the marriage between my sister and Percy Hay."

At the name of Mary Stuart, Elizabeth's entire face frowned, not just her thin, painted lips, but her eyes, etched brows, and even her high cheekbones seemed to pinch inward. But Kerr continued. "The Gordons and Hays have been feuding for decades, ruining the lives of men, women, and children on both sides. If Chief Hay is swayed to accept my sister's hand for his son, there will be a chance for peace."

"And my cousin will not support this unless you deliver her letter and gift?" Elizabeth asked.

"Aye," Kerr said. Norfolk cleared his throat, his brow furrowed as if prompting Kerr. "Your Majesty," Kerr finished.

"And why under heaven would I want to end a feud between two Catholic clans to my north?" Elizabeth asked, disdain in her words. "When they could join forces in an attempt to put Mary on my throne? Why would I do that?"

Kerr met her dark eyes with strength and honesty. "Because I am next to be chief to the Gordon Clan, and I do not follow the Catholic cause of my ailing father."

"Does my Scottish cousin know that?" Elizabeth asked her words snapping.

"Nay, 'twould have been foolish to admit when she tasked me with this mission in payment for her support. Although now that I have proclaimed it aloud, there is no doubt it will reach her. That does not change the fact that I love my sister and clan above any religion or prince. And so, at Mary Stuart's bidding, in return for her support of the union between Hay and Gordon, I beseech ye to let me read Mary's letter to ye and receive her gift." This was the time to look humble. Since Kerr knew his acting skills were terrible, he again looked at his boot laces in an attempt.

When he looked up, Cecil was whispering in Elizabeth's pale ear where a large pearl tugged on the lobe as if it were biting her. *Does it pain her?* The thought made him rub at his own ear lobe.

Elizabeth's gaze shot behind Kerr to the back of the muted hall. "Sacrificial Lamb," Elizabeth intoned. "Come forward."

Sacrificial Lamb. The fact that the English queen had given her a name showed that she favored Maggie, but the title made Kerr's jaw ache.

Maggie wove slowly between the courtiers, coming forward. Kerr held the gift and letter by his sides, wishing he'd been allowed to wear his sword in the hall. Not that he'd have drawn it but holding onto the hilt helped him contain his anger.

"Your Majesty," Maggie said and lowered into a curtsey with such grace that her dress belled out around her, the air underneath escaping little by little to let the blue velvet encircle her on the paved floor.

"My sweet lamb," Elizabeth said with warmth in her voice. "Rise and come to me."

Maggie rose and walked forward, letting the queen take her hand. "This Scotsman saved you from a depraved rogue in the stables?"

Would she admit he had saved her?

"Master Gordon assisted me, yes," Maggie said, and Kerr's frown faded as the side of his mouth rose at her choice of words.

"And he helped me retrieve the stolen gloves," Maggie continued. "And assisted me in testing them for poisons, of which there were none found."

Elizabeth looked over her to Kerr, assessing him. "And you believe this man to be one of honor, even though he is a Catholic Scot on a mission from Mary Stuart?"

Maggie turned to study Kerr with her monarch, the entire room focusing on his back. Kerr felt pinned by all the gazes and stood straight and tall, his legs braced as if for battle. He was like a mighty stag surrounded by hounds, or vipers. His hands fisted, itching for a sword. Perhaps one above Elizabeth's head.

Maggie looked back to Elizabeth. "Your Majesty. I have labored to discover any substance that could harm Your Majesty for my entire life, having been schooled by my father who guarded your own father, the great King Henry. I have developed a critical and sensitive sense of what is dangerous, and my heart tells me..." She looked back at Kerr, "that Kerr Gordon is not a danger to Your Majesty. His desire to help his sister and prevent bloodshed is honest. I do not see him leading or participating in any revolt against Your Majesty."

Elizabeth kept her small eyes tethered to Kerr, judging him against her knowledge of people and politics and her natural instincts for survival. As if thawing with an early spring, her tight lips relaxed into a smile, a flirtatious glint sparking in her dark eyes that were said to be so like her own mother's. "You may have saved my lamb from the clutches of evil, but she now has saved you from the clutches of a queen. See that she is rewarded."

Kerr exhaled slowly. "May I read this letter and deliver the gift?"

Elizabeth waved her long fingers at the musicians who began a lively tune. "After you reward my lamb with a dance." One of her arched brows rose higher. "I hope that you know more than a country jig, Master Gordon." Elizabeth turned to her favorite, Lord Robert Dudley, and he immediately presented his arm to lead Elizabeth down to the dance floor.

The queen left Kerr standing there with his letter and wrapped box in his hand. *Daingead.*

Maggie walked closer. "She chose la volta," she said, low. "We can wait for another."

"I know the dance." Kerr secured the letter in the folds of his wrap and the box back in the leather satchel flung over his shoulder under his short cape.

"La volta?" she asked, surprise in the largeness of her lash-framed eyes.

He presented his arm. "I endured several lessons from Rhona before I traveled to court." The dance steps actually reminded him of the patterns he practiced in battle training. Lightness of foot and the ability to move one's body were as important as physical strength in battle. That way the entire body became a weapon. Years of feuding had prepared Kerr for battle on a misty moor, but now the battle had moved to a golden hall.

Kerr led Maggie into the center where Elizabeth and Dudley had already begun the dance which required the man to grip the woman around the waist and lift her, turning them both. Rhona had said the dance was considered scandalous in some places, but apparently scandal was not something that worried Elizabeth overly much. She still paraded around with Lord Dudley, her favorite who had never fully rid himself of the whispered guilt over his first wife's mysterious death ten years earlier.

Three other pairs had also come forward, Elizabeth's ladies, dressed in dull colors to allow their queen to shine. Although Maggie was by far more beautiful than any of them, even if she'd been wearing gray and not the brilliant blue of the gown Elizabeth must have gifted her. Perhaps since Maggie was of a lower class, the vain queen did not see her as competition in her royal circle.

Kerr turned his mind to the steps of the dance. *Like with Rhona. Like a bloody battle.* He took a full breath and gave a shallow bow to Maggie as she lowered into a small curtsey. Then she hopped, and Kerr's feet moved in time with the musician's fast pace. Where Maggie's voluminous skirt hid most of her steps, everyone watched his. It was almost unnerving. People didn't watch when he battled, although they did when he trained. Kerr imagined his warriors in place of the judging courtiers and turned in a dandy circle, his feet moving through the hops and steps of the dance. His back remained straight, and his shoulders back and broad.

"You are doing well," Maggie whispered as she passed him, their backs nearly coming in contact. She sounded surprised.

Now for the lift and turn. Kerr placed his hands on Maggie's narrow waist. He could feel the rigid boning that gave a smooth line to her bodice, like a set of armor. How would her waist feel bare under his hands? The thought nearly made him lose count of his steps, but his constant battle training saved him.

He lifted her, turned, and set her down a quarter circle to the right. Even with the heavy layers of material, she was much lighter than the stones he moved to build muscle. He lifted her up again and down, three more times to bring them back around.

Maggie's smile caught his gaze. "You dance like you are warring," she said, a bit breathless.

They came together. "Is that bad?" he asked and slowly twirled her away from him. He caught her fingers to reel her back in. The blue gown belled out in sweeping grandeur, showing off its rich embellishments and layers of rich fabric.

She stopped before him, still attached, and smiled up into his face. "You can relax a bit," she said, looking at his hand that held hers. "'Tis a dance, not a battle." Unguarded and breathing fast, she seemed to tease.

"I know much more about battle than dance, but in both instances, quick feet keep one alive," he said, studying the way the light played across her high cheekbones, the shadows unable to mute the spark of fun in her eyes.

"Alive?"

He leaned closer toward her ear. "Surrounded by hunting hounds, court is a battleground." She smelled lightly of jasmine. He noticed that her inhale caught, and he backed up slowly, keeping her close while music for another dance began.

"You worry about your person here?" she asked, her words a bit breathless.

"I keep on guard always. Like ye."

She swallowed, her long neck free of the ruff that so many wore. "We are alike then," she said. "Always watching for danger, because we are placed where hounds roam."

He caught her fingers. They were slender and strong. Their

gazes locked. "Aye," he said, marveling in the way little flecks of dark color cast out from her pupils, making her eyes so much more beautiful. It seemed, the more he studied Maggie Darby, the more fascinating she became. Her lush lips were parted and pink. They looked as soft as her touch.

Suddenly Norfolk appeared at his side. *Mo chreach!* Kerr guided Maggie slightly behind him.

Norfolk grinned. "Exceptional dancing," he said. "The queen will receive Mary's gift and letter, unless you would rather continue to stare at one another and cause more tongues to wag."

Kerr glanced across the room where most people were watching Maggie and him standing on the edge of the cleared floor. "Of course," Kerr said.

Before he could move away, Maggie placed her hand on his arm and lifted onto her toes near his ear. "'Tis best we stay on guard together then." The pressure of her hand, voluntarily on his arm, as they walked forward together sent heat through his body.

"Your Majesty," Norfolk intoned, nearing the throne Elizabeth had retaken after la volta. "A gift and letter from your cousin, the Scottish queen, Mary Stuart," Norfolk continued. "Appropriate perhaps on this day devoted to love."

Elizabeth snorted softly. "Love? That she would declare such when she speaks from the other cheek with slander on her tongue." But she beckoned Kerr with her hand.

Maggie let go of his arm, and he withdrew the box and letter again. "I was instructed quite severely to read the letter myself," he said.

That made the queen grin. "Quite severely? I can imagine. My cousin is not a timid mouse." Her fingers moved through the air. "Very well. Read at will but give me the box to hold."

Kerr set the wooden box on the intricately embroidered petticoat covering Elizabeth's lap and showed her the unbroken seal of Mary Stuart on the parchment. Then he broke it with his thumb, already knowing what it held since the Scottish queen had made him rehearse reading it with heart. Although, he could not bring himself to deliver it with Mary's high theatrics here before the English court.

"Dearest sister, my gracious Queen Elizabeth.

I remain in this block of gray stone, a prisoner watched by dour-faced uncompromising dogs. I beseech you for release or at least a longer tether and have no evil plans or forethought of tyranny and betrayal. Those who say otherwise tell falsehoods, and God, in his ultimate power, will see them burn. For I am loyal to my sister-queen, women and royals together, and decreed by God to govern their lands as sovereign peoples, supporting one another and loving one another as sisters of royal Tudor blood.

I send with this warrior of Scotland, a gift rendered by my own fingers from my heart to yours. They hold love and goodwill for Your Majesty. May you live long and remain strong and true to us. Your fond sister, Mary."

Elizabeth's face took on the lines and pinching of her growing years when Kerr looked up to meet her gaze.

"She calls you sister, though you are cousins," Dudley said next to her.

Elizabeth's looked down at the box with painted swirls on its lid. "'Tis affection she wishes to build between us, affection I offered years ago, but her rash actions and mutinous melancholy have turned my affection cold."

Dudley patted her bare hand. "See what her fingers have wrought while she waits on your forgiveness."

Elizabeth beckoned to Burghley who pulled a short blade to cut through the knotted ribbons keeping the box tightly locked. He had no idea what the gift was and really did not care. His mission had been accomplished. Mild curiosity kept his eyes on the queen's lap. What would fit in the medium-size box? A thin pillow for her arse? A pair of embroidered stockings? A prayer cloth or veil? Jewels to bite her earlobes?

Elizabeth's agile fingers lifted the lid, and she pulled out white-bleached leather, rolled tightly together. Wide cuffs of fabric were stitched with initials and birds flying free from iron cages. As the queen unrolled the gift the rest of the way, exposing long tapered fingers, Kerr's stomach hardened. *Daingead.* He did not look at Maggie who stood by his side.

Elizabeth's one brow rose as she held up the long pair of lady's gloves. "Well now," she said, meeting Kerr's gaze with renewed suspicion. "A gift of perfumed gloves at the exact time I am in need of a new pair."

CHAPTER SEVEN

*"If you prick us do we not bleed? If you tickle us do we not
laugh?*
If you poison us do we not die?
And if you wrong us shall we not revenge?"
William Shakespeare – *Merchant of Venice*

"**G**LOVES?" MAGGIE SAID, her whisper loud with her
incredulity.

"I did not know the gift was gloves," Kerr answered as his
wide strides kept up with her rapid steps back up to her room.
She carried Mary Stuart's gift, back in its box. The queen wanted
to wear the gloves this Valentine's night, so Maggie needed to
wear them first. Fortunately, the queen had allowed Maggie to
leave the hall to check the gift for poisons before donning them.

"What did you think it was then?" Maggie asked. "A bird
cage? A lap dog? A gem encrusted amulet?" Maggie threw her
arm out as she spoke, letting it swing down by her side with
vigor. "It was small and made no sound when shaken to denote a
jewel."

"It could have been stockings or an altar cloth." He shook his
head. "I do not know ladies' accoutrements. Mary is said to
embroider to speed the passing of time."

"And just when the queen suddenly has had all her gloves
stolen for no apparent reason other than making it necessary to

wear your gloves immediately."

"They are not *my* gloves."

She flapped her empty hand. "You brought them."

Stopping before her door, Maggie glanced around to see where she could set the gloves, and Kerr took them from her hands. She reached down to pluck the undisturbed holly leaf that sat three inches from the floorboard and stuck the heavy key in the iron lock. "You can leave me here. I will test them for poison and wear them for an hour before returning to the queen." She pushed into her room, barring the way with her body.

"Ye should not be left alone," Kerr said, his ruggedly handsome face tightening with anger and concern. Concern for her? Or concern for what she would find?

There had been something between them during the dance. Hadn't there been? Some said la volta tricked couples into thinking there was passion between them by teasing them with a touch and rousing the pulse to mimic love. What she had felt, the warmth, the giddiness in her middle, it could all have been a farce.

"I will be well alone," she said and tried to shut the door, but Kerr's boot remained in the gap.

"I will wait for ye," he said.

Could he care for her? Her stomach did a little flip, but she squashed it. His mission was done anyway, and her vanity would make her vulnerable heart squeeze when he rode away. Tomorrow perhaps? He was the next in line to be a clan chief and must return to his beloved Scotland. She hadn't known all of that. *Foolish.* She should know more about a man she'd let into her confidence.

She tipped her chin upward. "Surely you have more important things to do than wait outside my door." She flipped her free hand about. "Save your clan, feed your horse, use the privy—"

"Your safety is more important than taking a piss and my horse's belly," he said, cutting her off.

She met his eyes, searching. For what? Some hint that he

truly did not know Mary had sent gloves? A glimmer of true concern for her?

She forced a smile. "So I fall somewhere above your horse and below your family. If I had a horse, that's where you would fall too, unless, I suppose, I'd drank three goblets of wine. Then the privy might move ahead."

Was she angry or teasing? Kerr's brows gathered as he studied her. He was confused, but then so was Maggie.

Kerr rested his hands on her straight shoulders as he bent to look in her face. "Nothing has changed since before the queen opened the gift."

Did he mean during la volta when he held her so firmly? She met his eyes, searching. "Everything has changed," she whispered.

"Not my honor," he said, his words hard.

Her inhale caught as he leaned in, and the faintest tickle of his breath touched her lips, almost like a kiss. "I swear, Maggie." He paused for a moment, as if a kiss hung in the air between them, but then he backed up. "I swear that I did not know what was in the box. Mary gave it to me tied."

Maggie drew in breath to feed her thumping heart, wetting her lips. She cleared her throat, trying to shake the feeling that they had in fact kissed. "Did she ask you not to open it?"

He blinked as he stared at her, his frown intensifying. "I do not recall. It was surely inferred if not said."

Staring into the stormy gray of his eyes, Maggie felt she could lose herself there. Did she want to lose herself? Her daydreams of running away from court bloomed more and more often. She'd become a simple country woman and live where no one depended on her to keep the queen from poison. But right that moment she had a job to do, not only to protect the queen but since she must don the gloves, she must protect herself.

She searched his hard features. He certainly looked honorable when he stared at her so intensely. "You could escort me and the gift to Her Majesty when I am done." She took a step backward and broke the tether of Kerr's stare, looking down to the floor as she slowly shut the door.

Closing her eyes, she took a full inhale. *The queen is depending on me.* The mantra she told herself daily filled her head, and she turned, her skirts belling out with the force.

Rushing to her laboratory table, Maggie set the box down and unfolded the gloves. She had two glass vials ready, one with acid and one with water. Those who poisoned gloves usually pushed the lethal substance down into the fingertips with hopes it would get under the wearer's fingernails. Then when the victim pulled the gloves off and ate, the poison would transfer to the food and enter the body that way. Although some poisons could be absorbed through the skin too, so Maggie would swab all ten fingertips and the interior cloth that would touch the palms and backs of the hand.

She sniffed gently. No smell of bitter almonds. She smelled only a slight tang of animal urine, used to tan the leather, under the sweet smell of jasmine imbued into the gloves. A glance inside revealed no obvious residue. Maggie took long sticks with cotton tied at the ends, sliding one into each finger of the glove and swirling them around before removing them to inspect. Nothing that she could see. No bluish white or pure white powder. Nothing damp.

One by one she set the ends of the cotton swabs into both the water and the acid vials to see if anything came off them. She saw nothing unusual. Jotting all her observations she saw or didn't see into her journal, Maggie took the acid vial to the apparatus to clamp near the flame. She would heat it and see if a gas was produced that would make a brown spot on a small square of glass that she had clamped over it. It was a test for arsenic that her father used.

Had Kerr returned to the banquet? *No concern of mine.* Did he really not know the gift was a pair of gloves? *He seems so honorable.* If only there was a test that she could perform by swabbing him and testing to see if he was up to treachery or not.

Maggie paused, glancing at the wall beyond as a smile overtook her. *Swabbing Kerr Gordon!* She snorted softly and looked back down at the vial she was heating over the candle.

The liquid bubbled, emitting a gas over which she held the glass. Condensation frosted it, but no brown spot emerged. Maggie released her breath. No one poisoned the gloves. At least not with the commonly detected poisons.

"He wouldn't let me put the gloves on knowing they were poisoned anyway," she whispered. At least she felt sure of that. She sighed, letting her head hang as she slid through all the information she had gathered on Kerr Gordon. "He is honorable," she whispered and picked up the gloves, shaking them one last time. Nothing fell out.

They were slender and long with three layers of thick embroidery encircling them at intervals from the wrist up to the elbows. "Beautiful," Maggie said as she inspected the stitches that Mary Stuart had made depicting a bird in a cage and a bird flying free. The message was not subtle, but then nothing about the Scots queen was subtle.

Mary Stuart was the bird locked in the cage and she wanted desperately to be free. But freedom for Mary made war for England as the Catholics tried to dethrone Elizabeth Tudor. One woman's imprisonment prevented a civil war that would kill thousands.

Still, Maggie knew everything about this mess with Mary upset Elizabeth exceedingly. Elizabeth preferred for them to be monarchs of their own countries, working together for the benefit of both Scotland and England. But with Mary's son on the throne of Scotland, the only thing Mary could do was incite a revolt. The woman was much more likely to try to take Elizabeth's throne than her own son's throne.

Maggie slid the left glove on, wiggling her fingers into their spots. No itching or burning. "Well, there shouldn't be after I tested," she said, chiding herself. She believed in the science her father had taught her.

Maggie slid her right hand into the matching glove. Her fingers slid deeply into place before she froze. Her breath caught, all the hairs standing on her nape. Hard, steely teeth pressed cold against the skin of her wrist, right where her pulse beat like a bird's desperate wings as it tried to escape the snare.

She moved instinctually to rip her arm back out, the blades embedded in the wrist cuff angled so that they sliced into her skin. Instantly blood began to seep through the embroidery. Maggie screamed.

⟫⟫⟩⟨⟨⟨

KERR CIRCLED THE perimeter of his room like a lion in a cage. His gaze raked across his few belongings that he'd set on the washstand. Nothing seemed out of place, yet someone had disturbed the leaf in his door. He'd had nothing to steal except his long sword and *sgian dubh* that he'd been ordered to leave behind before attending the banquet, and they were still present.

The only thing he found that may or may not have been there before was a needle and spool of white thread set under his bed. He looked once more at the strange leaving that he'd set on the writing desk. Why the bloody hell would someone break into his room to leave domestic items?

The scream tore straight through Kerr, and he snapped around toward the wall that separated their rooms. "Maggie!" He surged out of his room and pounded on her door. "Maggie. Maggie, open the door. What's wrong?"

He heard the key turn and pushed forward around the door to see Maggie holding her arm out before her. Face pale, her eyes looked too big in her beautiful, heart-shaped face.

"What's happened?" he asked. She backed away as if she were afraid or uncertain.

He looked down at the arm she held out, covered with one of the gloves. The red stain of blood seeped through the embroidery at her wrist. "Daingead. Ye are bleeding."

"There are blades sewn into the wrist," she said and blinked back what could be tears, either of disbelief or rage.

He reached to pull the glove off, but she yanked her arm back. "'Tis so tight that if you pull it farther off, it will slice deeper, maybe severing a vein," she said.

"Bloody hell," he murmured and yanked his *sgian dubh* from its sheath at his belt. "I will cut it off ye."

"You will ruin the glove," she said, snatching her arm to the side.

"'Tis no good if it has been tainted by an assassin. Give me your blasted arm, woman."

"If the blades were soaked in poison, I may be dead soon anyway." Her words were straightforward without emotion. "Arsenic, Oleander, Monkhood, Hemlock, Nightshade." Her eyes shut. "I feel dizzy."

Kerr re-sheathed his blade and swooped Maggie up in his arms. She gasped, her eyes flying open as he carried her to sit on the edge of the bed. "Hold your arm out straight," he said. He gave no room for arguing in his order, and he drew the hewn blade.

Maggie held her arm out, propped with her other hand to steady it. Kerr positioned himself by her side and slid the blade upward carefully at the cuff, slicing the bleached deer hide leather all the way down to her wrist.

"Fok," he cursed low at the damage the tiny blades, like sharp teeth, had done to Maggie's skin. Ignoring the swelling of blood, he continued to slice down each finger in case there were more blades sewn into the leather.

She breathed rapidly. He rattled off a series of curses in Gaelic. Was there poison on the blades? Was Maggie's heart racing from some elixir meant to steal the queen's life or only concern? He couldn't stop to ask. "Blasted glove," he murmured, opening the thin chambers that held her pale fingers. Finally, the last one was parted, and he let the entire glove drop off Maggie's wet arm.

The blood dripped from her, thick and dark. He yanked off a cloth he carried from his belt. "Hold this on the cuts." When she didn't immediately do it, he lifted her other hand that was still in its glove to press it on the wound.

Kerr ran across the room to the washstand, bringing the pitcher of water and the linens closer to her.

"I've gotten blood on my gown," she said, her voice small.

"How soon would any poison affect ye?"

"I... I am not sure," she said, meeting his eyes. "I didn't detect any poison in the gloves with my swabbing, so it may have been blades alone."

Dammit! How did blades get into the glove? Had Mary meant them for Elizabeth or did someone else sew them in? Was it meant to kill Elizabeth or just to implicate Mary in an assassination plot, so Elizabeth would be forced to sign her death order? Could the Hays have secretly sent Kerr on this quest, knowing the outcome would prevent any alliance with their enemies? There were too many questions and no answers, and at that moment none of it mattered except getting Maggie's arm to stop bleeding.

"Is the other glove safe to remove?" he asked as he applied pressure to Maggie's bleeding wrist.

"I think," she said, the words breathless.

Kerr pulled on each finger, waiting for Maggie to nod at each step along the way, until the tight-fitting glove slid off, leaving her left arm unmarred. He tossed it on the floor and knelt next to her.

She had placed one of the linen towels on her lap, resting her long, slender arm there as he held pressure on the cuts. They didn't say anything for long minutes. Kerr listened to her inhales and exhales.

"Do ye feel faint?" he asked.

She shook her head. "The cuts sting. I'm glad I tested for poisons first."

"I need to look at your cuts." He waited for her nod, before lifting the towel. Two rows of three slices each marred the delicate skin of her wrist over her veins. If she had tugged the glove off quickly, the blades could have bit deeper, severing her veins. His gut tightened with fury, and he peered closer. "If we wash and apply a poultice and keep it wrapped tightly, they should heal without the need for stitching."

Her head brushed his as she bent over her wrist to inspect the red-stained skin. "Six cuts in a most sensitive place. An assassin's attempt." She tipped her head to meet his gaze. "Of which you know nothing?"

Fury still twisted Kerr's stomach at the risk to Maggie, and it bled into his answer. "I did not know the gift was a pair of gloves. Mary did not say. And I surely would not have let ye don them if I'd known they were laced with blades."

She let out a long exhale, her face relaxing into what looked like belief. "I had to ask," she said. "'Tis my duty to the queen."

He stared hard at her. "'Tis also your duty to report this."

Her lips tuned inward as if she fought to hold back her answer.

Kerr shook his head. "Why would Mary give Elizabeth reason to execute her in such a blatant way? Mary would not be so obvious if she were to attempt an assassination. She would want nothing tied to her name."

Maggie let him hold the pressure on her wrist. "Would anyone want to see you hang, Kerr?"

Kerr's inhale stopped. The spool and needle under his bed. He let his exhale out long. "It seems the answer to that is aye."

Rap. Rap. Rap.

"Mistress Darby, are you done with the testing?" called a man through her door. "The queen is asking for her gloves."

Maggie's eyes snapped wide, her gaze going between the door and Kerr.

Rap. Rap. Rap. "Mistress Darby?"

"Good God," Maggie whispered, her eyes wild. "'Tis Walsingham, Elizabeth's spymaster."

CHAPTER EIGHT

*"I call God to witness that as a private person I have done
nothing unbeseeming an honest man, nor, as I bear the place of
a public man, have I done anything unworthy of my place."*

Francis Walsingham – Elizabeth I's Spymaster

M AGGIE'S HEART BEAT so hard that her head swam. Poison or
panic? Both could see someone dead. She looked down at
her arm covered in blood. There were blood drops on the floor
along with a mangled, massacred, bloody glove with blades sewn
into it.

"Mistress Darby? Are you well?" She could hear him jangling
keys. Of course, the head of Elizabeth's security would have a set
of keys to all the rooms in the palace.

"I am well," she called, loudly. "Please give me a moment.
I've…" Her gaze snapped to her laboratory table and then to
Kerr's *sgian dubh* laying on the floor, tinged with blood. "I've
made a terrible mess."

Maggie tugged away from Kerr who followed her to the
table.

"A mess?" Walsingham asked. "I will enter and help you."

"No!" she yelled. "Wait one moment."

Maggie turned to her table, grabbing a glass vial. She walked
quickly to her bed, grabbed a pillow and went to the place on the
floor where the glove and blood lay. Next to it she crouched.

Good God! What was she doing? It was her job to report all suspicious activity, and a glove with blades sewn into the wrist was definitely suspicious. She should be throwing open her door to show Walsingham.

She glanced at Kerr who retrieved his blade, wiping it clean. He watched her closely, probably thinking the same thing. Would she throw him to the hounds of Elizabeth's court? They would tear him apart, torturing him, blaming him or Mary Stuart. There were many at court who wanted the Scots Queen executed, including Lord Walsingham.

"Open the door," Walsingham said, obviously noting the panic in her voice.

There was no time to think clearly, only go on instincts. And instincts told her Kerr had nothing to do with the lethal glove. If she opened the door and told all, Kerr would be taken directly to the Tower of London.

"What are ye doing?" Kerr whispered near her.

"Saving us both. At least for now," she whispered. Placing the pillow over the glass vial, she stepped on it. The cracking glass was muted by the feather-filled pillow. She threw the pillow back on her bed and pushed the pieces near the glove with her slipper. Grabbing one pointed piece, she held it high on her arm, above where the glove would sit.

"Maggie," Kerr whispered, but she shook her head.

Maggie took a full breath and sliced quickly across her skin, opening up a long cut, which swelled with blood. Kerr grabbed one of the white linens from the wash basin and held it on the new cut.

"Shall I hide?" Kerr asked.

Maggie's gaze snapped back and forth between the door and Kerr. "No," she said. "Go along with what I say. Open the door."

Kerr met her gaze. There were no questions in them, only respect and acceptance. Was that trust? For he was clever enough to know how all of this would look, sending him to the gallows or block.

He turned the key, opening it for Walsingham and two

guards, one of them Henry. They pushed into the room.

"Gordon?" Walsingham said, but his gaze went to Maggie. "What mischief is this?"

Maggie's face was tight with distress, distress she didn't need to pretend. "I was testing the gloves," she said, motioning to the cut one on the floor. "I slid it on before placing the vial securely back on the table." She shook her head. "I am so clumsy. Not only did I drop the vial, but when I bent to pick it up, I tripped on this gown." Her voice quavered. "I should have hemmed it before wearing."

"Go on," Walsingham said, crouching to pick up the glove.

Lord! Don't look inside.

Maggie stepped around the glass and blood to get to him, taking the ruined glove from his hand, keeping it closed. "I fell on the broken glass, and it cut my wrist. I screamed, and Master Gordon heard me from his room next door."

Walsingham frowned at the wall and Kerr. "Your room is next to Mistress Darby's?"

"Aye, 'twas where I was assigned," Kerr said.

"Not by me," Walsingham said and turned back. "Continue."

"Master Gordon ran inside, saw me bleeding and crying and thought something was wrong with the glove."

"Is there anything wrong with the glove?" Walsingham asked. He indicated the other discarded glove on the floor and Henry picked it up by the tip of one finger as if it might be poisoned.

"Well now there is," Maggie said, adding a bit of a wail to her tone. "I tested it for all poisons, and it was clean," she cried. "But Master Gordon cut it off me, thinking the worst. In so doing, my blood from the glass cut got all over it."

She held the white linen away from her arm. Her pounding heart kept the blood flowing, and she covered them before Walsingham could inspect them, seeing the evenly spaced cuts on her wrist. "The point of his blade hit the skin of my wrist too." She pinched her lips tightly closed. Too much fabrication, and Walsingham would see right through it.

I am lying to the queen's security. The thought ran through her like real poison, making her stomach turn as she glanced at Kerr. *He's not guilty. He's not. He wouldn't have let me put the glove on.*

Walsingham made a movement as if trying to retrieve the mangled glove. She turned abruptly away. "'Tis ruined!" she said, wailing. "Her Majesty will never forgive me! Her new gloves from her precious cousin! Ruined!" She let her tears run out over her cheeks.

Walsingham looked at Kerr. "You thought Mistress Darby was in peril?"

"She screamed," he said. "When I ran in, she was on the floor and bleeding. I have heard of poisoned gloves that burn the skin, so I cut it off her." He indicated the weapon tucked into his side.

Walsingham's dark eyes moved around the room and down to the broken vial on the floor with the drops of blood. "'Tis unfortunate you did not lock your door, Mistress Darby. You would have been able to tell Gordon what had happened before he chose to tear apart the gift he'd brought to the queen."

Maggie sniffed loudly while keeping pressure on her upper arm and wrists. "I will attempt to fix the glove, bleach it and sew the length that was cut. But I cannot have it done now and the queen expects it."

A gasp came from the doorway where Cordelia and Lucy appeared. "Maggie!" Lucy called and rushed inside. "You've cut yourself."

"And ruined Mary Stuart's gift to the queen," Maggie said, a fresh set of tears swelling from her eyes. Would the sisters question her emotion? Maggie hadn't cried before them since her mother died five years ago.

"What happened?" Cordelia asked.

"Oh my, Maggie, you poor dear," Lucy said.

"Blood is so hard to get out of leather," Cordelia said, and Lucy began to list ingredients to a recipe that might remove the blood stains.

"Perhaps," Kerr said, his voice like a calming flow of reason into the cacophony of women's voices in the room, "one of the ladies could gift the queen with a pair of gloves for this evening, and Mistress Darby can try to remedy the ones from Mary Stuart to present this week if they can be salvaged. Otherwise, I will take whatever punishment Queen Mary would demand of me for ruining her gift."

Walsingham studied him, his eyes narrowed and brow furrowed, as if he wished to crack open Kerr's mind to root around and pluck out his secrets. "Mary Stuart," he said, leaving off the title of queen, "may consider your mission a failure, Highlander, and not support your sister's suit to marry a Hay."

"That would be unfortunate," Kerr said solemnly. But it would be worse yet if Kerr was hanged, drawn, and quartered as an assassin. Or blamed for setting Mary Stuart up as if she meant to kill her cousin. Her supporters would try to kill him.

Maggie's hand went to her chest as if to keep her heart from bursting forth. Kerr was trapped on both sides.

"You will get more blood on your gown," Cordelia said, her voice chiding as she pulled Maggie's arm away and tried to look under the rag.

Maggie yanked her arm back, unwilling to let the sisters see the cuts on her wrist. How would she explain them? Six cuts in two rows, all the same width and deepness. The sisters would not believe they were from Kerr's dagger as he cut off the glove or the shards of glass. And neither would Lord Francis Walsingham. Lies led to a tangle of lies, and this tangle was twisting tighter and tighter.

"Your record is impeccable," Walsingham said. "Perhaps Her Majesty will forgive this. It depends on her mood." He looked to Lucy and Cordelia. "Find the best pair of gloves among the court ladies for Her Majesty to don this evening for the Saint Valentine's Day banquet."

They gave brief curtseys, and glancing at Maggie, raced from the room. A moment of awkward silence settled as Maggie waited for Walsingham to decide what was going to happen next.

"I will help Maggie clear the broken glass," Kerr said, "and assist her in cleaning and mending the glove since I am responsible for slicing it off her."

"The queen will want to see firsthand that you are unharmed," Walsingham said to Maggie. "Clean up as much as you can and return to the festival."

"I can start on the glove tonight," Maggie said.

"After you are properly bandaged," Walsingham said. "Lord Burghley would be sure you are cared for." He looked at Kerr. "And you will go now to explain the mishap to the queen."

Kerr looked like he might argue, but Maggie shook her head. "I will catch up to you, Lord Gordon. Thank you for your gallantry."

He exhaled through his nose, fists at his sides, and finally stepped into the hallway. He looked like he'd rather battle an army than go back to the festival with the queen and courtiers. One man's court was another man's hell, and Kerr Gordon did not belong here.

Walsingham turned toward her. "Now let me see those cuts."

"The lower ones are small from the tip of Lord Gordon's blade, hardly worth tending. 'Tis the cut from the glass shard above that will need to be wrapped."

"Hmmm," he said and motioned to the one remaining guard. "Find the queen's physician."

LAUGHTER CAME FROM the gilded, sparkling hall where the queen still sat amongst her Saint Valentine's Day revelers. Lord Whitt stood in conversation with Lord Norfolk. A glance his way told Kerr that he was their subject. Had they heard about the glove mishap already? Kerr had only stopped into his room to leave his blade and lock the door.

"A pox on you and your family for not allowing this match of the heart," said a man on a raised stage that had been erected halfway down the length of the hall. He wore a flowing toga of an ancient Roman. Wings had been fashioned out of goose feathers that were tied to his shoulders.

"Ho dear Cupid," said another man, clinging to a lad dressed to portray his wife. "Let it be as you have said. Our daughter is in your command."

Cupid nocked an arrow, and two guards stepped before the queen where she sat on her dais, but she peered out from the side to see the arrow fly. It hit its target, a red, velvet heart pinned to a wrapped hay bale near two more actors dressed as a couple. They hugged each other, prompting a smattering of applause while some shushed them as one actor began to talk.

"Take me away, dear Cassio," the lad playing the daughter said, purposely making his voice higher. Were there no better actors in London?

Elizabeth laughed as the man playing the suitor scooped up the lad, nearly dropping him. The room broke into applause and laughter as they exited, and the musicians began a lively tune to end the play.

"Bravo, Sir George," Elizabeth called loudly as a man, obviously the director, came forward with a flourish. He took his bows, and then called out the characters who took their own.

Had Walsingham ordered them searched before entering? The queen sat with her courtiers, in the open, with people all around her, including an assassin. Either one working for Mary Stuart or apart from her but in her name, it didn't matter. Both scenarios would probably see the Scottish queen dead in the end.

The guard, Henry, that Walsingham had accompany Kerr back to the hall, bent to say something in Elizabeth's ear. Her gaze snapped up as the man spoke, her eyes focusing on Kerr. "Our slashing Highlander is here." Elizabeth's voice rang out, and the guard straightened, stepping away. "Come," she called, motioning to Kerr with her naked fingers. Her long face was painted with the white she favored, making her look as if chiseled from pristine marble. Her red lips turned down as he approached, her sharp gaze full of judgement.

Kerr bowed low. "I beg your forgiveness, Your Majesty. I thought only to save Mistress Darby from what I thought was poisoning her."

"While wearing a glove you brought into my court," Elizabeth said. "For me."

The room behind him hushed, although the musicians played low in the background, covering any sounds of shifting on the braided rush mats covering the paved floors. Although Kerr doubted any dancing would start while the hounds salivated for a show of a different kind. Candlelight flickered from a hundred candles as the shadows grew from the lowering light that filtered in through the wavy glass panes in the large windows.

He met her steely gaze. "I was not privy to the contents of the boxed gift. It was handed to me by Mary Stuart before I departed, along with the letter I read. When I heard Mistress Darby call out in pain or panic, I thought the worst and reacted to save her."

"Again," Lord Burghley murmured beside the queen, making her look at him and then back to Kerr.

"That's right," Elizabeth said, tilting her head, the red curls pinned with pearls. "You are my little lamb's savior from the other night as well." She narrowed her eyes. "What designs do you have on Margaret Darby, Lord Gordon?"

Beside Burghley, Whitt made a slight noise. "The Highlander is no lord, Your Majesty, but some rabble who is likely hoping to put Mary on your throne."

"Hush," she scolded, annoyed at being corrected. "Kerr Gordon will be the chief of the Gordons of Banffshire once his father is no longer. That makes him a lord in my eyes." She cut Whitt a glare and returned to Kerr. "Perhaps we can talk about my cousin," she said and pointed to a seat she had nearby to be brought closer for him to sit. The musicians started another dance, and the courtiers turned back to the floor.

Kerr sat, and with the placement, the queen's face was strategically several inches above him. He waited, wondering where this conversation would land him.

"My cousin is beautiful, younger than me by nine years," Elizabeth said, tipping her head to gaze at him. The full ruff tipped upward high behind her head, framing her brilliant red hair. The color sat in stark contrast to the paleness of her face and the lace of the ruff. "Do you find her beautiful?"

Kerr had heard that Elizabeth worried vainly over losing her youthful bloom. There were still some of her councilors who hoped she would marry and produce offspring, although her time to do so was quickly slipping away. A dangerous bout of smallpox years earlier had left her scarred, hence the thick white makeup. There was no doubt she was jealous of her younger, unscarred cousin who had produced a son for Scotland.

"Mary Tudor has been confined for three years," Kerr said slowly. "She gets little exercise aside from pacing in the hall. She rages with frustration, weeping loudly, and swooning at times dramatically. 'Tis difficult to be in her presence for long."

The space between Elizabeth's eyes narrowed. "But is she beautiful?"

He was not about to tell the jealous queen that her cousin was tall, graceful, and still in the prime of her womanhood. And beautiful in her overly dramatic way, although he always felt like he needed a gulp of whisky after meeting with her. "The two of ye queens are made from similar blood, both bonny lasses indeed."

Burghley made a choking sound that turned into a cough. Elizabeth looked between Kerr and her advisor, but then she smiled. "I like the way you speak, Highlander." Her smile faded. "Tell me... My cousin is said to be enchanting, especially to men. And you, Highlander, seem easily enchanted if you are spending so much time with Maggie Darby even though you have only been here three days." She leaned forward. "Are you enchanted by my cousin? Under her spell, as some would say."

"Ye seem to have several questions in that statement, Your Majesty."

Her painted lips tipped in amusement. "Feel free to answer them all."

He thought for a moment. "Perhaps to some men. Nay and like ye said, we have only just met," he said.

Elizabeth blinked. "You are immune where other men are not, and you are not enchanted by Mary and have only recently met Maggie Darby."

He kept her gaze, giving the slightest of nods.

"For whom do you act then? The truth now, Highlander. On your loyalties."

"My loyalty is to my kin. My quest is peace between the Gordons and the Hays to bring happiness to my sister and an alliance that will allow me to lead my clan once again to prosperity instead of being constantly on guard against murderous neighbors. Despite the tangles of possible assassins, troublesome queens, and a lass who puts herself in harm's way out of duty to ye, my cause is simple."

Elizabeth's small eyes widened the slightest amount, and he could see her ire rise like steam starting from a simmering pot. "Troublesome?" One of her brows rose. "I prefer that to ineffectual and meek."

Elizabeth placed her palms together, the fingers steepled up. "You speak plainly, and so will I," she said. "I have survived the Tower and house arrest, longer than three years. I rule with strength despite the threats from disgruntled Catholics who wish to see me burn for heresy so they can put my cousin on the throne of England. But my kin are important to me too, and so despite the pressure..." She glanced at Burghley, giving him a little glare. "From my advisors to do away with my wretched cousin, I am charitable enough to keep her alive. Even with Catholics plotting constantly." She studied him as if he were one of those popish plotters. "So although your cause is simple, like a rock thrown into a pond, the waves ripple out causing tangles amongst the weeds." She straightened in her seat, looking out at the room. "Nothing in this life is simple."

"Guards!" came a man's voice from the arched doorway into the hall. "Protect the queen." Several gasps rose in the room, a flutter of people moving out of the way of potential violence. The guards on either side of the dais, stepped up, placing themselves before Elizabeth where she sat, very much like when Cupid shot his arrow during the theatric.

Walsingham pointed at Kerr with one hand, the bloody glove in the other. Behind him, Maggie was held firmly by a palace guard, her face ashen. "Maggie," Kerr murmured, his gaze going to her arm which was bound tightly with linen.

"Arrest Kerr Gordon," Walsingham yelled.

Elizabeth stood, stepping out from behind the human shield. "On what grounds?"

Walsingham held the bloody glove up into the air. "On grounds of attempting to assassinate Your Majesty."

CHAPTER NINE

"A strength to harm is perilous in the hand of an ambitious head."

Queen Elizabeth I of England

S HAME TO YOU *and your family name.* The memory of the queen's harsh words reverberated through Maggie like thunder between mountains. *To let your heart get in the way of your duty.* Something the queen had proudly resisted for the thirteen years she'd been on the throne.

Maggie stood at her father's door, her fist poised to knock as the last hour of her life churned through her mind. Lucy and Cordelia crying, holding each other as Maggie was rushed into her room only to take a cloak over the gown she wore. Cordelia's tears poured out of wide eyes as she hugged Maggie goodbye. "I am sorry," she had whispered at her ear, squeezing Maggie hard.

Maggie's hand uncurled for her palm to rest on the wooden door. She swallowed hard past the tightness in her throat that led all the way down into her chest and middle, all of it a tangle of worry and embarrassment and remorse and... Kerr. They'd hauled him away with much less courtesy than they'd shown her, even though he did nothing to resist. Where was he now?

Night was falling fast, casting shadows everywhere. She forced another breath in and coughed on a gasp when the door suddenly flew open. "Are you going to stand there all night, girl?" her father, Reginald Darby, asked.

Maggie's hand lowered, and she bravely met his gaze. "Father, I need your help." Truth was she had nowhere else to go. Lord Burghley hadn't been able to stop Walsingham from throwing her out of Whitehall immediately.

Her father ushered her inside and glanced up and down the street, shutting the door behind her. William was drying his hands and threw the rag on the table, coming over. "Did that Highlander do something to you, Maggie?"

She shook her head but stopped. Kerr had most definitely done something to her. He'd given her gloves with blades sewn in them. Walsingham had brought her the spool of thread and the needle that he'd found in Kerr's room next door. But Kerr's reaction to her scream was so genuine. Could it have been a farce? "I... I don't know."

Her father and brother looked at each other and William pulled out a chair for her to sit. "We need details, Maggie," William said. "And why are you here at this time of day? 'Tis not safe to wander the streets of London in the dark."

Maggie looked at her father instead of William. Her fists bunched in her lap under the fall of her cape. At least she'd been allowed to take it for warmth. "I have been relieved of my duty to Her Majesty." She held her breath, waiting for the explosion.

"What?" William yelled, and she steeled herself against the storm of anger. "Except for Elizabeth's Spanish-loving sister, a Darby has always been a poison tester for the queen or king." The strength of his voice had grown with each word until he was shouting. Both of his hands had found his head, holding it as if it might explode with the thought of their family ruin.

Maggie ignored him as best she could, choosing to focus on her father. "Father... There were blades in the queen's glove." She pushed aside her cape to show her bandaged arm. "I... I know he didn't put them there." She shook her head. "It all happened so fast. I had to make a decision, and I chose to not cast blame on an innocent man, but Walsingham found thread and a needle in his room, and—"

Her father raised his hand, and she stopped. Would he slap her? Maggie stared into his aging eyes, but he only lowered his hand to his side and sat in the chair opposite her. He stared, examining her like he did with evidence. "William," he said, without moving his gaze. "Your sister needs a hot bath and clean clothes."

"I have no other clothes," she whispered and blinked against the pressure of tears. "And this gown has my blood on it." She pulled back the cloak to show the drops marring the blue silk.

"God's teeth, Maggie," William said. "What have you done?" He took up her arm but couldn't see past the white bandages to the cuts beneath. His tone suggested he was more upset about the sacking and lack of clothing than her arm. So was she.

"Go on, boy," Reginald Darby said, his voice stern as he waved his hand toward the buckets of water they kept ready inside for visitors. "And get my slate and chalk. I need to get the details straight from the tangle Maggie has in her head." He bent a bit to make sure she met his eyes fully. "That she is about to tell me very slowly, without leaving out a single detail. Because..." He paused to claim her complete attention. "The answers are always in the details."

Maggie sniffed, feeling very much like the little girl who'd been granted grace after admitting to some foul deed. She blinked past the ache of tears. "Thank you."

Her father's face relaxed somewhat. "And how many times did King Henry throw me out of the palace?"

"At least four," she whispered, and he nodded.

She took a square linen from the pocket tied under her petticoat and wiped her nose. "But you didn't do anything wrong, and I... I did." She'd trusted Kerr, a Scottish Catholic she'd only known for less than a week. Was it his rugged looks and strength that made her turn her back on her family and the queen? Perhaps it was the fact he'd saved her when he arrived, or the dance in the hall in front of everyone? Or the near kiss in the corridor?

He is innocent. The thought surfaced, twisting in her as her instincts screamed that he knew nothing of the blades.

William set the slate down and turned back, his shoulders stiff, to start water over the fire.

"Details, Margaret Isabella Darby," her father said. "Your heart is good, and your brain is clever. Court intrigue is tricky, so let's figure this out. This has to do with those missing gloves for certain. Gloves that went missing before your Highlander arrived."

Her breath halted, and she lifted her eyes to his. Chest loosening a bit, she inhaled. "Yes," she said, sitting up straighter. "They were gone when the guard walked us up to my room upon his arrival. The guard assigned him to the room next door."

"Which guard?" William asked. Having spent six years at court as a boy with the young King Edward, William had made friends with many of the guard staff who had remained. He also made it a habit to continue to track those who worked in the royal household.

At her father's urging, Maggie started unhooking her hood and took off her cape. "I did not recognize him."

"Have you seen him since?" William asked, hauling a large bucket of water for the small oak tub.

Maggie thought as she removed her stomacher and outer sleeves. "I do not think so, although I have been in my room inspecting the clothes over again after my room was broken into."

William huffed. "Someone has set the Highlander up to take the blame for a failed assassination." He set the bucket down. "He arrived after the gloves were stolen. He was placed in the room next to yours by an unknown guard, and you said something about Walsingham finding needle and thread in his room."

Considering that her brother had been furious, William certainly held onto details. Apparently much better than she. Maggie nodded. "Yes. I think so too. So I... lied for him."

Her father tapped the chalk on his slate as he finished writing some notes. "And that's where you made your mistake."

Was attempting to help an innocent man a mistake? Even when it meant you took the blame too? "At least I'm not in the Tower like Kerr," she said.

"William Cecil, Lord Burghley, no doubt," William said. "He has looked out for you like he did for me, thanks be to Father for that."

"The man owes me his life," Reginald said and waved off the rest. Maggie and William had heard the story many times about how their father had warned a young William Cecil not to drink the wine until the king's taster did. It so happened that night, the taster fell over dead.

"We will go over each detail while you wash," her father said.

William set a privacy screen around the tub. He would pour the steaming water from the small caldron, which still rested in the hot coals, into the cold water waiting for her in the tub. Lord, she needed a warm and soothing bath. But the guilt made all her muscles tighten again. Surely Kerr was not getting a warm bath this night. Nor any type of forgiveness.

THE TOWER OF London. Kerr had heard nightmarish tales of the dungeons, so he was surprised when he was led into what looked like a room in his father's castle. The Bloody Tower, which was what the guards leading him had called it, had low stone ceilings, cold walls, and rush-strewn floors. Kerr felt confined to a tomb, but there were two windows, a small rug, table, chair, bed with blankets, and a washing station. There was even a bloody pillow for his head. This was not at all like the prison cells he knew held the majority of the Tower inmates, levels below him. He had no heat, but his woolens and the blankets left to him would keep him alive in the extremes of February.

Kerr stood at the window studying the view of the early

morning change of guards in the bailey before the soaring White Tower. The large structure was built during the reign of William the Conqueror from Normandy over five-hundred years ago. Several large ravens hopped around the yard, being followed and watched by their keeper.

Footsteps sounded on the steps leading up to his cell, making Kerr turn.

"I made certain Walsingham remembered your rank," a man said from the corridor.

Kerr's hand raised to his hip where he kept his sword, which wasn't there, of course. The long face of Thomas Howard, the Fourth Duke of Norfolk was framed by the small, barred window set in the door.

"Open the door," Norfolk said. Keys jangled before one slid into the iron lock, turning. Norfolk, wearing his courtly hose and voluminous breaches, strode inside, his fur-lined cape giving him a kingly look. He glanced around and nodded. "Not terrible. I was imprisoned in a different tower, equally well appointed. My grandfather spent some time locked in this, the Bloody Tower." He walked over to the bed that Kerr hadn't bothered to make and then turned to study him.

"It used to be called the Garden Tower," Norfolk said, "but the name changed with its history. Henry Percy killed himself here, and the two young princes, Edward V and Richard, the Duke of York disappeared from here, never to be seen again."

Kerr stood with his legs braced in a battle stance. He kept silent, glaring at the pompous arse. After a long pause, Norfolk took the seat at the table. "I am here to question you for the queen and her council," he said, his voice carrying. No doubt there was a guard listening outside the heavy door.

"My words will not change from last night," Kerr said, leaning back against the jutting stone wall. "I tire from retelling the truth when it is not believed."

Norfolk stood and walked closer to him, lowering his voice. "The truth has no place in this." He searched Kerr's face. "We are

HEATHER MCCOLLUM

two Catholics trying to survive in this Protestant country. We are on the same side, you and I."

Never. What was Norfolk's purpose? "From how I see things, ye are on that side of the door and I am on this side."

Norfolk waved his hand. "I mean supporting Queen Mary."

Kerr had already explained to Walsingham, with Norfolk present, that he had not known of the blades in the glove and had no idea if Mary had sewn them in or someone here in England. The gift had not been left unattended except in his room. And his leaf in the door trick had revealed that someone had placed the needle and thread under his bed but had not taken out the package of gloves before he'd given them to Elizabeth.

Either Mary or someone, before she gave them to Kerr, had sewn the blades in. But the left needle and thread showed an obvious associate at Whitehall who was knowledgeable and ready to protect Mary Stuart from blame if the assassination attempt was thwarted.

"So you truly did not sabotage the gloves yourself and do not know who did?" Norfolk asked, his voice low. "They were placed in the perfect spots to slice the queen's veins open when she went to remove it in panic after feeling the first bite."

Mo chreach. That could have happened to Maggie if she had lost her head and yanked the glove off. The thought tightened Kerr's gut even more.

"I know nothing except that it was done without my knowledge, and I have been made to look like the culprit."

"With the needle and thread in your chamber," Norfolk said and began to pace, looking up at the rough stone ceiling, hands clasped behind his back. "It was sitting on your desk."

"I found it under my bed," Kerr said, watching the man. "And I set it on the desk."

"Under the bed," Norfolk repeated, nodding. "To make it look as if you wanted to hide it, but not hidden enough to be hard to find."

"Ye do not believe that I sewed the blades in the glove?" Kerr asked, crossing his arms. He didn't trust Englishmen or most Scotsmen for that matter. Norfolk's actions were not purely to find the truth.

Norfolk stopped near Kerr. "It is whispered by some that I should wed Queen Mary. I am Elizabeth's cousin through her mother's mother, Elizabeth Howard. The queen is actually named after her." He paused momentarily as if losing his thought. "And of course Mary Stuart is Elizabeth's cousin through Margaret Tudor, Elizabeth's aunt. So the joining of the two of us, with our strong royal blood, is supported by the Catholics.

"Indeed. We have more right to the throne than a Protestant woman, who in the eyes of the great church of Rome, is illegitimate."

Kerr already knew the players in this chess match. He'd studied the pedigree before coming to England. This was old information he cared little about. Instead, Kerr's thoughts kept moving to Maggie, but before he could say anything, the man continued to talk, filling the room with his whispers.

"I do not know whom to trust. There are others at court trying to depose the English queen, but of course they do not reveal themselves."

Norfolk was obviously one of them, although he hid it from Walsingham somehow.

"I sent word to Mary about the whole incident with the glove, so she would be forewarned about being questioned." Norfolk stopped and looked at Kerr, offering him a smile. "If you die in Mary's service, even if you were not successful in killing her cousin, she will fulfill her promise to aid your family. I am certain of her kindness and loyalty to those who support her. But if you turn on Mary..." he paused for effect, "she will not support the marriage of your sister with the Hay lad. You will fail, not only your queen and the true religion, but your family as well."

"Do all Englishmen talk as much as ye?" Kerr asked and turned to the window to look out. A sky of swollen clouds filled with drifting snowflakes.

"You must know the consequences of your further actions," Norfolk said. "No more implicating Mary in any of this or your death will do nothing to help your family."

Kerr watched the people beyond the tall walls hustle by, trying to get to their destinations through the cold. "What happened to Maggie when I was taken away? Was she arrested?" Kerr turned to Norfolk. "Is she here somewhere in one of the towers?" Would she be afforded the warmth and comfort of a noblewoman's cell because her family had been so loyal to the Tudors through the years?

"Maggie?" Norfolk asked, as if the simple-minded man couldn't keep up.

"Aye, Maggie Darby. The one who tried on the glove." Kerr's voice was terse. "The one ye spoke to a number of times with Lord Whitt."

"Yes, of course," Norfolk said, his hand gesturing in the air. "She was let go. Sacked. Turned out with merely a cloak over her gown. I suppose she's returned to her father's house if he will have her. Poor thing might be on the streets if he wouldn't take her in."

Was that a possibility? Would Reginald Darby be so cruel as to turn his back on his only daughter?

"I want ye to retrieve my things that were taken: my sword, daggers, horse, and take them to Maggie, wherever she may be. Tell her she may..." He swallowed hard. "She may sell my sword and dagger to keep herself well. She can ride my horse, Caspian, into Scotland to Auchindoun Castle in Banffshire to live with my family there. My sister, Rhona, will take her in."

"For your service to my Mary, I will try," Norfolk said softly, his gaze moving to the bars at the door and then back. He shook his head. "I see that you are a good Catholic supporter of Mary, and I will do what I can to see your sentence reduced from painful death to a quick one."

"How gracious," Kerr murmured. "Or better yet, find me a way out of here."

Norfolk pressed his beringed hand against his doublet. "And risk ending up in here myself." He shook his head. "Someone must be at fault for the blades in the glove, and it cannot be Mary. So it must be you."

"Even after I tell Walsingham everything ye now told me?"

Norfolk frowned as if annoyed. "He won't take the word of a Catholic Highlander over mine." The lack of worry on the easily read face made Kerr frown. "And if you do anything of the sort, Mary will turn against your cause in the north of Scotland. Your sister will not marry her Hay, and your clan will continue your bloody feud, all because you were selfish enough to try and save your own life." He shook his head. "Nay, Gordon, you must take this blow for your honor and to save your family."

Norfolk stared at Kerr for a long moment, waiting to see if he would agree or possibly be of more annoyance to him. Finally, Norfolk gave a swift nod. "Good day, then. I will tell Mary of your loyalty, and your family will benefit."

He tugged at his doublet and righted his cap. He leaned into Kerr for a moment as if they were co-conspirators. "I must be off to dine with Roberto Ridolfi, a very influential and wealthy man. He is a banker and has funds to pay an army to support Queen Mary." His smile seemed almost giddy with the want of power. Married to the Scottish queen, Norfolk would become the King of England, Ireland, and Scotland. He was playing a very dangerous game with his ambitions.

"May God forgive your transgressions," Norfolk said loudly and stepped to the bars. "Guards, I am finished."

Kerr momentarily considered rushing the door, but the number of guards in the corridor was high, and he was without a weapon. He exhaled. Norfolk was right. Clan Gordon would not benefit if Kerr convinced Walsingham and Elizabeth that he had nothing to do with the lethal glove, for then the blame would fall on Mary Stuart, and she would be of no help to his clan.

"Norfolk," Kerr yelled, his rock-hard voice a command. The man stopped, his face in the door's window after the guard relocked it. "Help Maggie Darby," Kerr said. "Swear to me or my tongue will continue to cause trouble."

Norfolk frowned, meeting his unblinking gaze. "I swear it."

Kerr watched him turn and walk away. A guard's face appeared. He glared as he jangled the keys before Kerr, placing them on an iron hook several yards away where he could see his way to escape but could never reach it.

Quarter of an hour later, Kerr watched Norfolk walk out of the base of the Bloody Tower, talking to the keeper who had welcomed Kerr with a grim face the night before. Kerr squinted, making out that Norfolk wore the Gordon family sword. Would he keep it as a prize or actually carry it to Maggie? Kerr had little hope that she still held for him any of the warmth he'd felt when dancing with her, not after looking so damn guilty of not only the attempted assassination of her queen but also of lying and manipulation. He huffed. She had likely given up on him completely.

The wind blew whistled as it found the cracks around the glass panes of the windows, snow hitting them. He pulled one side inward, and the sting of snowflakes hit his face. They didn't bother him, but to a soft-skinned lass used to heat and comforts, the cold could kill. He curled his hand around one of the bars, his strength useless against stone and iron. Kerr's eyes searched the landscape beyond the tower walls that was growing white quickly. "Where are ye, lass?"

CHAPTER TEN

"For there is nothing lost, that may be found, if sought."
Edmund Spenser, *The Faerie Queene*

"**B**RING ME MY supper," William said, thumping his fist on the table in the dining room. He laughed and called toward Maggie in the kitchen. "I've been wanting to say that since you left to live at the palace."

"If you want burned poultry and watery soup, you can come find some yourself," Maggie called back from the hearth where she struggled to remember what herbs would make a pleasant stew. "I know more about poison than cooking herbs. You have been the one to make meals these past seven years."

She heard William grunt and push his chair back. "I will teach you, so you don't poison us." Her brother had remained to take care of their father, and they'd lived without a maid to save money.

Now that she was back, her brother could leave home. It was time for him to find a wife and start his own family. She would be left behind, trying to make stew out of water and dried thyme. The thought twisted inside Maggie. It twined around the constant worry over Kerr.

After combing through the minute details of the past week with her father and brother, Maggie was certain her heart and instincts had been correct. Kerr did not alter the glove, but he had been made to look guilty to take the punishment.

Would Walsingham believe him when he pled his innocence? Would Kerr implicate his Scottish queen when she was the one who could help his sister and family avoid further war? Was he suffering in a cold, dark, rat-infested dungeon?

"I feel ill," she murmured when William came over, brandishing several more bunches of dried herbs before him. "You make the stew."

Maggie walked out of the kitchen to the front room that served as a hall and dining area and lowered into her brother's vacant chair. Her father looked across at her as he chewed some brown bread that William had taught her to knead and bake that morning. It was slathered with fresh butter that she'd churned, her palms still raw with blisters. She didn't remember when she'd gotten them during the process, her mind on whether Kerr was chained and without bread. *Good Lord.* She needed to get him out of this mess.

"'Tis too dangerous," her father said.

She blinked. Could her clever father read minds now? "What is?" she asked.

"Whatever you have swirling around behind that frown. If the Scotsman is in the Tower, there is no getting him back. The queen has banished you from court. You are lucky to have your freedom and life."

He was right, of course. She could have been sent to the Tower too. In fact, she still could if the council decided she was dangerous to the queen.

Rap. Rap. Rap.

The sharp knocks at the house door made them both turn to stare at it. Maggie's heart jumped to match the repeated knocking.

Rap. Rap. Rap. "Mistress Darby?"

"You best open it," her father said, standing.

William appeared beside her. "I will."

"Nothing foolish, my boy," Reginald said.

Maggie looked between them, her eyes wide. Did they think

it was the queen's guard come to haul her away? While William went to the door, she ran to collect her warm cloak. If she was to be hauled off, she needed whatever was on her to survive.

William opened the door while Maggie peered out a crack in the shuttered window. She could only see one man through the wavy glass pane.

"Lord Norfolk?" William said, and Maggie hurried over to stand by her brother. A large horse was tethered at the front post of their modest house. It looked like Caspian, Kerr's horse.

"I see you are still in your father's house," Norfolk said, looking at her. "Fortunate that he took you in."

Maggie felt her cheeks warm. "He is a forgiving man," she murmured and noted the sword at Norfolk's side. "You have Kerr Gordon's sword," she said, her words as tight as her stomach.

"Ho now, good lady, you certainly have an eye for the detail of dress." His hand stroked the hilt. "He gave it to me to show Queen Mary that he supports her and deserves her help for his family." He turned slightly. "However, Gordon's horse is without a home. He bade me bring him to you so that you may ride to his family castle in Banffshire if you so desire. He says that his sister will take you in."

Maggie's breath caught, making her heart pound hard once more. "Is he well? Where is he? What has the queen decided about his guilt and fate?"

Norfolk frowned down at his sleeve where she had grasped it. He gently pulled his arm away as if her hands were dirty. "He is held, due to my intervention, in the luxurious cell in the Bloody Tower." He waved his hand. "A misnomer started a century ago. There is no blood there."

"But those escorted out of the Bloody Tower have their blood spilled upon the executioner's block," her father said from right behind her.

"Rightly so," Norfolk said. "And if Gordon is found guilty of attempted assassination, he will also."

"He did not put the blades in the glove, nor did he know

about them when giving it to the queen," Maggie said, conviction making her words sharp.

Norfolk looked over his shoulder. Was he avoiding her eyes? "The Scotsman will confess and hopefully die swiftly with honor."

"Has he been tried already?" she asked, hand pressed against her chest.

"Nay, but it will occur soon enough." Norfolk finally met her eyes. "But my duty is done bringing you his horse and telling you that you will be welcome in Banffshire. In fact, you might want to leave London before your name gets tangled more with his. Elizabeth is, after all, a Tudor. They are known to cut off any loose threads," he said, the meaning obvious. She might still be arrested, tried, and executed.

He leaned in right before her face. "I would leave soon if I were you." The side of his mouth, over his pointy beard, hitched up.

"You are being hailed," William said from beside Maggie. It was only then that she realized she was flanked by both her brother and father. The show of support helped her find her strength.

"Good eve," Norfolk said and turned on his leather-crafted court shoes. He strode across the cobbled road toward a man in the shadows who lowered his hand. He was wiry looking, his arms moving about with his speech as Norfolk approached.

Maggie squinted into the night. "That is him," she whispered.

"Who, him?" her father asked.

"The guard that day when Kerr arrived," she said. "He led him to the room next to mine in the palace."

"The man who is speaking with Norfolk?" William asked, and she nodded.

William snorted softly. "That is no guard for Elizabeth."

"You know him?" Reginald asked, the three of them peering out into the night.

"Roberto Ridolfi, a well-known banker. He travels abroad

often for his work, but some say his work involves more intrigue than tallies of coin. He was arrested once but released."

"He looks quite involved with Norfolk," Reginald said and pulled them inside the house.

"Aye," William said, the two of them thinking. "They are plotting something."

"The horse?" Maggie asked.

"William will stable him with our mare, Clover," her father said, tugging gently on his wiry beard. "Nothing devised between Norfolk and Ridolfi can be good for our queen."

The sound of horses in the street made her hurry back to the shutter, but they rode past the house. If she were arrested, she couldn't help anyone, not the queen and not Kerr.

While her brother and father stared at one another as if communicating in silence, Maggie looked between them. "I cannot flee to Scotland." Their grim faces and silence made her swallow hard. "I would never survive the winter woods anyway," she murmured. And how could she leave Kerr to face the executioner's block?

William's hand came down on her shoulder. "We will help you, Maggie. Our family may be small, but we are as loyal to our family as your Highlander is to his."

She met his gaze without blinking and took a deep breath. "Loyal enough to follow me into the Bloody Tower?"

⋙⋘

LIFE WAS A battle until the end. Kerr's warrior blood ran fast as he paced in his cage that was made to resemble a noble's room. His mind churned over details that had landed him there. How could Walsingham's network of spies miss that Norfolk was an active traitor? And who was Ridolfi? Kerr hadn't heard his name mentioned at court. Could he have sewn the blades into the glove?

Kerr ignored the low cursing of the two guards in the corridor beyond his cell. They had relieved the two men who had stood watch over his locked door since midday. Did they really think he could bend iron and force his way through the door? With locks and iron bars, it was a waste of manpower. One guard glanced in through the bars as if to ascertain he hadn't flown, and then he shuffled off, perhaps for the night.

Kerr went to the window, opening it inward, and let his gaze fall over the night outside the walls of this fortress. Lamplight flickered, and the soft glow of hearth fires outlined windows of cottages lining the narrow streets.

Maggie. The thought of the trust she had gifted him, her cleverness and brazen attempt to shield him from blame, the closeness they'd shared before this mess unfolded... He exhaled long. Why the bloody hell hadn't he kissed her?

She must flee to his clan. For even if her father took her in, Walsingham may decide that she was more involved and drag her to the Tower too. "Ye need to get far away from the Tower, Maggie lass," he murmured, "and from me."

Footsteps sounded outside his door. Light ones hurrying up the steps. He listened in the heavy silence of the vault surrounding him.

"Kerr?" The voice came on a whisper but thundered through him.

Bloody hell. He strode to the door, grabbing the bars, his heart pounding, to stare into the face that lurked behind his eyes every time he closed them. "Maggie?"

She smiled widely and spun away, grabbing the keys from the hook mortared into the wall. "We need to hurry," she whispered, shoving the key into the iron lock.

"Ye shouldn't be here. Good God, lass, I would not see ye caught up in these treasonous lies anymore." His words were low but forceful. Yet she ignored them, turning the key.

"Make it look like you are sleeping in the bed. We can relock the door, and it will take until morning for them to miss you," she said as she jerked the heavy door open. She walked in and stopped before him.

Her cheeks looked flushed in the candlelight, her dress cut low, exposing more skin than she'd dared to at court. Hair fashioned up in curls, her head was bare. Some tresses flowed down around her strong, slender shoulders. She was the most beautiful thing he'd ever seen, and Kerr felt something he'd never truly felt before. Fear.

"Maggie, lass," he said, pulling her into him. "So ye know. I swear to ye I –"

"Had nothing to do with the glove," she finished. "I know. 'Tis why I'm here. I will not let an innocent man die, especially one…" She tipped her head back. "One I'd really rather get to know better." She seemed to wait, as if there was a question in the words. A question Kerr would not allow to go unanswered a second time.

He leaned over and pressed his lips to hers. The fear that had pounded through him at the thought of her being found moved over as a rush of want made him lose himself to the sweetness of her kiss. She tasted of honey wine and boldness, and he tipped her face to deepen the kiss. Her fingers curled into his shoulders, holding him to her. The tension that had clenched within him dissolved. She was alive and whole in his arms, and she believed his innocence.

They broke apart, but his large hand still cupped the side of her face.

"You kissed me," she whispered and looked up into his eyes.

"Something I should have done sooner," he said.

"Must have been something I ate."

The distant whisper of a voice from down the stairs threw Kerr into action. He left Maggie, striding to the door. The key was still jutting out. *Mo chreach!* He glanced to the hook where it had been. He held his breath as he pulled the key, reached to hang it back, and then pulled the door closed. It was still unlocked but looked undisturbed.

"Hide," he whispered, his gaze whipping around the room. He pointed to an alcove where the privy pot sat. Privacy was a perk of being locked in the luxurious cell.

Maggie turned and threw herself into the space, pulling back her petticoats so that nothing stuck out.

"I think another bout is coming on me," the second guard groaned, and his footfalls echoed as he ran back down the steps.

"Bloody awful night," the first one said, his words grinding out as if he battled pain.

Kerr laid in his bed, pulling the blanket over him as if he slept. He listened to the lumbering footfalls of the guard as he came close. As long as the man didn't pull on the outward opening door, he wouldn't know it was unlocked.

"You asleep, Scotsman?" he asked from the barred window.

Kerr made no movement, concentrating on letting his shoulder rise slightly as if he breathed evenly. He could hear the guard's stomach make a loud rumble.

"Blasted mutton," the guard said. "Must have been turned already."

Despite his blood rushing, readying his muscles to act if the unlocked door was discovered, Kerr lay quiet, listening. The guard cursed again, and his heavy footfalls thudded down the steps.

Kerr rolled from the bed. "Maggie," he said, and she peeked around the corner at the door.

"Make it look like you are still in the bed," she whispered, going toward him.

"Ye take too much risk," he said shoving the hay in the tick into a lump that might look like a person in the dark. He shook his head. "The Tower is full of guards. I don't know how ye got inside, but ye need to get out the way ye came in. I will let ye know if I make it out myself."

She shoved his pillow under the blanket. "We are going out together."

"Nay," he argued, lifting the blanket to settle it over the mass. "Ye need to ride to my home in Banffshire. Did Norfolk bring ye my belongings, my horse?"

She grabbed his hand, dragging him toward the door as if she'd pick him up and carry him herself. "He brought me your horse. Caspian is waiting at my father's house."

Daingead! Her father was helping and probably her brother. They would all lose their lives if caught. "Ye must go. Take my sword and dagger. Sell them to find safe passage if your brother will not take ye to Scotland."

Maggie rose on her toes to look out the bars in the door. "Norfolk kept your blades. He only brought the horse."

"Bloody thieving bastard," Kerr said.

She ran over to blow out his candle, throwing darkness around them. Only the few sconces in the corridor beyond showed her outline in the shadows. "Come, before the guards revive themselves." She pressed the door outward.

"Revive themselves?" he asked. "Ye poisoned them?"

"A bit. 'Tis a potent potion that will keep them busy until their bowels stop clenching."

"Hurry." A man's terse voice came from near the stairs, making Kerr's hand go to the missing sword that used to sit at his side. The face of Maggie's brother seemed to float in the darkness there, lit only by the taper he held before it.

Maggie grabbed the key from the hook, fumbling it in her haste. Kerr took it and relocked the door. He would drop the keys on the stairs to make it look like one of the sick guards had misplaced them in his haste. Anything to delay them realizing he was missing from the locked cell.

"Here," William Darby said, thrusting a set of breeches and hose at Kerr. "To get you out of London, 'tis best you look like an Englishman."

Kerr set the clothes down and unbuckled his kilt, letting the heavy wool fall. Maggie turned away, her skirt rustling in the darkness. He quickly pulled on the hose and beeches. Luckily William had included a large tunic to replace his, which stunk of sweat. "I still say this is too dangerous, Maggie. To sneak into the Tower of London just to—"

"Save you like you saved me in the stables," she finished, for the first time admitting she was in dire peril. "If you stayed here, your throat would be in as much jeopardy as mine was."

His mouth softened. "And ye without your chastity belt and me without my sword."

She did smile then. "Ah, but I have a purging potion." A whispered laugh came from her. "And this time I had to hide in *your* room."

"Chastity belt? Hiding in Maggie's room?" William asked but Kerr was already moving, pulling Maggie behind him down the stairs. Halfway down, Kerr set the key along the wall on a step.

"Is there anyone ye did not poison that we should be watching for?" Kerr asked.

"The soldiers at the gates," Maggie said, her breath coming fast as they hurried. "I gave them the same type of tarts, but without the potion, so it won't be obvious that it was the tarts."

"And they let ye walk right in?"

"I am a lady for hire," she said, which explained the low-cut gown. "For the Tower's governor. William says it is a well-known occurrence."

"I may not work in Whitehall Palace anymore," William whispered, "but my eyes and ears are open for royal rumors. 'Tis habit from my time with King Edward."

They moved down the empty stairwell to the bottom without encountering any guards. Were they all in the line of privies for the soldiers? Hopefully Maggie's cleverness at poisoning some of them and letting others remain fit would throw off their concern that the little beauty who'd come to entertain their commander could be at fault.

"Walk normal," William said, shoving a rectangular card and a mason's string toward Kerr. "Show them this, your guild badge."

Kerr glanced at the stitched leather badge that was marked with the name *Jared Grigg* and an emblem design of a rock and trowel. "You were here to measure stone to cut to replace the damaged stone making up the Bowyer Tower on the inner wall," William said.

"There is damaged stone on Bowyer Tower?" Kerr asked.

William frowned. "Try not to sound so damn Scottish, and

yes. Artillery mistake that happened last week."

The man apparently kept his ear to the ground. Kerr could use him in Banffshire.

Maggie squeezed Kerr's arm. "We will wait until you are out. If no alarm is sounded, then we will meet you in an alley behind the tower's back wall."

"If there *is* an alarm, get the bloody hell out of here," Kerr said, pulling her back to look down into her face. Heart-shaped and framed by curls, even in shadow her beauty showed. "I will always remember how ye tried to help me."

She frowned up at him. "If there *is* an alarm, run out and meet us at the back side of the wall. Your horse waits at our home with one of ours. We will race toward Scotland." The woman thought they could outrun Walsingham's guards all the way to Scotland.

"Let us just pray there is no alarm," William said. "If you all play your parts, all will be well."

He took Maggie's arm, but she stayed before Kerr. "All will be well," she repeated and placed her hand on Kerr's cheek. "But if not…" She hesitated. "You are a fine man, Kerr Gordon, an honorable man." She reached up onto her toes and brushed his lips with hers.

"Winnie Anderson, we need to go," William said. "Now. And you, Jared Grigg, will follow us after a count of twenty. Head out from around that corner." He pointed. Maggie let William tug her away.

Kerr rubbed his jaw, watching her clutch her shawl around her arms. "Where the hell do ye get your false names?"

"People who've wronged him," Maggie whispered and took a big breath before stepping out into the bailey on William's arm. There was a definite sway to her hips, and she kept her head held high.

Kerr watched from the shadows as they approached the two guards standing at the exit gate. "Halt," called one of the guards, and he lifted his musket straight at Maggie.

CHAPTER ELEVEN

"All the world's a stage,
And all the men and women merely players;
They have their exits and their entrances;
And one man in his time plays many parts,
His acts being seven ages."
William Shakespeare, *As You Like It*

"**B**IT O' LUCK," Maggie called as they approached. With her heart thumping hard, it was difficult to keep her flirtatious smile. "I gets to sleep tonight." She could see the spark in the darkness that indicated the musket was lit and ready to fire. Straight at her and William.

"Commander is dining with Lady Percy this evening," William said and held up a coin. "Gentleman, he is," he said with the thick Cockney accent he liked to use around town. He flipped the coin up and caught it, pushing it back into his pocket. "Still paid us for the trouble of coming out in this blasted cold."

The musket lowered.

"The lady is welcome to stay with us," one of the guards said, coming closer to slide a hand down her arse. The bum roll stopped him from feeling much, but Maggie was still tempted to use her poison-tipped boot on the rogue. She wore it with a cover that William had helped her fashion, so she wouldn't accidentally poison anyone. But she could flip the cover off easily.

Her brother pulled her away, and the guard dropped his hand. Lucky for him.

"You blokes are on duty," William said. "I ain't getting thrown in the Tower for helping you forget your post." He pulled her past them and out under the archway that would be closed soon with a thick, barred portcullis.

Two guards stood above where the thick chains raised and lowered it. "You barely made it out," one called down. "Else you'd have to stay." He smiled broadly at her, making a chill of dread spread through her very core.

As they made their way under the stone arch, she heard the chink of the heavy chain begin to crank. "Oh no," she whispered, glancing over her shoulder. Kerr walked up to the guards inside. Would he make it out under the portcullis? *Hurry, Kerr!*

Maggie and William rounded the corner, and she pulled away from him to peek back inside. Kerr was walking too slowly. He twirled the measuring string William had given him around a finger as he walked with confidence.

"Tell them to stop the gate," she said to William.

"It will be all right," William said, eyeing the lowering port-cullis with a frown as if he thought it might *not* be all right.

Nearing the gate, Kerr tipped his cap. "Jared Grigg, mason," he said, his voice leisurely. "Going home for the night. Back tomorrow at noon."

The foul guard who had groped her backside squinted at him. "I don't remember you coming in."

Kerr shrugged. "'Twas early. But I've finished taking the measure of the stone on the Bowyer Tower to cut it in the morn." Kerr talked slowly, trying to hide his accent, but she could still hear a bit of it. "Was it you who blasted the rock right off?"

The other man laughed and punched the guard in the arm. "How did he guess it, Danbury?"

"Go on," Danbury said, rushing him out.

Kerr took the extra time to coil up the string as if he hadn't a worry of getting trapped inside and discovered. He walked slowly toward the lowering iron teeth cranking down. Maggie held her breath as he had to bend over to duck out under the points. He whistled some notes of a tune as he walked out into the dark, February night.

Maggie let her breath out, and sucked in the cold air, her rooted body relaxing enough to move. William tugged her arm, leading her to follow the wall around the tower. A few people moved like silent shadows back into the night. Poor creatures who had to scrounge in the city streets for food or coin.

"Here," her father called in hushed tones. He stood alongside a dark building opposite the tower wall.

She and William melted into the shadows with him. "He got out," she said, her whisper on a shallow exhale. She peeked around the edge of the building to see three men dodge out of Kerr's way as he traipsed along toward them, not even bothering to try to stay hidden. In the dark, his bulk seemed amplified. She stepped out from the alley enough so that he could see her, and then slid back between the buildings.

Kerr veered across the street and into the darkness. His gaze moved from Maggie to her brother and finally stopped on her father. "I will not forget this kindness," Kerr said to him and turned to William and then Maggie. "From all of ye. Ye are all welcome in Banffshire if it is unsafe for ye here."

Her heart picked up at the thought of leaving all this behind. To be with Kerr, away from the intrigue and guile of court, they could learn to know one another. Despite the danger now, it sounded like a dream that was within her reach.

Her father nodded and spoke with quiet conviction. "To save an innocent man from poison, whether that poison be made of lethal plants or slander and falsehoods, has always been my mission in this life."

"I thank ye for it, Master Darby," Kerr said, and stepped over to Maggie, taking her hand to squeeze. "Ye risk too much."

She threaded her fingers through his. The hold was intimate, more so than their brief kiss. She inhaled, willing her mind back to making her dream come true. "We should flee the city tonight," Maggie said. "Your horse is saddled and waiting at our house."

"They will comb the city for you once they discover you gone," her father said and looked to her. "And Maggie and William now."

The moon filtered down between the buildings, illuminating Kerr's handsome, serious face. He looked out at the night. "There could be another way," he said, turning back to Maggie. "Ye could stay."

Worry hit Maggie's stomach like a fist. "Stay?" she said.

"There are things about Norfolk that Walsingham must know to save your queen."

"Like that Norfolk is planning to wed Mary Stuart so he can become king of England, Ireland, and Scotland?" Maggie asked.

Kerr hesitated. "Aye. Did Norfolk say as much to ye?"

William snorted. "No, or she'd be in The Tower or already dead."

Maggie kept her fingers in Kerr's warm grasp as her brother spoke fast. "He is a known Catholic even if he hides it from Elizabeth. And we saw him speaking with a man known to travel amongst European nations for banking. They are planning something, I am certain. Something soon."

"Roberto Ridolfi," Kerr murmured.

"You know of him?" her father asked.

"I only know Norfolk said he was meeting with him, and he insinuated that the man would help him become king."

"What a fool to admit such a thing," Maggie said.

"He thinks I will not jeopardize the wedding of my sister to our enemy clan," Kerr said, the words coming slowly as if they pained him. "That Queen Mary won't support the union if I say anything against him or her."

"It will jeopardize the peace between your families," Maggie said.

Kerr met her searching gaze. "But if Norfolk's plans are uncovered by someone other than me…"

William reached the end of the scenario quickly. "If Maggie uncovers the plot, she could be re-instated as the queen's protector," William said, his words coming fast. "We would not have to leave London."

"Or she could be thrown in The Tower as a conspirator trying to throw the hounds off her scent," her father said. He looked to his son. "She cannot go running to tell Walsingham all this without more evidence. She will look guilty enough when Kerr is found missing."

Maggie pressed closer to Kerr. Did she want to be re-instated at Whitehall? Her brother and father were counting on her position there, so the answer must be yes. Her hand pressed against the muscles evident under the linen of Kerr's shirt. "No matter what, you need to leave London," she whispered. They had only known each other for a week. How was it that she couldn't fully inhale with the thought of him riding away? She had only a taste of him, the briefest of kisses in the tower, but she wanted more. So much more. She swallowed past the ache in her throat. "Walsingham has spies everywhere. They will find you if you stay in London."

William shook his head. "He must suspect Norfolk. The duke isn't clever enough to hide his treason well."

"I would not leave ye until I know Walsingham believes ye," Kerr said, and the back of his finger slid along her cheek.

"You need to ride away," she said the words, even though they seemed to stick to her tongue.

"Once I know ye are safe. 'Twas my fault ye were thrown out of Whitehall and your position." He released her hand before she could argue and turned to William. "Do ye know where Norfolk frequents when he is not at Whitehall?"

"He has a well-appointed house on the Strand," William said. "If he's scheming with Ridolfi, I doubt he would retreat to his manor in Waltham Forest, at least not yet. He will stay close to the queen."

Maggie inhaled fully, throwing on the cloak of duty she'd worn her whole life. "Then we go to the Strand," she said and looked at her father. "You should go home to keep things ready in case we must flee."

Shuffling feet in the street made them all flatten against the rough side of the building. "Do you think Jane would take us in tonight," a man said, his slurred words cutting through the quiet where he walked arm in arm with another man. The two of them staggard along the cobblestone road.

"We can only hope," the second man said. "Her thighs are like the softest milk puddings."

Milk puddings? Like a lady's thighs?

They passed, and William spoke to their father. "Stick to the shadows."

Her father nodded to William and then came silently to Maggie, kissing her forehead hard. "I will see you both at home." He turned and walked away.

Kerr followed William out into the night, still holding Maggie's hand. They turned in the opposite direction that their father had gone. They walked in silence for half an hour through winding roads that cut right along the two- and three-story houses of wattle and daub until they finally turned onto the Strand where the wealthy built or refurbished the town homes and small mansions.

"The narrow one that is lit," William said, pointing toward a three-story home with precisely cut stone lining the façade and a slate roof. A small, pebbled walkway led up to the house. The other houses on the road were mostly dark, but Norfolk's house was lit dimly from within despite the lateness of the hour. They stopped up against the one side of the dwelling near a tall, glassed window. Voices could be heard inside, although they were muted by the heavy glass.

Maggie jumped, her hand pressing against her heart, when the front door opened, and they all flattened up against the side.

"Fortunate for your friend, the Highlander lingered at court instead of merely dropping the gloves off. Otherwise, you would have had to place the needle and thread in her room instead." The man's voice was familiar, but it lacked the affable condensation that marked everything Lord Norfolk spouted.

"I would never have left Lady Darby to be blamed."

Maggie's breath caught as her hand flattened against the pain in her chest. That voice she knew very well. It had bid her good morning for years during their growing friendship. It was Cordelia Cranfield, and she was a traitor.

CHAPTER TWELVE

*"Do not tell secrets to those whose faith and silence
you have not already tested."*
Queen Elizabeth I of England

"WALSINGHAM MAY HAVE blamed Queen Mary herself if no one was to be found that he could torture and kill," Lord Johnathan Whitt said as he stood with Cordelia Cranfield under the front eaves of the Duke of Norfolk's house.

"Maggie Darby is trusted by the queen," Cordelia said. "She never would have believed her to be guilty of sewing blades into a glove."

"'Tis why she needed to die that night in the barn," Whitt said, his voice rough. "If the Highlander hadn't ruined that, if he'd only come a day later, there wouldn't have been anyone yet assigned to try on the gloves. Elizabeth might have succumbed to the bloodletting then."

Maggie's world felt too dizzy for her to move, and she leaned into the stone at her back, letting it hold her from dropping into a pile on the ground.

Cordy. How could it be? Her mother, Lady Agnes Cranfield, was Catholic but practiced in private. Maggie had never seen a rosary anywhere near the Cranfield sisters. Not that being a Catholic was the problem. It wasn't the knife that cut into Maggie, slashing her inside as she thought of the laughter they'd shared together each day. Was Lucy also part of the conspiracy?

"'Twas you," Cordelia said, her words weak. "You would have murdered Maggie?"

Cordelia yelped as Whitt grabbed her arms, giving her a shake as they stood near the doors of the house. "She's a heretic, Cordelia, like the bastard queen. With her removed, we would have had access to the queen's clothing."

"You sent the man who was going to rape her first?" Cordelia sounded like she was going to swoon.

Lord Whitt held her up by the elbows. "I do not condone such things, of course. When I saw he was planning such vileness, I had planned to slice his head from his neck, and kill Lady Darby myself." His whispered confession of the evil in his heart made Maggie unable to draw breath. Her fingers curled into the stone as if the sturdiness could keep her as strong.

"But then the Highlander showed up," Whitt said. "I still sliced the fool's throat, but your friend lived another day."

"I do not feel well," Cordelia said, but Maggie could no longer see her as she stared at her own boots.

The sound of horse hooves and a carriage came from the opposite side of the house, and Kerr helped Maggie pull back against the house into the deep shadows.

"Since my plan was foiled by poor timing," Whitt continued, "we must follow through with Ridolfi and Norfolk's plan tomorrow. You must lure the queen to the chapel."

The sound of wheels cracking on cobblestone announced the carriage's arrival. Kerr let go of Maggie and began to step out. William grabbed him, struggling to hold him back. Maggie clasped her hands before her as Kerr picked William up, ready to throw him into some winter-bare bushes, but William clung to his arm, his legs trying desperately to hold on to him.

Whitt looked back at the shadows by the house and hurriedly climbed in after Cordelia, rapping on the roof to get the carriage moving quickly.

William let go of Kerr's arm. "You Highland fool," William

whispered.

Kerr looked from the carriage as it fled down the road and then to Maggie, his chest heaving. "He planned to kill Maggie, hired that fiend who was going to rape her, and wanted her to take the blame for the gloves."

Maggie sat down on a short wall running alongside the house. *Cordy.* Cordy was part of this.

William stood up, brushing twigs off his short breeches. "Kill him after we have evidence, otherwise, you will add murder of one of England's viscounts to your charges and possibly link Maggie's name in there as well."

The sound of the wheels faded. Kerr stepped up to Maggie, lifting her to his chest. "She didn't know he wanted ye dead," he whispered, guessing at her weakness. Maggie felt Kerr rest his chin on the top of her head. She inhaled his scent. It somehow calmed her racing heart like some potent mixture of lemon balm.

"A friend's betrayal is the sharpest dagger," she murmured.

William scratched his fingers through his hair. "Well damn, Maggie. She sounded regretful to me. Perhaps coerced. If I hadn't kept a level head," he frowned at Kerr, "I would have snatched her away from that bastard, Whitt." He rubbed fingers back and forth across his mouth. "But we need to know where they are going, where the explosives are set, to prove they are the ones behind it."

"She may have been the one to steal the gloves from your room," Kerr said, letting her step back.

The door opened again, stopping her from any speculation. Norfolk and the man she'd seen talking to him in the streets hurried down the steps. Roberto Ridolfi, William had said. Another carriage came around the other side of the house and stopped.

"King Phillip of Spain will help once the heretic is dead," Ridolfi said. "He but awaits my word." They stepped up into the carriage, and it rattled on down the cobblestone road.

"I suppose killing them would also give me more charges,"

Kerr grumbled.

"Without proof, Norfolk would be seen as an innocent victim," William said.

"They must be going to the chapel Lord Whitt mentioned," Maggie said and took another calming breath.

He *tsk*ed. "There are a hundred chapels in London. Without knowing where it is, it would be like finding a grain of poison in an hourglass of sand."

"We could follow the queen on the morrow," Maggie said. "And then somehow stop her from going near the chapel."

"She may have us arrested," William said.

Maggie squeezed Kerr's hand. "You need to leave London tonight."

The shadows seemed like a curtain around them, and Maggie could not look away from the man who had saved her twice, first in the stables and then by safely removing the lethal glove. "William and I are still able to get close to the queen, but they will arrest you immediately if they see you." Her chest hurt, and she drew a deep breath. "You really should escape while it is still dark."

He reached up and gently clasped her chin. "But Maggie Darby, ye are someone I'd really rather get to know better."

She swallowed, remembering her words to him in the Bloody Tower. He lowered his head and feathered a kiss along her lips. His mouth was warm in contrast to the cold creeping through her clothes. The snow of earlier had changed to a light rain, which seemed colder. But all of that melted away under the warmth of his gentle kiss.

"What the hell does that mean, Gordon?" William said, his voice too loud in the silence.

Kerr pulled back but didn't look away from Maggie's eyes. "It means I'm not leaving London tonight."

"SHE WON'T TAKE us in," William said as they stood before the intricately wrought door.

"She said I could come anytime I had need," Maggie said, remembering Agatha Cranfield's words from her mother's funeral. "And right now, I am very much in need, partly because of her own daughter." She raised her hand and knocked briskly. "Countess Agatha Cranfield will give us shelter and a meal; I am certain of it."

The door opened enough to allow a wrinkled face to appear. Countess Cranfield's faithful butler, Simmons. "What mischief is this?" he asked, looking over Maggie's head to William and Kerr. Maggie had stayed overnight many times in the house with Lucy and Cordelia. She knew the butler to be one who adhered strictly to the rules of loyalty, and that loyalty belonged completely to the Cranfields.

"I know it is late, Master Simmons," Maggie said. "But we are in dire need of shelter from this drizzle. Countess Cranfield said I was welcome any time I needed a place to stay."

"Her ladyship has retired for the night," Simmons said, his tone brisk as he waved a candle before him to peer closer at the three standing on the stoop.

"Come now, Master Simmons," Maggie said. "Countess Cranfield said anytime I needed a mother, I must come." Although the cheerful woman had invited her back, this might push the limits of propriety too much for her butler.

Maggie gave the man a stern look. "*Anytime.*" The words came slow and drawn out. "She said so at the grave of my mother, and right now I am certainly in need. Would you turn away Lucy or Cordelia on a cold night like this?"

"And who are they?" Simmons asked, scowling at Kerr and William.

"My brother, William Darby, and... my friend from the north, Jasper Grigg."

"And why are you not at your own home tonight?" Simmons asked. He held the flame out like he might try to set them on fire if they pushed forward.

"'Tis my father," Maggie said, and gave William a little kick with the blunt toe of her boot.

William glanced down at her boot even though he was the one to help her make a cap for the blade. He raised his head. "Ah yes," he said and frowned. "He's gone quite mad."

"Mad?" Simmons asked.

Maggie lowered her voice. "'Tis embarrassing to say, but he is going around inside the house… naked."

"As the day he was born," William added. "But with much more hair." He made a face as if imagining their father running up and down the steps naked.

"And our friend from the north having arrived, we cannot take him there," Maggie said. She glanced at Kerr. "Be assured that madness does not manifest itself in William nor myself."

She waited for a reply, all eyes on Kerr.

He cleared his voice. "I am not mad either and rarely run about naked as the day I was born."

William smirked. "Well, there was that time after you had too much whiskey."

Kerr frowned. "I do not drink spirits in excess."

Maggie looked at Simmons. "Best lock up the whiskey just in case."

Simmons looked flummoxed, which was what they were going for. If he was confused enough, he might lower the candle and let them inside without them causing a scene.

"All the inns are closed at this hour," Maggie insisted, taking a step closer to the butler. And like people do when wavering and confronted, he took a step back. "It would be for this one night only."

"By tomorrow, Father will have put his clothes back on," William said.

Simmons' mouth pursed. "I suppose Mistress Darby may sleep in Lady Cordelia's room above."

Luck was with her. Maggie could search the room for any

letters with details of the upcoming attack. If they discovered the chapel name, they could find it early in the morning before the queen even left Whitehall. Maggie smiled broadly. "Wonderful," she said, taking another step forward, and Simmons backed up again. "And William and Jasper can take the guest room down the hall."

"Spot on," William said, not waiting for the butler's agreement. He wiped a hand over one eye as if exhausted from running about London. It was nearing midnight, so they all needed to find some rest.

Maggie dodged around the butler, making him turn, and Kerr and William followed her inside. Kerr shut the door behind them. And they were in.

"No need to wake the maid," Maggie said. "I can find us refreshments in the kitchen. Good night to you, Simmons. I will show the gentlemen where the guest bed chamber lies down the hall from Cordelia's suite."

The elderly man blinked at her rapid words. "I … can be of assistance," he murmured.

Maggie held a hand slightly before her mouth and yawned broadly. Seeing the action, Simmons fought his own yawn, trying to hide it behind his fist. Next to her William yawned again, sniffing as if trying to revive himself.

"No," Maggie said. "Go on to bed, kind sir. You are clearly exhausted from the day." No doubt, the man was tired of caring for Countess Cranfield, who could be overly dramatic for no reason except that she was bored.

Maggie beckoned William and Kerr to follow her to the kitchen that she knew sat at the back of the house.

"Lord Cranfield does not live here?" Kerr asked as they carried a lantern into the dark room where coals still glowed in the hearth.

"He died five years ago of Smallpox," William said.

"Lucy and Cordelia's mother is Countess Agatha Cranfield," Maggie said. "She lives alone except for her servants."

Kerr strode to the hearth to kindle the glowing coals and add some dry peat that sat in neat squares next to it. As the coals caught and the flames flickered up from the kindling, light illuminated the tidy room with long worktables and dried herbs hanging from above like in her father's kitchen.

"Well done with Simmons," William said, giving Maggie a nod.

She took a full inhale. "It will afford us one night to rest and eat and think." She found some rolls, cheese, and cooked pheasant for them to eat, and they sat at the small table in the corner.

William swallowed some weak ale and set his mug down. "When the glove did not kill Elizabeth, Whitt joined the plans with Norfolk," William suggested.

Kerr sat opposite him, next to Maggie. His leg brushed her skirts every now and then. "From what Norfolk asked me in The Tower," Kerr said, "I don't think he knew who was responsible for the glove, but he had devised a different plan with Ridolfi, an explosive plan."

William nodded and stifled a yawn.

"I will never really know if Queen Mary was involved or not," Kerr said. His face was grim. "She will beg innocence, but she is drawn to drama and intrigue of any sort."

Maggie swallowed the small piece of roll she'd been chewing. "'Tis a trait in the peerage and royalty," she said. "When one must find food daily to stay alive, intrigue and drama are not a priority."

William went to bank the fire and sat down on a pallet laid next to it. "Do you snore, Gordon?" He tipped to one side, his cycs already closing.

"Nay."

Maggie stood. "William does."

"I think I'll lay right here for now," William said. "'Tis warm."

Maggie took up the lantern and stepped around her brother.

She tugged Kerr's hand. "Let's search Cordelia's room," she whispered. "If the name of the chapel is written on something, we will have evidence to show Walsingham before they arrive."

The house was dark, but she maneuvered easily having spent last Christmas making merry for several days here. Which added to the sick feeling of betrayal in her stomach. Was Cordelia truly trapped in Norfolk's plan?

Kerr followed behind her, their footfalls quiet. An occasional squeak of the stairs made her halt, but no one seemed to be moving in the sleeping house. The warmth of Kerr's hand in hers sent a flutter of nervousness through her middle. She was leading him up to a bed chamber, and William seemed quite comfortable before the fire in the kitchen. She had never put herself in a position that could make her look compromised, because there had never been anyone by whom she'd like to be compromised. Until now.

Chapter Thirteen

M AGGIE OPENED THE door to Cordelia's pale-colored room that had two rich tapestries gracing the walls. Thick curtains surrounded the large bed, and a silk coverlet, filled with goose down, covered it. Kerr held a taper to the lantern to light two oil lamps on the mantel and set about making a fire in the swept hearth.

"Thank you," she murmured as she watched him take off his cloak and bend down to the grate. The muscles of his back stretched William's shirt to nearly bursting the seams. Kerr's shoulders were massive, the same with his biceps. "Do you practice with your sword often?" she asked, her voice stark in the quiet room.

He glanced over his shoulder at her, his brow raised. "Aye. Every morning when I am at Auchindoun." He turned back to his task. "With feuding and raids happening at any moment, a warrior must stay fit, strong, and quick."

She frowned. "And Norfolk kept your sword and dagger."

"I aim to get them back," he said and bent his head to let out a long breath to feed the spark in the firelit wool he set in the peat.

Maggie walked to the writing desk in the corner. The room

was cold, and she tugged her shawl closer. Using the lamplight, she flipped through the pieces of parchment left there, but they were all blank.

Even so, her heart beat faster. She was in a private room alone with Kerr. She had been before while at Whitehall, but that was before he'd said that he'd rather get to know her better. Could that truly be why he wasn't riding away tonight?

"Your weapons are important to you." She watched him rise, straightening. "You must wish to stay in London to reclaim them."

His gaze met hers. His features were in shadow with the fire at his back, the light illuminating her where she stood before the four-poster bed. "They could be replaced."

"Oh," she said and turned back to the desk, flipping over two books there to search if anything fell out. Nothing. Her inhale came in jagged little pulls, her whole being very aware that Kerr stood across the dark room.

Must focus on the task. She glanced under the desk and in the drawers, pushing her hand to the very back, but she felt only a few unused quills and jars of ink. Maggie turned around, leaning against the desk.

Kerr stood before the one set of bookshelves. His fingers moved over the leather spines, pulling them out and sliding them back. She could imagine him reading with her before a fire. His deep voice would bring the Greek gods, from her father's book on legends, to life. *Good lord! Focus!* Maggie walked the perimeter of the room, looking in storage chests, empty cups and pitchers, and under the bed.

"Nothing," she said and turned to find Kerr watching her. He held what she imagined was a battle stance, like when he fought the villain in the stables. Muscular legs braced, arms full of strength, large hands cradling a book. She swallowed. Kerr Gordon was pure male. Able to kill and survive through cunning and skill. He was also clever and listened to her ideas. And he could render her breathless with his gaze. She had never met anyone like him.

She cleared her throat. "There is nothing here to give as proof to Lord Walsingham," she said and looked away. "You really should leave tonight to be ahead of him." Her inhale felt ragged, her heart clenching at the thought of him riding away.

"Nay," he said.

Her voice was softer with her shallow breath. "The only thing I could think to keep you here when there is so much to send you away is your need for revenge on Norfolk and Whitt."

He closed the book, sliding it back onto the shelf. "I could do that by alerting Walsingham anonymously so that Mary did not know I foiled the plans of her conspirators. Send a child with a carefully worded letter warning him of the false christening."

Kerr took a slow step toward her. Her mouth suddenly quite dry, she touched her tongue to her bottom lip. His gaze dropped to her mouth, then returned to stare into her eyes. He didn't move forward anymore, and time seemed to hang in place between them.

"Ask me why I am really staying in London, Maggie Darby," Kerr said, the words drawn out in his thick Scottish accent, that reminded her of water burbling over rocks in a wild river. "Why I can't seem to ride away." They stood completely still as the fire crackled in the hearth. Maggie felt a nearly physical pull between them, as if they were magnets attuned to come together. Did Kerr feel the pull?

"Elizabeth is not your queen nor your responsibility," Maggie said, sensation tickling through her, making her shift.

"She is not," he said.

As the fire grew in the hearth, Maggie could easily see the strong line of Kerr's jaw and his generous mouth, the intense look in his eyes. The house was asleep, and they were alone. There was a lock on the door, and William slept like the dead once he succumbed for the night.

"Ask me, Maggie, why I am still here in London, if ye truly wish to know. Otherwise, I will leave ye to sleep." He spoke slowly, and she saw him swallow. His hands fisted next to his legs as if he fought for control. What could rob him of his obvious discipline? *Me?*

"'Tis your choice," he said. "One ye can change at any time."

Her choice? Was he asking to kiss her again or more? Much more?

The thought released heat within her, heat fanned by the flutter of awareness she'd been trying to ignore. She shifted against the ache that surged at the crux of her legs. She was a virgin, but having lived at court, she knew the workings of physical love, and that ladies were ordered to remain chaste until marriage.

She also knew that life was short. How many times could she have been killed in the last week alone? Too many to worry about social dictates. If she returned home to care for her father, and William left, she would probably never marry. Everyone said physical love was grand indeed. There were innuendos, jests, and whispers with smiles. Cordelia wasn't waiting to find out by a husband, one who would likely be old or possibly cruel if he was chosen to enhance her family's interests.

Maggie pulled in a breath. "Why are you still here in London, Kerr? Tonight, when you could be riding away to safety?"

As if being released from shackles, he moved toward her with powerful grace to stand before her. She tipped her head back to reach his gaze, her breath catching at the hunger in the intensity of his eyes.

"Because of ye, Maggie Darby. Because ye are clever, and courageous, and..." he reached the back of his fingers up to her cheek, gently stroking her. "And ye are so incredibly soft. I will never leave ye in jeopardy, and if ye meant what ye said before, I too want to know ye better. Very much better."

His words held longing, mirroring her own, and a type of languid relief settled over her.

She wrapped her hand around his fingers at her cheek, holding them there. "Then by all means, Kerr Gordon, get to know me better."

Kerr's warm mouth met Maggie's lips. This kiss was softer than the one in his prison cell but no less desperate. A soft sound of pleasure escaped her as she opened her mouth, slanting against him, her hands rising to hook onto his shoulders as he bent over her, surrounding her with his powerful arms.

She slid her palms down the thickness of his arms as their kiss deepened. Breathing against him, he swept inside past her open lips. He tasted of honey ale and dark promises of pleasure. More heat barreled through Maggie like a wave of molten rock, and she pressed into him. Her thick garments were in the way, but their mouths slid together, giving and taking. She ran her fingernails up through his thick hair and clung to his neck.

His hand slid down her back to the petticoats, but with her bum roll and thick layers, there was nothing to feel except padding, and she so much wanted to feel more.

Her hands slid up his chest, exploring the muscles under the linen. Without breaking the kiss, Maggie untied the knot at his neck. Lips clinging to each other in frantic longing, she tugged his tunic out of the breeches, her fingers finding the ties that held them together over his hips.

He stopped her hands, lifting them to kiss. "Maggie, ye are a maid still. I would not…"

She shook her head even before he finished the sentence and placed her hands on his chest. "I have decided that life is too short, especially when trying to protect a queen." She offered him a small smile. "I want to live and live well."

Her voice dropped softer, but she kept his gaze. "I want to know what this ache is within me, an ache that grows every time you look at me, and even more with your touch." She took his hand, uncurling the fingers. "We do not know what tomorrow brings, Kerr. Let us live for tonight." She placed his open hand on her chest that lay bare above the neckline of her gown. "Touch me, Kerr Gordon, and feel how you make my heart fly and my blood rush."

"Maggie," he said her name like a tortured warning.

"Shhhh," she said, raising her palms to his stubbled face, the roughness of it in tantalizing contrast to her own. "I want you, Kerr. And now that I know that you…" She slid her hands under the tail of his shirt and up over his hot skin. "Want to know me…"

"Aye, lass, I want to know all of ye."

Kerr stepped back, and she almost tried to stop him when he walked away from her. But he went to the door and turned the iron key, locking them in. He removed it and dropped it on the floor. The sound of it hitting the floorboards sent a shiver through her, and she watched as he turned slowly, pulling his tunic off as he did.

The fire sent shadows and light across his skin. A sprinkling of hair covered the tanned skin of his chest. With the breeches untied, Maggie could see the angular lines of muscle showing his strength all the way down to where his jack bulged.

Kerr quickly untied his boots, slipping them off along with the hose that looked out of place on a warrior from the wild north country. He straightened, his shoulders massive, and he walked toward her with a predator's grace. His gait was full of slow confidence as he watched her. He stopped several steps away, assessing her, a small frown growing.

"Do you think I am frightened?" she whispered. "That I might dash around you to scoop up the key and flee?"

"Perhaps," he said, his straightforward gaze sliding down her fevered body.

The swell of her breasts pressed upward against the neckline of the low gown. Maggie pulled the pins from the triangular stomacher, holding it in place. She stepped to the washstand without taking her gaze from Kerr, and placed the long, sharp pins there, letting the stomacher come away to show her stays. She reached up to untie the long sleeves tied at the shoulders, letting them slip down her arms. Her petticoats followed quickly with a tug of the ties around her waist. They billowed out around her ankles as they dropped, and she stepped out of them.

She walked toward him. "I am not going anywhere," she said, her voice soft, "until you teach me about this fire inside me."

Her words made him shift, his hand going to the front of his breeches, cupping the largeness there. "Ye are certain, Maggie?"

"I am this certain," she said, pulling the ribbon that laced her stays in the front. They opened, releasing her torso, and she slid them down her hips until they lay as neglected as the petticoats, bum roll, and stomacher. She stood in her white linen shift, moving so that the fire glowed behind her. She reached up to pull the three long hair pins holding up her mass of hair. The fragrant curls toppled down around her shoulders as she walked toward Kerr, knowing full well how the fire would reveal her body through the thin material.

"I know things from books and my laboratory," she said, her voice a whisper. "The way chemicals work and plants that help and hurt us. But I know almost nothing about this ache within me. This fire." She reached up to touch his cheek. "Teach me, Kerr Gordon. Teach me about this fire."

CHAPTER FOURTEEN

"Graze on my lips; and if those hills be dry, stray lower, where the pleasant fountains lie."
William Shakespeare – *Venus and Adonis*

KERR GROANED LOW and took a long, deep breath, letting it out with words said in his deeply accented ancient language. "Och but ye are the loveliest lass I have ever seen, Maggie."

He stepped closer, his arms wrapping around her. Her hands slid up the hot skin and muscles of his chest, through the sprinkling of hair and up to his neck to pull his face to hers. But she needn't tug, for his mouth swooped down to capture her lips.

Heat and longing swirled around Maggie, wrapping her up as surely as Kerr's arms. Free of most of her clothes, she could feel every part of his strength against her, including the thick length pressing between her legs. It seemed to fit perfectly there. She raised and lowered on her toes, rubbing. It was as if her body wanted to make certain she knew exactly what part of her needed him. Even if she hadn't heard and read about the workings of love, her body would have guided her.

Her hand slipped down over his taut stomach, reveling in the displayed strength, to press against his rigid length. Kerr groaned against her mouth. She reached between the ties of his breeches and found him. Hot and heavy, his jack stood erect as if seeking her heat. A shudder of longing made her tremble at the thought, and she felt weak in her legs. Stroking up and down his length,

Kerr's breathing became more ragged, and his breeches fell to the floor, leaving him naked.

"Ye will unman me, lass," he whispered against her mouth. He drew her hand away from him, although she couldn't imagine anything making him seem less of a man, a powerful, mighty man.

Stepping back, she took in his entire naked body. The glow of the fire playing along hewn muscle emphasized his ruggedly carved form. She'd seen the drawing of Michelangelo's masterpiece sculpture of David, but Kerr's body was so much more. She swallowed, feeling her body clench below with hunger. She wanted him, all of him.

His gaze never left her as he walked over to the washstand and back, like a beast tracking its prey. Standing still, her hands rose to the swell of her breasts under the smock, palming them, her fingers plucking at her hard nipples as he watched.

One of his hands went to his jack as he stared at her. "Och but ye are lovely, Maggie."

The reverence in his words gave her courage, and she bent to ruck up the bottom edge of her smock, lifting it slowly as he watched. Her legs, still wrapped in silk stockings and gartered above her knees, were exposed first. Once she reached her hips, she lifted the linen up and over her head, letting the white material trail off her fingers to float to the floor. She bent to untie the garters.

"Nay," Kerr said. "Leave them." His voice sounded hoarse, making her smile.

She stood totally bare except for the stockings. Kerr strode to her, gathering her form up against him. The contact of his skin against hers sent another wash of heat through Maggie, and she moaned. His strong hands caught her head, tilting her face so that his kiss covered her already open mouth.

Tasting, touching, breathing in each other's scent. Her whole consciousness was flooded with Kerr and their combined senses. All of it fed the fire spreading inside Maggie, and she pressed the crux of her legs against his hardness.

She tipped her head back as he kissed along her neck and moaned as he took her nipple into his mouth, sucking as he palmed her other breast. His talented finger caressed a path to the ache between her legs, and she opened her thighs, giving him any access he wanted.

"Oh God, Kerr," she whispered as he touched her heat, pressing up inside her where she had never been touched before. "Yes," she gasped as he moved there, exploring, stretching, and stroking. She shivered as his thumb grazed on the outside of her, finding the nub she stroked herself some nights, bringing such aching pleasure. He seemed to read her desire like it was his own, stroking her inside and out until the fire grew wild and her legs trembled.

His kisses moved back to her lips. "Ye are drenched with sweet heat, lass," he said against her.

"I can barely stand."

His arms wrapped around her, and he carried her against him, one arm under her backside, the other supporting her back, and set her onto the edge of the bed.

She looked at him standing over her, magnificent. "Oh God, I want you, Kerr," she said, and felt her legs spreading, welcoming him in.

He groaned, and she watched him stroke himself. "Ah lass, we will take pleasure in each other for certain." He climbed into the bed, kneeling before her opened legs. She held out her arms to him, but he pressed against her shins, raising her knees. "Relax, Maggie, lass," he said, and she watched his head dip between her thighs. His tongue touched her, and she nearly jumped at the pulse of lightning that shot through her.

"Oh my lord," she whispered as he claimed her below, loving her with tongue and fingers. She had heard of women placing their mouths on men but did not know it was reciprocated with such carnal power.

The pleasure in her built higher until it was sweet torture.

"Oh Kerr," she said, barely able to keep her breaths from growing too loud. The crest of her pleasure began to break over, her breathing fast as he worked her open flesh. "Yes," she hissed. "Oh yes." The pleasure exploded within her, pulsing wave after wave.

Kerr raised his face to her, his expression tortured and full of lust. She saw his hand working his jack as she continued to feel the waves of her own pleasure slowly ebb. She reached down to her wetness and touched herself.

Kerr groaned low and turned, grabbing a small towel he'd found at the washstand and had thrown onto the bed. His eyes squeezed shut as he groaned. For long seconds he breathed, and then climbed up the bed next to her.

He pulled her against his chest, and she nuzzled her face there, inhaling his scent. Her leg slid between his, and he kissed her. Gentler now, and she kissed him back with slow reverence, until they broke apart, and he tucked her head under his chin. Their skin began to cool, and he pulled the blankets up.

As her breathing slowed, her rational mind caught up to her. Maggie blinked, feeling tears press against the backs of her eyes. "You did not compromise me," she whispered.

For a long moment, Kerr said nothing, only stroked her hair. "Ye must decide when we both aren't full of heat."

Maggie lay her hand against his chest over the thud of his heart. She closed her eyes as she lay in the arms of a man so honorable that he would not take his own pleasure in her. For the first time in Kerr's arms, she was afraid. What would the future entail? And if Kerr was not in hers, would she be able to endure the pain?

THE CURTAINS HAD been closed around the bed, but the top was open. Kerr stared up at the scene painted on the ceiling over him. The saints had watched him lose himself to the fragrant arms of

Maggie. He turned his head to the pillow where she lay, beautiful and undone in sleep. Her hair tumbled about her heart-shaped face, a frame for the exquisite smattering of freckles over her pale skin. Her dark lashes lay against the softness under her almond-shaped eyes under perfectly arched brows. He could stare at Maggie until the sun was high, but it was nearly dawn, and he must get to the bedchamber he was supposed to be sleeping in.

He forced himself to look upward, away from the beauty before him, and met the condemning eyes of the artist's rendition of God looking down from a cloud. "I do not regret any of it," he whispered. He might regret the outcome, but he could not wish away what had passed between Maggie and him. It was too exquisite a memory.

Clop. Clop. Clop. Clop.

Kerr pushed up out of the warm, Maggie-scented covers at the sound of horses stopping before the house. He padded across the room to the curtained windows. Cordelia and Lucy Cranfield stepped quickly from a hired coach, which rumbled off. *Mo chreach.*

"What is it?" Maggie asked, pushing up, her hair like a soft cascade over her shoulders.

"The sisters have returned," he said, grabbing the English breeches that lay in a heap on the floor.

"Good Lord," Maggie said, throwing back the covers. She was naked. Sometime during the night, he'd even unrolled the stockings down her legs, one at a time while kissing the skin along her calves.

She ran around the room, snatching up the stockings and her smock. Despite the dire situation, Kerr stood there taking in her loveliness. He remembered the taste of her as he trailed kisses over her skin, listening to her soft mews.

"Kerr," she said, and he followed her gaze to his rigid jack. "You will never get that into your breeches." If she didn't look so panicked, he would have laughed.

He adjusted himself, tying the rope at his waist. "Englishmen must have smaller jacks than Scotsmen," he said, trying to stuff his tunic in with his erection.

"Or Scotsmen are more randy," Maggie said.

Below, the door opened, and Kerr could hear Simmons talking. How would Cordelia react knowing they were in the house? In her room? Naked?

Footsteps pounded up the steps, answering his thought.

"She is coming here to find ye," he said. "Shall I hide?"

Maggie's wide eyes slid about the spartan room. With most of Cordelia's things at Whitehall, there was nowhere to hide except behind the curtain. She shook her head. "Help me first," Maggie said, throwing her stays around her middle. There was no way to dress a lady quickly in court clothes, yet she was trying. He tugged the ties tightly closed, thanking God for making him a man yet again. She ran for her shoes, jamming her feet in them, and he set her bum roll around her hips for her to tie at the front. He brought her shoes over and held her petticoats for her to grab from him.

"We have much to discuss, Cordelia," William said, his stern voice carrying from the hall. "Maggie is up in your room."

"God's teeth," Maggie swore, flapping her hand at Kerr. "Get dressed!"

"Cordelia, is that you?" said a sleepy voice down the hallway. "Heavens, sir. Who are you?"

"Countess Cranfield," Maggie whispered, her eyes wide. Was she realizing that there was no way to hide the fact that she'd spent the night in this room with him? He hadn't even been able to get back to the guest suite to muss the blankets. If William walked in there, the game was over.

There was no time to get his boots or tunic on before the latch on the door rattled. "Maggie. Wake up," William called.

"A moment, please," she answered, but her voice sounded strained. She flapped a hand at Kerr to get him to put on his tunic. Heavy footfalls went down the hallway in the direction of the guest suite.

"The Highlander does not seem to be in there," Simmons' voice came from that direction.

Maggie placed both hands on her cheeks, her eyes closing as the thunderous sound of William racing back to Cordelia's room preceded his fist hitting the door.

"Gordon!" William's voice filled the house as Cordelia's mother and the sisters started talking behind him all at once. Somewhere in there, Kerr thought he heard Simmons trying to answer questions.

"I am not—"

"They were afforded two rooms."

"No, I was told to retire. Of course—"

Kerr looked at Maggie. "I think we should stay in here. What say ye?"

His question had the desired effect. Maggie's panicked face relaxed, her brows going up as she held a hand to cover her mouth. "I agree," she said from between her fingers, and they both looked at the sturdy oak door.

"Open up, Gordon," William yelled. "Maggie, open the door. I know he's in there."

"He is rather frantic," she whispered. "I have to speak up."

Kerr shrugged his shoulders. He would go with whatever she would like to do.

"I am fine, William," she called through the door. "Stop yelling."

"Is he in there with you?" William asked, his voice a near growl.

"Who?" the countess asked. "Simmons, who is in there with Margaret Darby?"

"A Scotsman, milady, from his accent," Simmons answered.

A gasp came from either the countess or one of her daughters or both. "How unseemly," the countess said.

Maggie's palms slid down her very pink cheeks. "Yes, William. Kerr is in here."

"Foking hell," William said, bringing about another chorus of gasps.

"Not before the ladies, sir," Simmons said.

"Open the door, Maggie," William demanded.

Maggie drew closer to the door, her hands clenching into fists. "Not until you stop sounding so angry."

"Gordan, are you in there hiding behind her skirts?" William asked, obviously taunting.

Kerr opened his mouth to say something about Maggie's skirts not being on to hide behind but stopped himself from adding fuel to the wildfire, even if it would have been humorous.

"I would hate to have to slice ye through, Darby," Kerr said instead. "Before the ladies. Simmons would have blood stains to contend with then."

"With what, Gordon? You seem to be missing your sword and daggers," William said.

Maggie held up her hands to cut off Kerr's return strike and turned to the door as she yanked on her second petticoat. The stomacher still sat across the room. "Everyone, calm down. I will unlock the door, and you, William, will step away," Maggie said.

"I will thrash him," William said.

"Ye can try," Kerr said.

"Neither of you will thrash anyone," Maggie yelled. "William, you will go retrieve Kerr's horse while I talk with Cordelia and Countess Cranfield."

"I am here too," Lucy called from farther down the hall.

"Good Lord, help me," Maggie whispered, her palm now pressing against her forehead.

Kerr couldn't help but chuckle softly, and she turned to glare at him. "You may lose your freedom to a forced marriage to me," she said, her voice soft and forceful. "Therefore, none of this is humorous."

Marriage? To Maggie?

William continued to pound. Simmons yelled for him to stop. The sisters asked questions, and the mother made ponderous exclamations about dishonor. But all that faded as Kerr thought of how perfect it was to wake up next to Maggie.

"Maggie," he said, and she turned back to him. He gazed into her blue eyes, all traces of his earlier jest gone.

"I must open it," she said, turning back to the door.

"Wait." He walked up behind her, placing his palm flat on the door. He inhaled the fragrance of her hair, felt the softness of it brush his lips as he neared her ear and spoke. "Will ye marry me, Maggie Darby?"

CHAPTER FIFTEEN

"There is nothing more dangerous than security."
Francis Walsingham – Queen Elizabeth I's Spymaster

M AGGIE SPUN AROUND, her back against the door. Her mouth dropped open, and they stared at one another for a long moment. William continued to demand they open the door, and the ladies chattered away behind him. Was Kerr serious? Or was this part of the jest? She closed her mouth with a clank of her teeth. "I…" Her face pinched. "What?"

Kerr ran his hands up through his hair, which looked very much like he was serious and a bit unnerved by what had just popped out of his mouth. He dropped his hands and gave a quick nod. "Will ye marry me?"

"You are serious?"

"Maggie, I am going to break this door down," William yelled, his fists returning to the door.

"No, young man, you are not," Simmons yelled. "'Tis sturdy English oak."

"It will not stop me! Maggie, stand back."

"I am going to find a constable," Simmons said, his words the loudest Maggie had ever heard from the dignified old man.

Maggie turned back to the door. "No, I am coming out now."

"Maggie," Kerr said. She glanced at him while grabbing the heavy iron key that she'd placed in the lock. He ducked his face so that she had to meet his gaze. "Whatever happens after ye open that door, know that my proposal stands."

He reached around her and turned the key, pulling her backwards as her brother barreled into the room like a bull. Even his nostrils flared. Kerr pushed Maggie behind him, and she curled her fingers into his tunic, steadying herself.

"Let her go!" William yelled, apparently not seeing that Kerr wasn't holding onto her but rather, she was holding onto him. "You… You dishonorable scoundrel!"

Maggie took a full breath and stepped out from behind Kerr, but her rumpled appearance did nothing to calm William down. "I am still a maid, William. Kerr is an honorable man."

"Honorable? To sleep in the same room, a locked room, with you, Maggie…" William shook his head. "He has ruined you."

Maggie's hands went to her hips. "And Kerr has asked me to wed."

Everyone stopped talking at once. Cordelia and Lucy stood with wide eyes next to Simmons. Countess Cranfield held her robe tightly wrapped around her thin body as she eyed Kerr up and down. Hopefully the bulge in his pants had receded. Maybe Scotsmen did have larger jacks. The thought of Kerr heavy in her hands made a rush of heat weave down between her legs, and she shifted, pushing the inappropriate-at-this-time thought away.

The countess's lips turned into a smile, and her hands clapped together once, making Cordelia jump. "We can have the wedding at our country estate. It will be lovely." She turned to her daughters. "We can do this charity for your dear friend who has lost her mother and from what Simmons says, her father to insanity."

"Have you given him an answer?" William asked. Although his question was for Maggie, he glared over her head at Kerr.

Maggie planted her hands on her hips. "I thought that with all the issues abounding, it would be prudent to wait to see where we are tomorrow before answering."

"Tomorrow?" Countess Cranfield asked. "What is tomorrow?"

Maggie's gaze moved to Cordelia. "We hear that there is a christening to attend today, which may impact tomorrow greatly."

Cordelia's eyes widened, her face paling in the low light of the sconces in the hall. Her hand when to her chest.

"Are you attending, Cordelia?" Maggie asked and looked to the other sister. "And you, Lucy?"

Lucy's brows drew together. "Cordelia told me the christening is next Sunday. That is why we are visiting Mother today and tomorrow instead of staying at Whitehall."

Maggie looked back to Cordelia. "So you've managed to keep your sister out of it."

"We need to talk," Cordelia said, eyeing her mother. "Alone." She strode forward and pulled Maggie with her into her room. She paused when she saw the rumpled bedding. "You should change," she said. "Where are your things?"

"I have no things," Maggie replied curtly. "Because I was thrown out of the castle with the clothes on my back for not reporting an innocent man."

"Dear me," Countess Cranfield said from the corridor. "Cordelia, are you involved in something, something I should know about?"

Cordelia looked to her mother and then back at Maggie, who stood with her arms crossed before her. "Let me talk with Maggie first, Mother."

Kerr was still in the room, William breathing heavily in his face. Maybe it was good Norfolk had kept Kerr's weapons, because her brother might push him past his restraint. "William," Maggie said, "find us all some breakfast below. Kerr, do not find a weapon. I will be out shortly."

Kerr kept his gaze locked on her brother. "I don't need a weapon."

"You bastard," William said.

"Enough," Maggie yelled. "Everyone, calm down so we can figure out what to do."

"What to do?" Countess Cranfield said. "I don't even know what is going on except that I hope to start planning a spectacular wedding."

Everything was happening so quickly that Maggie couldn't even take a moment to consider Kerr's proposal or what it meant. Was it even real? *It stands.*

Cordelia shut the door as the two men left. The window curtains were drawn back, allowing in the sun that had risen despite all the upheaval.

"Do not lock the door," Kerr called. "Or Simmons will be quite furious when I break it down."

Maggie turned to Cordelia who paced, her hands before her. The usual confident air she cloaked herself in seemed skewed to the point of tatters. "I didn't mean for you to be involved at all," she said, stopping to look at Maggie. "Johnathan asked me to place the needle and thread into your room. When I told him that you already had some in there, he insisted I still do it. It was only then that he drew me into his confidence about…"

When she didn't continue, Maggie did. "About trying to kill the queen of England."

Cordelia's hand flew to her throat as if she could already feel the cut of the executioner's axe. "Oh Maggie. I… I didn't know what to do. Johnathan… well we had been…"

"Lovers? I think I knew that."

Her hand still rested at her throat, and she blinked. "It was a mistake I should never have made." She took a deep breath. "Johnathan… Lord Whitt and Lord Norfolk were so insistent that I help them since we are a Catholic family, and the pope wants Queen Elizabeth dead. Pope Pius says that she is a heretic, and if we don't kill her when given the chance, we will go to Hell." She swallowed hard as if truly believing her soul was in jeopardy. "I don't want to go to Hell, Maggie. I have already sinned with Johnathan." Her words held a tremor.

"You do not pick lovers well, Cordy. The man was going to kill me."

Tears erupted from Cordelia's eyes. "I know. I mean, I didn't know then, when you were attacked. I didn't know he could be so cruel."

Maggie had been friends with the Cranfield sisters since she arrived at court seven years ago. Cordelia was the strong one of the two, always dignified and cool. To see her rattled showed the truth of her fear. She was stuck between two terrible fates: a painful execution and forever in Hell. If Maggie was only given those two options, killing the queen seemed like the right course to take. And from Cordelia's reaction last eve, it seemed she truly didn't know about Johnathan Whitt's murderous plans for Maggie in the stables.

Maggie squeezed Cordelia's hands. "But you didn't put the thread and needle in my room, you put them in Kerr's."

Cordelia nodded briskly, like a bird, and then changed directions shaking her head. "I swear I wouldn't do anything to risk you, Maggie. I knew nothing of Johnathan's horrible plans in the barn or that there were blades in the glove. Or that..." She motioned to the door. "That you cared for the Scotsman."

"He is innocent, Cordelia. Kerr knew nothing of what the gift to the queen even was."

Cordelia's eyes swelled with tears. "And now you are tangled up in this mess, especially when it is discovered that Kerr is missing from the Tower. Did you break him out last night?"

Maggie nodded.

"Oh Lord, Maggie," Cordelia said. "You are the bravest woman I know."

Maggie looked directly into her eyes. "For us to get out of this without going to the block, you need to be brave too, Cordy."

Her eyes grew wide. "What do I have to do?" she whispered.

"Start by telling me everything."

WILL YOU MARRY me? The question churned in Kerr's head, weaving between all the details that would save the English queen's life as well as Maggie's. She hadn't answered him, not even silently with a smile. Over the course of a week, she had turned him into a hound, begging for a scrap of an answer to the most important question he'd ever asked anyone in his life. "Bloody hell," he murmured.

"Do your part, Highlander, and this will work," William said, misinterpreting Kerr's curse. "I won't revenge my sister's honor until after we save the day."

"I can kill with an English sword as well as a Scottish one," Kerr said, his hand on the borrowed rapier that William had found for him. It lay hidden under the mid-length cloak he wore.

They walked together down the cobblestone street, dodging vendors hawking their wares in the early afternoon. Maggie's brother had turned from a jovial ally to a hateful arse. Although, how could Kerr blame him when he'd probably have acted the same way had he found his own sister, Rhona, locked in a room with a half-dressed man?

They headed toward Saint Vedast Chapel next to Saint Paul's Cathedral where Cordelia said the explosion was to take place. Apparently, the Catholics who were scheming to kill the queen like Queen Mary's husband, Lord Darnley, didn't want to harm the great cathedral. Therefore, the assassination had been planned for the smaller chapel next door.

From what Cordelia had revealed from the planning meeting between Whitt, Norfolk, and the Florentine banker, Roberto Ridolfi, Saint Vedast had been stuffed with enough gunpowder under the floorboards to blow the entire chapel to bits, including anyone inside it. The schemers had used the child's christening as an excuse to have the queen come out from behind the protection of Whitehall. It was a great honor to have her as a godparent. Cordelia didn't think the parents were involved.

William and Kerr were dressed in workman's clothing: breeches, tunics, and caps to blend in. In contrast, Maggie would be dressed as one of Elizabeth's ladies in muted gray colors, which the queen mandated so as not to be outdressed. Countess Cranfield had argued with the force of a concerned mother for both Lucy and Cordelia to stay away from the chapel. Finally, Simmons had promised to make certain Cordelia was out of harm's way. She was expected by Norfolk and the queen.

Ridolfi's plan was for Cordelia to make certain Elizabeth was in the chapel, and as many of her ladies were out of it before Norfolk gave the signal to Whitt to light the fuses. Cordelia was to try to trick as many of the queen's advisors into the chapel as well. If they could also kill Walsingham and Cecil in the explosion, the way would be open for Mary Stuart to be freed and to take the throne of England.

Shovels thrown over their shoulders, Kerr and William walked up to the whitewashed chapel with its main tower steepled and pointing up to God. Innocent people walked around it without an inkling that if chance happened to bring them by when it exploded, they would die too, leaving families grieving and possibly without a provider.

Kerr walked directly inside, his boots clipping on the inlaid floor of white and black marble set in geometric square patterns. Walsingham and the two palace guards, Henry and Giles, stood in the middle, inspecting the location. Chances were, they hadn't looked in the crypts underneath where the gunpowder had been smuggled in and set.

As planned, William took the lead. "Sirs, we ask you to vacate the chapel while we set about making repairs."

William and Kerr were not naïve enough to expect the head of Elizabeth's security to walk amiably out with them, but they would give him a chance.

True to form, Walsingham drew himself up. "The repairs must wait. Her Majesty, the queen, is about to arrive for a christening."

Kerr gripped the shovel that still rested on his shoulder. One, two, three steps, and he swung at Giles. *Wham*. The shovel hit his face, knocking him down onto the marble.

"Nay!" Henry yelled, but William hit him before he could sound much of an alarm, and the young guard crumpled to the ground. Luckily, the rest of the guards were surrounding the queen as she rode through the busy streets of London.

To his credit, Walsingham drew his sword and did not cower. His stoic face turned straight to Kerr. "Highlander. I heard you had escaped with the help of a man and woman." Walsingham glanced at William. "William and Maggie Darby will hang for their part in your schemes."

Daingead. He should have made Maggie leave. "Your queen is in jeopardy," Kerr said, meeting the man's cold suspicion with a heated gaze. He must convince Walsingham that he was telling the truth before Norfolk showed up.

"From Mary Stuart and her supporters," Walsingham said with a haughty sneer.

"I will keep watch on the doors," William said. He passed a look to Kerr and gave a small nod. Despite his fury at Kerr, the two had made a plan. If all went to hell that day, William would take Maggie away to Kerr's family in Scotland. William strode back down the aisle toward the ornate doors of the chapel.

Kerr stepped closer to the queen's head of security. "Lord Norfolk and Lord Whitt are working with a banker, Roberto Ridolfi, to assassinate Elizabeth. Today. By blowing up this church."

Walsingham's brows lifted, and he let out an annoyed sigh. "I know about Ridolfi, and I am collecting evidence on Norfolk. And Whitt is a fool who is only interested in the next skirt he can breach."

Even with the confidence in his voice, the man's gaze shifted amongst the rows of pews running the length on both sides up to the pulpit. "I would have heard of such a plot unfolding today."

"And yet, there are no parents nor bairn here."

"We came early to review the location and threats. Norfolk is even planning to attend. I doubt he will show if that is his plan."

"The real christening is scheduled for next week," Kerr said. "Norfolk, Whitt, and Ridolfi sent false invitations. This is a ploy to get Elizabeth and ye here."

"If you have dreamt up a slaughter, my loyal guards, who are currently surrounding Her Majesty will outnumber any small pockets of Catholics seeking the Pope's blessing by killing her," Walsingham said with confidence.

"There is gunpowder in the tombs below us. Enough to bring this entire chapel down."

Walsingham's face lost some of its superiority. "And why should I believe you, Gordon? You are a known supporter of Mary Stuart from a family of Catholics in a country who disregards the authority of England."

Kerr leaned closer until his face was directly before the man's. "Because I did not leave London." He didn't blink. "Why would I bother to warn ye, risking my freedom and head, if we were not currently standing over barrels of gunpowder with Johnathan Whitt at the fuses outside?"

Walsingham's brows pinched. "You have seen him plant these explosives?"

"I have my own spies who have told me their plan. Norfolk will come in. Ridolfi has already flown London, and Whitt will light the fuses. When Norfolk leaves the building after the queen steps inside, the building will blow."

"And you stayed to warn us because you support Elizabeth and not your Mary?" Walsingham said, obviously still suspicious.

Why did he stay? The answer was easy now. "I stayed because Maggie is involved by helping me. The English queen is important to her, and... Maggie is important to me. She would not leave, and so I have taken up her cause."

"Where is Maggie Darby now?" Walsingham said. "She poisoned half the men at the Tower last night."

"None died."

"No, but their bowels kept them busy so you could escape."

"And yet we are here, risking it all, to warn ye and the

queen," Kerr said. "Who would be the fool then if they did not heed a warning when there is no other explanation to justify the risk?"

The door of the chapel opened, and Norfolk strode inside, a smile on his face. "Walsingham," he called and then stopped when he saw the two guards laying in heaps on the floor. "What goes on here?" he asked, pulling his sword, Kerr's sword. *Blaigeard!*

"Where is Lord Johnathan Whitt?" Walsingham asked.

"Back at Whitehall, I presume," Norfolk said and shrugged. "I have only just arrived." He turned in a small circle, his feet shuffling, as if looking for the shorter man. "He was not invited to the christening." He stopped, his eyes widening. "What is this traitorous Scot doing here? Assaulting your men and spouting lies?"

"I have been informing Walsingham about your plans with Whitt and Roberto Ridolfi," Kerr said.

Norfolk's brows pinched, and his eye twitched. "Plans? My plan for the day is to attend this boring christening because our queen bid it, and then see about a good meal. Where your plans, Gordon, should involve paying the executioner to make a clean cut."

"Ye play the part of an innocent, but ye are guilty of treason," Kerr said. "Elizabeth has been warned and is not walking into your trap."

Norfolk blinked rapidly, his face then tightening in anger. "You would ruin the christening of a child and my good name in the service of Queen Elizabeth in an attempt to shift blame onto someone other than yourself. How dare you, you dirty Scot!"

"There is no child or christening here today," Kerr said. "Only your conspirators and ye." He turned to Walsingham. "Shall we take a look around the chapel?"

Norfolk's face had turned red, and he twisted toward the door as William stepped inside. He nodded to Kerr, the signal that Maggie had stalled Elizabeth's arrival.

"Ho now," Norfolk said and gave a bark of dark laughter. "Another traitor asking to lose his head, William Darby, our dear Maggie's brother. It seems that the Darbys have turned traitor." His words came faster as if he was seized by panic.

Walsingham cleared his throat. "I believe we should talk, Lord Norfolk, in order to clear your name once more."

"Clear my name?" Norfolk yelled. "My name, as always, is pristine with genuine affection and love for my queen."

"And which queen would that be?" Kerr asked. "The one ye swore to serve or the one ye plan to marry so ye can climb upon the throne of England?"

"You are mad, man," Norfolk said. "I have no involvement in this plot you say has been made."

"There is proof—" Kerr started, but Norfolk cut in.

"Are there letters written in my pen?" Norfolk asked. "If there are, they have been forged. Any gunpowder stored below has been there since King Henry's rule. If Lord Whitt is involved in some schemes, then that is his business and yours, but I am completely loyal and loving toward my queen, Her Majesty Queen Elizabeth."

Walsingham stood straighter, his voice coming soft and even. "No one mentioned gunpowder."

"PLEASE, YOUR MAJESTY, come away from here," Maggie urged as she stood, along with Countess Cranfield, beside Queen Elizabeth who wore a voluminous gown of green velvet and brocaded silk.

"What are you playing at, Little Lamb?" Elizabeth asked, handing her horse's reins to the groom before the chapel.

Under no circumstances was Maggie to let Elizabeth or any of her ladies enter Saint Vedast chapel. Cordelia's mother, still dressing all in black from the death of her husband, had come along with Simmons to help sway the stubborn monarch.

"There is talk of treason," the countess said, but she waved her beringed hand as if she wasn't sure the talk was valid. Through the whole explanation at their house, the countess refused to think that Cordelia had any dealings with anything remotely traitorous. But if her daughter was going to try to sway the queen, she demanded to go too. Cordelia stood with the other ladies, dressed in pale colors, behind the queen. Her guard surrounded them all.

Maggie let out a long breath. There was no time to explain, and the countess's gesture had only weakened the intensity of her warning.

Queen Elizabeth took several steps toward Saint Vedast, but Maggie dodged in front of her, nearly trampling one of the ladies. "The christening is happening at Saint Paul's Cathedral instead, Your Majesty. The crowds are expected since Your Majesty will be Godmother to the child."

Elizabeth glanced around at the empty square. Small groups of onlookers stood, having caught sight of the royal entourage, but it was not enough to support Maggie's words.

Elizabeth turned narrowed eyes on Maggie. "First you show your disloyalty by trying to protect Chief Gordon when the glove was obviously meant to shred my veins. Then I hear that you might have been involved with his escape last night. You follow me here, and now you are telling me I must go to St. Paul's instead of the place that my security minister plans to meet me." She looked Maggie up and down in her haughty way that usually made her subjects crumble to her will.

Maggie took a full breath, fortifying herself against the strong woman. "I know this seems quite odd, but there is a plot to see you dead."

Two of the ladies with the queen gasped, holding lace handkerchiefs to their mouths. Cordelia stood toward the back of the group, her face pale.

Elizabeth waved off Maggie's words. "There is always a plot to see me dead, and yet here I am. I will not let idle threats from discontents stop me from doing my duty to this child, his parents, and my kingdom."

"Of course not, Your Majesty," Maggie said, curtseying low. She rose. "But I beg you, there are explosives in the tombs under the small chapel. They are set to blow when you and your ladies enter. Killing you all and Lord Walsingham and Lord Burghley."

The ladies behind her began to whisper in panic. Cordelia grabbed Lettice's arm, pulling her toward St. Paul's Cathedral.

"Have you seen these explosives?" Elizabeth asked, her voice loud, stopping all chatter.

"No, but I—"

"Then how can you know about such things, Mistress Darby? Either you are part of the conspiracy but have thought better of it, or you are leading me away from safety into the cathedral where there will be worse consequences for me."

"Perhaps we should investigate ourselves," Countess Cranfield said, making Maggie itch to tell her to shut her mouth. The closer they got to the chapel, she seemed to reconsider the validity of her own daughter's claims and what Maggie, William, and Kerr had overheard. Was the woman losing her mind?

"Lord Norfolk and Lord Whitt are planning to see you dead, Your Majesty," Maggie said. "They are working with Roberto Ridolfi to dethrone you through your murder so Mary Stuart can take your place."

"Ridolfi," Elizabeth said. "I know that name. He is a banker whom Walsingham is watching. He travels between countries often."

Several of the queen's guards jogged ahead to see if Walsingham was inside. If all had gone according to plan, Kerr should have already convinced Walsingham of Norfolk's guilt and had exited the chapel through a back door so as not to signal Lord Whitt at the detonator.

"Your ladyship," Simmons said, striding up to the countess. He stopped and bowed to Elizabeth. "Your Majesty. Perhaps until this is figured out, we should not be standing in the road where anyone can reach Your Majesty."

The countess frowned at Simmons, but she took his arm when he offered it. His cleanly tailored, black and white livery looked as fine as any lord's suit. "I would get the countess to somewhere warm," he said. He had been loyal to the countess and her family for decades, like the Darbys had been loyal to the English monarchy.

"Where is my Sweet Robin?" Elizabeth asked, glancing back toward the gentlemen and guards that remained around her. Robert Dudley, Earl of Leicester, was Elizabeth's favorite, even if she would never wed him.

"Remember, he rode back to Whitehall," Lettice said, "to fetch your fur muff."

"Oh yes," Elizabeth said, frowning as she rubbed her bare hands together. "I will wait here for Lord Robert then."

Cordelia made her way through the ladies. "We really should get you into the Cathedral, Your Majesty, until this is all reviewed for your safety."

"Very well," Elizabeth said, clearly annoyed. "Lord Geoffrey, go find Lord Walsingham in the chapel, and bid him come to me near St. Paul's. Tell him of this."

The man was walking closer to danger. Where was Kerr now? Had he exited yet? Maggie gave the queen a brief curtsey and opened her arm wide to indicate the cathedral.

The queen looked disdainfully at Maggie's appendage as if it offended her. "I know in which way the cathedral lies, Mistress Darby. You do not—"

Kaboom!

The queen's words were cut off by the explosion behind Maggie, the blast slamming against her back. She fell forward into the queen, blocking the billowing smoke and crumbled pebbles that fell from the sky.

KERR WAS THROWN to the ground by the explosion. He covered his head with his arms as chunks of mortar fell around him, one slicing his arm like a lance.

"Get off me," Norfolk yelled, having leaped up to run, but Walsingham held fast to his ankle. William staggered upright, going to help.

But Kerr was not interested in Norfolk. He could even keep his sword, for all Kerr cared. Kerr pushed out of the rubble at the back of the chapel where they'd surprised Whitt. Brushing the blood from his left arm, Kerr he searched through the smoke for his true target, the bastard who had tried to kill Maggie.

A movement through the smoke caught Kerr's eye. "Foking tolla-thon," he swore as he leaped forward toward Johnathan Whitt. Dodging a whole section of crumbled wall, Kerr raced after the viscount. He didn't even bother to see if he still had a borrowed sword. He'd kill Whitt with his bare hands for orchestrating Maggie's abduction, near rape, and near murder.

"Whitt!" he yelled, and the man glanced over his shoulder, his eyes widening. He turned back, running with all his might.

Johnathan Whitt's meandering through gardens and indulging in royal feasts were no match to Kerr's daily sprints, horseback riding, and battle training. Kerr's boots ate the distance between them, gaining on the viscount until he reached out, grabbing his arm.

Kerr spun Whitt around. Whitt swung his fist. Kerr caught it easily in his palm and leaned into his face, his lips pulled back in a snarl. "Ye, Whitt, are a traitor to your country, a murderer, and ye almost caused Maggie's death. For that ye will die. Painfully." Kerr let go of him, and Whitt tried to yank out his sword. Kerr took two steps forward and slammed his fist into the man's jaw. Whitt spun around, falling unconscious to the ground.

Kerr spat near him. "And I'm sure your queen will make it painful indeed."

MAGGIE COUGHED ON a dust-filled inhale, spinning to see that the back part of the chapel was engulfed in dust and fire. She still clung to the queen. Elizabeth looked dazed, dust coating the brilliant red of her hair.

"Quickly, Your Majesty," one guard said, rushing her, along with the ladies toward St. Paul's Cathedral. The rustle of skirts was soon replaced with wailing from the ladies as they lifted their hems and ran on their slippers over the rock-littered cobblestone.

"Everyone inside," Simmons called, as he beckoned the ladies, his arms flapping. The guards had run the other way toward the wreckage in hopes of finding villains or victims and survivors. *Please let Kerr and William be out of it. Please God.* Maggie's prayers played over and over above the ringing in her ears from the blast.

People had run onto the streets to see what had happened, many of them giving curtseys as Elizabeth rushed past.

"My good people," she called. "Save yourselves."

"This way," Simmons said, ushering the queen and Maggie through the doorway first, followed by the countess, Cordelia, and the queen's ladies.

The cathedral was large with white marble arches and gold accents that ran down the sides of the interior. Cold and silent, it stood like a large tomb that smelled of dusty velvet drapes, smoky oil lamps, and scented kneeling pillows. Maggie's boots clicked along the marble floor as she rushed with the queen and the countess into a vestibule off the main room.

"I will lock you in and guard the door," Simmons said as Cordelia caught up to her mother. They had no way of knowing how many traitors were part of the plot.

"The room is too small," Cordelia said, looking for another place they could hide.

"The other ladies will be fine out here," Countess Cranfield said. Maggie caught a glimpse of them clustered together, some of them kneeling in desperate prayer. But she was right. They must protect the queen immediately, and the antechamber would be small and secure.

Maggie led the queen into the square room with Cordelia helping her mother. "Bar it from inside too," Countess Cranfield said. "In case any of the infidels get past Simmons."

Did Simmons have combat training? He hardly looked it. Maggie bent to pluck off the cap she had secured that morning over the blade sticking out of her boot. If Kerr were there, he would defend the door. *Kerr.* Was he dead? He and William? Had they been caught in the explosion? Panic tightened in her chest like a fist, making her bend over, her hands finding her knees through the heavy petticoats. She sucked in several slow gulps of air and straightened. Cordelia was fanning the queen who also looked to be sucking in air way too fast. The countess stood with her back against the door, watching them with an odd grin as if she found the queen's panic humorous.

"We are safely out of harm's way," Maggie said going to Elizabeth. The queen met her gaze but did not say anything. She took another slow inhale through her nose, making the sides pinch in with the force. "And you are well and hearty, because you, our dearest queen, have the heart of a lion." Maggie nodded. "Like your father before you."

Elizabeth nodded, standing straighter with her next inhale, as if sucking in Maggie's confidence. Maggie nodded reassuringly. "And you have the love of your people, who will protect you to the end."

Behind Maggie, Countess Cranfield laughed. "And those loving heretics can join the bastard queen in Hell."

CHAPTER SIXTEEN

"You must be proud, bold, pleasant, resolute, and now and then stab, when occasion serves."
Christopher Marlowe – English playwright

M AGGIE WHIPPED AROUND to face the suddenly very spry Countess Canfield who lunged across the small space. The old woman held her hand high, a blade poised and ready to strike. Her aim was obvious.

Maggie threw her arms wide, blocking the queen from the front. Was Cordelia working with her mother? With a shove backwards, Maggie forced Elizabeth into the corner so that Cordelia couldn't reach her. But Maggie's focus was currently on the blade clutched in the old woman's hand.

"I send you to Hell!" the countess yelled, not caring who could hear through the door, which she'd barred from the inside. Her arm came down toward Maggie's face, but her gaze focused behind her where Elizabeth stood tall, her neck and shoulder exposed.

Maggie grunted as she struck the countess's arm, and the knife veered to the side. "Countess Cranfield!" Maggie yelled. "Stop!"

But the woman's other hand came up clutching a second knife. "Burner of good Catholics! Lover of damned heretics!"

"Mother, no!" Cordelia called, trying to get in front of her, but Agatha Cranfield had become a woman possessed with evil and lunatic strength. She knocked Cordelia down and surged again toward Elizabeth, who had followed Maggie's push to get into the corner of the antechamber.

"Get back," Maggie yelled, grabbing for one of the countess's knife-wielding hands. Maggie felt the sting of the other blade across her wrist. Still the woman came forward undeterred, both of her arms flying in a chopping motion with the knives. It was as if a demon possessed her. Eyes wide and wild, lips pulled back to show blackish teeth, her face was set in a snarl as she yelled. "'Tis time to end your wicked reign, heretic! Born from a witch! You will join your mother in Hell!"

She rushed forward at the same time Maggie lifted her skirts and pointed her toe at her. Countess Cranfield didn't notice or didn't care about the small blade protruding from Maggie's specially made boot. *One. Two. Stab.* Could she do it? The poison was in the tip, but it must be released by stabbing.

Draped in the black fabric of mourning, there was little skin exposed on the older woman. Only her hands and face. As she swung the blade toward Elizabeth in an arc, Maggie aimed her foot at the countess's hand. *Stab the tip in.* Her father's words pounded through Maggie's head like another heartbeat. The tip of the blade on her boot sliced the skin across the veiny hand.

The woman didn't notice, and the poison contained in the tip hadn't been released. Maggie blocked her arm again, dropped into a crouch to shove her hands against the woman's stomach. Agatha stumbled slightly, but came back, her arms swinging. If she would only hold still enough for Maggie to…

Maggie thrust her foot upward, her toes flexed. The tip of her boot pierced the countess's hand in the tender, fleshy part below the thumb. Agatha screamed as the point broke off, protruding from her wrist, making her drop the dagger to clutch her hand.

Maggie dropped her foot and held her hands ready for another strike, but Agatha Cranfield clutched her stabbed hand, yanking the point out. "What have you done?" she asked, staggering backwards. The effects of the poison worked fast, deadly fast. Once it hit the bloodstream, it paralyzed the heart, and death was imminent.

"Mother," Cordelia called, rushing over as Agatha dropped to the marble floor. She pressed a hand against her chest, and her face paled despite the exertion that had reddened her cheeks moments ago. The poison was delivered and working. Agatha Cranfield wouldn't get back up.

Maggie spun around to face Elizabeth. The queen stood tall, her fists clenched, ready to defend herself if Agatha had made it past Maggie. "Are you well?" Maggie asked.

Elizabeth looked from Cordelia, kneeling over her dying mother, to Maggie. Elizabeth swallowed, clearing her throat as if not sure how her words would come out. "You really must..." She paused and stood taller, regal. "You really must tell me who fashions your shoes, Sweet Lamb."

Maggie's face relaxed, her breathing slowing. "My father, Reginald Darby. He is brilliant."

Elizabeth nodded, keeping her gaze. "*My* father always said so."

"Get the bloody hell out of my way!" Kerr's voice from outside the barred door filled Maggie with such relief that she smiled fully, elation making a small sob come from her. Holding a fist to her mouth, she spun away from the queen, dodged Cordelia who sobbed over her mother, and slid the bar off the brackets on the door.

"Kerr!" she yelled. "Watch Simmons. He may be an assassin."

"What?" Simmons's voice came through the door. "Get your hands off me. I am the countess's servant."

The door swung inward. There was a mass of people in St. Paul's now, but all she focused on was Kerr. Dust covered his hair, his cap gone. Dirt and a bit of blood lay across his tunic, and his arm bled, but he looked hale and hearty. His chest filled quickly like he'd been running, and he grasped Maggie's shoulders. "Ye are well?" he asked, his gaze roaming across her, stopping on her hand, which sported a line of drying blood.

"Yes, and cleaner than you," she said, her hands rising to pat against his chest. "Thank God you are whole." She met his eyes, her smile fading. "William?"

"Sitting on top of Norfolk until Walsingham's guards bind the duke," Kerr said, and Maggie released her breath.

"Our queen?" Walsingham yelled from the doors of the cathedral as he rushed inside.

He was followed by Elizabeth's favorite, Robert Dudley, who had returned with her muff. "My sweet Bess," he called, striding toward Elizabeth as if racing against Walsingham to reach her first.

"Guards," Walsingham called and pointed to Cordelia and her mother. "Take them and the countess's man."

"She is dead," Cordelia cried.

"Leave the girl," Elizabeth commanded. "She did not know her mother was demented." The queen had no clue about Cordelia's other dealings with the fanatical assassins.

Cordelia looked at Maggie, tears running down her reddened cheeks. Maggie held her lips tightly shut and gave the slightest shake of her head. Once again, she was covering up knowledge to save someone for whom she cared.

Fresh tears flowed from Cordelia's red eyes. She stepped back as the guards came to carry Agatha Cranfield from the chamber.

"Countess?" Simmons called, grief seeming to tighten his face. "What has happened?"

"Your mistress was working with the assassins," Elizabeth said, her voice strong with no evidence of the hesitation she'd shown in the small room. "And Lady Darby defended me with her body, heart, and soul." Maggie met the queen's gaze. "Like all the Darbys have done for the reigning, God-appointed monarchs to the English throne."

Lady Darby? Not *Mistress* Darby? It was either a slip or, considering the queen's exceedingly clever mind, Maggie had just been raised to the peerage.

The queen turned to where a dust-covered William came to a

halt inside the cathedral, his chest heaving. "All the Darbys," Elizabeth said.

William ran to Maggie, pulling her greedily from Kerr's arms to hug. "I am well, William," Maggie said, her words muffled by his dirty tunic.

The queen continued, her voice strong. "I understand that there were barrels of gunpowder under the chapel and the christening is scheduled for next week, likely at a different location."

Walsingham cleared his throat. "When Norfolk ran out of the chapel he was detained. Lord Whitt was also captured."

The queen's eyes narrowed at Walsingham's flushed face. "The Highlander detained Norfolk?"

"Nay, Your Majesty," Kerr said, and Maggie pushed out of her brother's arms to hear. "I was busy throwing your spymaster over my shoulder and carrying him out while William Darby dragged out the two unconscious guards. The blast actually stopped Norfolk and then Walsingham and William made sure Norfolk didn't escape."

Kerr looked at Maggie. "I took care of Whitt."

"He is dead?" Maggie whispered.

"I left him alive for Walsingham to play with first," Kerr said, glancing at the queen's spymaster. "He might have other information about assassination attempts before he is killed as a traitor."

The queen's face tightened, her frown fierce. "Norfolk and Whitt will pay with their heads." She looked directly at Walsingham. "Have them questioned to see of Mary's involvement."

Her gaze turned to Kerr. Could she suspect him still? "And you remained in London to foil this plan."

Kerr crossed his arms over his chest, his legs braced in a battle stance. He opened his mouth, but Maggie found her voice first. "Yes, Your Majesty. Kerr Gordon is as determined as I and my family are about catching the assassins."

"Hmmm," Elizabeth said, her lips tight as her judgmental

gaze shifted from Maggie to Kerr.

Maggie cast a glance at Cordelia, her eyes wide over a handkerchief to her nose. Lettice Knollys wrapped an arm around her thin shoulders in support.

Kerr met the queen's stare. "Beware if the planners of this crime try to tangle innocents into this mess. They may wish to throw blame upon us."

Lettice gasped as Cordelia's knees buckled, and she sat down on the floor with her skirts billowing high around her. "'Tis been too much for her," Lettice said.

"Call my physician," Elizabeth said. "Lady Cordelia Cranfield must be seen." She grabbed up Maggie's bloodied hand. "As well as Lady Darby. Luckily the countess did not have such a clever craftsman honing her boots."

"No, Your Majesty," Maggie said.

Elizabeth released her hand, but she continued to hold Maggie's gaze. "I thank you for your service. I expect you will return to your station at Whitehall." Her gaze drifted to William. "And bring your family."

Without waiting for an answer, the queen turned away. "Take me home, Sweet Robin." Lord Dudley took up the queen's arm, gathering her close for a moment before escorting her toward the doors.

Queen Elizabeth paused and looked over her shoulder at Kerr. "I will bid the Highlander farewell at Whitehall at the banquet I will hold to honor the Darbys." The queen continued to walk regally out of the cathedral.

Maggie turned in Kerr's arms, her smile radiant. "It worked. It really worked. You are free." She grabbed his arms, but she couldn't shake him. She laughed at the attempt. "You can go to your beloved home. We will ask for your family sword back from wherever Norfolk stored it away. Was it on him?" she asked, her words tumbling like her thoughts. "Do you suppose he sleeps with it next to his bed?"

When she looked up, Kerr's face was serious. Nothing close

to humor or jubilation sparked in his eyes. "What is wrong?" she asked.

"Aye, the plan worked," he answered. "And now the Darbys are to return to Elizabeth's court. All the Darbys, which I believe includes ye." Kerr stared at Maggie, and the chatter, orders, clomping boots, and ladies sobbing around them, faded away. "Ye haven't answered my question, Maggie."

YE HAVEN'T ANSWERED *my question.* Kerr's words beat upon Maggie's heart. There had been no time to answer nor even think. He had asked her to marry back at the Cranfield house. At first, she'd thought it was a ruse to get William to back down and to save some of her pride when they'd been found together. Maggie hadn't let herself believe that his question was real, because if she did and it was not, there was no doubt her heart would break.

After two nights now of tossing and turning in her old bed at Whitehall, and covertly making certain Kerr hadn't left, Maggie was exhausted. She didn't even know where he'd been placed in the palace.

"I don't know if I can stay here at court," Cordelia whispered from her spot next to Lucy on Maggie's bed, the bed that was not really hers. Nothing here was hers in truth. Not the dresses or the few jewels. Not even her beakers and solvents for testing for poison. Everything belonged to the queen. *Even me.*

"Where would you go?" Lucy asked her sister.

"I do not know." Cordelia looked at Maggie. "Perhaps Kerr Gordon will let me return with him to Scotland."

Maggie's chest squeezed tighter, and her heart beat hard as if trying to break free of its hold over it. Kerr was going to leave London, there was no doubt. He must return to his clan to help end a bloody feud. He was the next in line for being the chief.

"I no longer feel safe in England," Cordelia continued. "Lord Norfolk's and our mother's associates may try to seek me out, and Lord Walsingham is suspicious of all my activities."

Over the last two days since the chapel explosion, both sisters had been questioned at length, along with Simmons, about knowledge of Countess Cranfield's associates. Simmons was still being held in the Tower, but it seemed he was as surprised by the countess's actions as the rest of them. The only thing saving him was his openness about the countess's comings and goings and with whom she dined. His information was giving Walsingham plenty of conspiracy efforts to chew upon, like a ravenous dog with many meaty bones.

Lucy squeezed her sister's hand. "Well if you go, I go. You are my only family left, Cordy."

The thought of losing her two trusted friends was the final punch to the wall Maggie had wrapped around herself. She blinked but could not stop the tears from rolling out of her eyes. "You both will leave me here?" she murmured.

Cordelia stood up, rushing over to hug her. "But Maggie, you and your family are heroes of the court. The queen has reinstated you and is finding you an assistant who will try on her clothes after you test them for poison and blades. She values you too much to keep calling you a Sacrificial Lamb now. She is even calling you *Lady* Darby." Cordelia smiled, tipping her head to meet Maggie's gaze. "I think she might knight you." She laughed lightly, although sadness pulled at her features.

Lucy came over, hugging Maggie too. "And the queen has given your brother and father their own workshop at Whitehall, with a generous stipend, to create secret weapons for Walsingham like your poison-tipped boot. I hear all the ladies want them now, and the queen has had to say no or there would be accidental poisonings at court."

Maggie nodded and sniffed, pulling her handkerchief from her sleeve. She should be happy. The Darbys were once again protecting the crown. It was everything she'd ever wanted in life.

Respect, security, her family cared for and honored. She'd been taught by her father early on that love and marriage were not things for which to strive. Both were far riskier in his opinion than working to uncover poisons.

But Maggie had grown up watching her parents working together, respecting one another, laughing together, and loving each other. Love was real, and it was within her grasp. *Will ye marry me?*

Yes. A thousand times yes. The words in her head made the tears gush out more, because they could not be true. They were the words she would utter if she were a simple Englishwoman, tied only to her family. But she wasn't, especially now. The queen was holding a banquet in her honor that night. She was showering her with security for her and her family. It was more valuable than gold.

Kerr deserved an answer. It wasn't possible for her to say yes. And her heart would surely break if she said no.

Rap. Rap.

All three of them looked at Maggie's bedchamber door, still like statues.

Rap. Rap.

Maggie hurried over, pulling it open. Disappointment at seeing William standing there instead of Kerr felt like a sodden wool cape draped over her shoulders.

William, with his talent for picking out details, frowned at her. "I am not the executioner come to drag you to the block, Maggie."

His gaze lifted to the sisters, and she saw the appreciation in her brother's eyes. Which sister interested him? "I've come to escort all three of you to the banquet. Father is still talking with Walsingham about the mechanism to make the boot tip release its load of poison." He shook his head but kept his smile. "It's like Father has woken from old age. I haven't seen him this spry and quick-minded in ten years."

Maggie moved numbly to find her short cape and handbag,

the silk petticoats of the green gown swishing softly along the floorboards. The ensemble was a gift from the queen and the only appropriate gown Maggie actually owned. It encased her form perfectly, unlike the gowns that were made to fit the queen. Pearls were sewn along the low-cut neckline to complement the smoothness of her skin. Long, fitted sleeves were embroidered with gold thread in the form of leaves and vines down to where her lace cuffs peeked out. The details were exquisite and rich. Both of which felt constricting, not by weight and tightness, but by what the gown meant. Maggie owed everything in her life to the queen. Poison might not stop her heart now but seeing Kerr ride away just might.

CHAPTER SEVENTEEN

*"It is absolutely necessary for me to
obtain this answer, having been for
above a whole year stricken with the
dart of love, and not yet sure whether
I shall fail of finding a place in your
heart and affection..."*
Letter from Henry VIII to Anne Boleyn while he courted
her

KERR STOOD NEAR the doorway of the great hall, watching lords bow and ladies curtsey to Queen Elizabeth. She sat regally on her throne in one of her ensembles that seemed so heavy with velvet and jewels that she probably couldn't stand in it for long. Had Maggie worn all the parts of it earlier to ascertain it wasn't poisoned or corrupted with sharp blades?

His gaze swept the gilt hall, but Maggie hadn't appeared yet, nor her family, nor the Cranfield sisters. Once more in his kilt, Kerr still felt restricted, like it was hard to pull in a full breath. Maybe that had something to do with Maggie not answering his question yet.

Will you marry me?

What had spurred him to ask such a doomed question? How could he think that she'd give all this up? Even if court life felt stuffy and ridiculously formal to him, she'd grown up here. Now that her family and she were being honored and given luxuries at Whitehall, how could he expect her to leave? He couldn't.

"Broody even though everyone considers you a hero," Lord Burghley said as he stopped next to Kerr. "Is comfort and riches not to your liking?"

"I prefer the fresh air of the moors," Kerr murmured.

"You are free to go," Burghley said, straightening the voluminous sleeve hanging from his arm. "I wonder what might be keeping you." His comment sounded like a question, one to which he already knew the answer. The answer suddenly appeared in the arched doorway leading into the hall.

Maggie floated with practiced grace into the room, her brother and two friends by her side. She was the gem that stood out among pebbles. The rich gown fit her trim waist. It sat low to emphasize her lush bosom and flared out with the underskirts over hips he knew were curved and covered with velvety skin. Skin that had been warm and fragrant under his lips. It was a good thing indeed that he was back to wearing his kilt and not the tight breeches the English preferred.

Maggie's hair sat pinned up under a court hood to match her gown, but several curls were left to cascade down to peek out along her shoulders. Her tresses were auburn like the queen's except without the brassiness of the dye Elizabeth used in her wigs. In the candlelight, Maggie's light blue eyes looked dark under long lashes. Freckles dappled her face, adding to her natural charm so unlike many other ladies at the English court with their caked-on makeup and coal-lined eyes.

Bloody hell, she was beautiful. She was more than beautiful though. Beauty he could leave. It was her strong spirit and bravery that lured him, her cleverness that intrigued him, her kindness and scent that wrapped around his heart, squeezing his chest when he thought about riding away without her. *She hasn't said nay yet.* The thought did not cheer him.

"It is said that you asked her to wed," Burghley said. "But that she has not yet answered."

"I would think that Walsingham's spies would have more important rumors to track down," Kerr said, his voice gruff.

"I personally have a fondness for Maggie Darby and an indebtedness to her father," Burghley said. "I would like to see her happy and secure."

Kerr looked to the queen's advisor. "And she could not be with a Scotsman from the wild north."

Burghley stroked his long, pointed beard. "I have a very hard time knowing the minds of females." His gaze moved to his beloved queen, leaning to the side to share some secret with her favorite, Lord Robert Dudley, Earl of Leister.

"Excuse me," Burghley said. The aging man walked away, bowed to his queen, and took up a station on the opposite side of Dudley on a small, padded chair provided for him.

The musicians played a light tune with two lines of dancers in the middle of the room. Elizabeth listened to something Burghley said close to her ear, her gaze taking in Maggie and her small group. Elizabeth stood, and the music stopped on cue. The dancers parted, all turning to hear what their beloved queen had to say.

"Come forward Lady Margaret Darby and your brother, Lord William Darby." Her gaze drifted to Kerr. "And our Highlander, Lord Kerr Gordon, the next Earl of Huntley and Chief of the Gordon Clan of Banffshire."

Kerr checked his steps so that he arrived next to Maggie. She looked well, the cut on her hand patched and cared for by the queen's personal physician. His own cuts and the burns on his back from the blast had been tended by the same man, which Kerr had been told numerous times was an honor. Only the queen's favorites received the best care she could command.

Maggie dipped into a deep curtsey, and William and Kerr bowed at the waist.

"For your great service to me," Elizabeth intoned, "and the security of my realm, I bestow upon you each, five-hundred pounds." Gasps, followed by applause, filled the hall at the large amount, which surpassed a lifetime of wages to a skilled tradesman. Would Elizabeth pay the exorbitant gift if Kerr carried off her most trusted lady?

The queen continued, and the room fell into silence as if everyone held their breaths. "At a ceremony on the morrow, I will knight both Kerr Gordon and William Darby. And to my once Sacrificial Lamb, who has proven to be as clever and determined as Lord Walsingham and as ferocious as a cornered bear when protecting my person, I raise you to peerage as Countess of Litchfield, with all the rights and privileges due to the station."

Bloody hell. Maggie would be a countess, a respected and revered lady of the English court. Maggie curtseying prompted Kerr to bow once again.

"Thank you, Your Majesty," Maggie said, "for such an honor."

"Thanks be to you, Lady Darby," Elizabeth said, a wry smile on her painted lips, "for acting as my shield and defender. If I had known you were so skillful with your lethal boot, I would have appointed you as my personal guard years ago."

A small wave of laughter grew among those who watched.

"Now let us dance," Elizabeth said, standing. She smiled, pointed at her people. "But beware that dancer who trounces upon Lady Darby's toes."

The room filled with laughter, but Kerr didn't join in. He felt more like slicing someone through on the battlefield. Without a letter from the Scottish queen, he would get many more chances once reaching Banffshire. *Damn.* Being an English knight meant nothing to the Scots. He will have failed his mission. His sister would sob, and his father would rage.

"May I have the honor of taking the newest lady at court out to dance?" Robert Dudley asked Maggie. He smiled graciously, bowing over her hand. Kerr wanted to punch him.

Glancing at the queen, Kerr saw that she also frowned. Perhaps she wanted to punch him too. Robert Dudley was the queen's favorite. Everyone knew this but also that she would never marry him. It would give him too much power. Since his wife had mysteriously fallen down the stairs and died, the scandal that he might have been involved in some way made any marriage with the queen unthinkable. But that didn't mean Lord Robert was free to make merry with other ladies of the court.

Kerr kept his spot, also turning to watch Dudley lead Maggie out to take a spot across from him in the line dance that had been underway when the queen made her announcement. Dudley said something that made Maggie smile, which made Kerr's hands fist at his sides. The queen steepled her hands before her as if in prayer, except she rested her chin on the point and stared with hostile eyes at the pair.

"Maggie Darby," the queen said. "Young and fair with hair the color of mine." She dropped her hands and leaned back in her high-backed throne. "It is said she looks like me except she still has the shininess of youth."

"You are still youthful," Lord Burghley said, and Elizabeth waved off his comment.

"Before she was merely a trustworthy servant to the crown," Elizabeth continued. "But now she is raised to the peerage and can attract any number of suitors for her hand."

"As can you, Your Majesty," Burghley said, ignoring the sideways glare she gave him.

"I do not have such luxury, as well you know, Spirit," she said, snapping. Burghley didn't flinch or glance her way. He knew the war that played within the aging queen between a desire to love and the repulsion of tying herself to a man and giving him a claim to her kingdom.

"Do you, Scotsman, like watching my Sweet Robin dance with your lady?"

Kerr inhaled. "She is not my lady, Your Majesty."

"Well, Robert is *my* man," she said. "And I will not stand for this." She stood, dropping her white-ostrich-feather fan in her seat. She stepped down, taking Kerr's arm. "Let us reclaim our partners."

Kerr escorted the queen out to the dance floor, people opening a path to allow them easy access. They stopped near the dancers, at the end of the double line. It was an awkward moment, the queen by his side, her vulnerability in the set of her frown as Robert danced down the middle with Maggie. Dudley had the good sense to stop, and he bowed while Maggie curtseyed.

"I have a desire to dance," Elizabeth said, and instantly Robert came to her side, moving in the space Kerr opened.

"I did not think your grand ensemble allowed for it, Bess," Robert said and kissed the back of her hand where a row of rich rings stood out like extra knuckles on her long, pale fingers.

She smiled at his gallant kiss. "Let us dance la volta and you can help carry it for me."

The words *la volta* carried across the room like a rumor of rebellion spread across a dissatisfied populace. It ended at the musician's corner where they stopped the jig and began a song that would accompany the queen's dance.

Maggie set her hand on Kerr's arm. He laid his other hand over it so no one else could claim her. Her hand was so small that he engulfed it and yet the feel of it against his palm reminded him how easily she could wound him. Never before had he been vulnerable. Not to the blade and surely not to the decision of a lass. But here he was.

They didn't speak as he led her to the floor where Robert whispered something into Elizabeth's ear to melt away her frown. The notes of the intimate dance began, and Kerr rested his hands around Maggie's trim waist. He turned, lifting her easily, and her petticoats billowed out as he set her down.

"You look dashing, Lord Gordon," Maggie whispered near his ear, and they parted with the steps of the dance.

They came back together, their palms touching in the most intimate way, reminding him of their interlude at Countess Cranfield's home. "Ye are the loveliest lass I have ever touched," he whispered close to her ear. She smelled of fresh flowers and clean woman. Did her father make her bathe everyday while at court too?

His hands encircled her cinched waist, lifting her easily in the pattern of la volta. She had a slight stain of red to her cheeks. They touched palms again, and he felt her fingers curl into his, threading in between. It was intimate, keeping them locked together until they must part again.

Holding onto Maggie felt so right, as if it was meant to be. They stared into each other's eyes as if the room were empty except for the two of them. He lifted and turned, setting Maggie down, sliding his hands along her waist. Maggie's skirts belled out, her fingers curling into his. He inhaled her smell of summer flowers. The rest of the court, with its scheming and gossip and condescension, lost all color as if fading into the gold and cream painted walls and tapestries.

But Kerr couldn't tell what he saw in Maggie's face. Confusion, passion, pain, and happiness tied so tightly that tugging on any one of them made her hurt. Without an answer to his question, he read only a "no" within her blue eyes.

Every time the dance brought them face to face, he would memorize another facet of Maggie. Her high cheekbones, stained a bonny pink. The smattering of freckles flung across her face like God flinging stars in the night sky. The red hues of her silky curls. The way her chin jutted forward when she raised her eyes to his.

The music ended, and a light applause brought Kerr back to the room. Everyone seemed to be staring at them, including Elizabeth who had apparently ended the dance before the musicians and now sat back on her throne. Perhaps the costume had been too heavy to perform la volta for long. She gazed out at them, a frown in place. Burghley bent to speak near her ear. Always scheming, always whispering, always worried about lethal implications. Although Kerr could hardly fault them after they'd nearly been blown to bits at the chapel the other day.

Maggie looked up at Kerr. "I think two dances, a handful of

conversations, and being present to accept her gratitude publicly is enough to satisfy my attendance requirements. She smiled lightly as if jesting, but Kerr guessed that she was not. "I think I will retire to my chamber," she said.

"I will walk you back," Kerr said.

Maggie glanced down at her slippers. "It would be unseemly for you to be seen leaving with me, alone."

"Then have one of the sisters come," he said, a thread of frustration in his voice. Damnable court rules. "Or your brother."

William was over talking with Lucy Cranfield who had a small group of men around her. They all laughed heartily at whatever she was saying. The woman had an irreverent sense of humor, which she seemed to use like a shield even more since her mother's death.

"I will not drag William away," Maggie said, glancing around. "I will ask a guard to act as chaperone."

Kerr looked down into her face. "Do we need a chaperone, Maggie?"

She cleared her throat. "The queen met with me earlier to question me about the night we spent together."

"What did ye say?"

"The truth," Maggie said and then shook her head. "Not all the details of the night of course, but that we merely fell asleep in there, and I am uncompromised thanks to your great chivalry."

The queen was now in conversation with both Burghley and a freshly entered Lord Walsingham. Robert Dudley, who could hear the conversation, looked out at Kerr. It was obvious from the look that his name was at least brought up. Perhaps Norfolk had convinced Walsingham that the Ridolfi plot, which the incident had been dubbed, was Kerr's doing all along.

Maggie asked the guard near the door to walk with them back to her room.

"'Twould be my honor, Lady Darby," the guard said, bowing his head. He walked before them as Kerr fell in line next to her. His boots echoed, along with that of the guard's, clipping on the stone floor. The swish of her skirts was the only other sound except an occasional hum of laughter from the great hall behind them. Portraits of English royals flanked the walls, lit here and there by glassed flames sitting in sconces.

Too quickly they stood at Maggie's door where he noticed a small leaf sticking out about a foot from the floor. She was using the trick he'd taught her. The thought helped his rigid jaw relax. She unlocked her door, ignoring the little leaf so the guard would not see her take note. The damn Englishman stood there like a sentry. Maggie turned, a small frown on her face as she saw that the guard had no intention of leaving until she closed her door.

Kerr took her hand anyway. Carefully, his lips feathered across the back as he kissed it even as his eyes remained connected to Maggie's. He straightened but did not release her hand. She left it in his.

"Are you leaving soon?" she asked, her voice soft as if hiding any emotion that might try to make its way into the tone.

"I must return to Banffshire to support the union between my sister and Percy Hay, even if I do not have the support of Mary Stuart." He frowned, exhaling.

"Queen Elizabeth will support your cause," Maggie said. "You but need ask."

"Support from a Protestant, English queen will only turn the Hays more against me and my demand for peace."

Maggie looked down at their hands. "It is a doomed mission for you," she whispered.

"Aye, but I must return and see where I can help."

She gave a small nod and opened her mouth to speak, her brows pinching. But then her gaze slid to the guard, catching whatever sat upon her tongue.

"I will at least see you at the ceremony tomorrow?" she said, but it came out as a question.

He nodded and squeezed her hand. "And then I must leave."

She slid her hand away. "Oh." He saw the delicate movement in her long neck as she swallowed. "Good eve then."

The door began to close, but Kerr placed his boot against the door, halting it. "Maggie." She stopped, a bit of light coming back to her face as she waited. "My question stands. I need an answer before I leave."

Before she could utter a sound or even change her expression, Kerr turned and walked away. He heard the door close behind him, slowing his gait until the iron key clicked in the lock.

Damn it all. He should demand an answer tonight. He wouldn't have to wait until the morrow to ride away. What did he care about being knighted? Although five-hundred pounds would go far in helping the people of his clan. It would give Rhona a larger dowry and entice the old Hay chief to stop the warfare.

Kerr stopped in the dark corridor, listening to the guard walk in the opposite direction back to the banquet. Kerr did not plan to return to the gaieties. What then did he plan to do? Go back to his room and gather his bag so he could leave as soon as the gold was his? He raised his hands to the sides of his face, rubbing the tension in his jaw and head.

Maggie needed to answer his question. Without the answer, he had no course of action. Kerr looked back down the corridor. It was empty and silent, no one about. Her brother had been given the room next to her, but he was entertaining the lasses back at the banquet. This may be the only time alone he could steal with Maggie.

Kerr walked back to her door. With a full inhale, he raised his knuckles and knocked. "Maggie, 'tis me, Kerr."

The key turned in the lock. The door cracked open, and her lovely face appeared. Glancing behind him to see the corridor empty, she opened it farther.

Maggie was already partly undone, her stomacher, sleeves, and outer petticoat off, leaving her in her stays over her lace-edged smock and one petticoat. The lacing pushed her breasts high, the embroidery lying against her creamy skin made Kerr ache.

"Maggie," Kerr said. "I—"

Before Kerr could get out another word, Maggie reached up to his neck, pulling his face down to hers, planting her lips on his. It was as if she'd shot him with poison, a poison that caused fire to erupt within his body, coursing down with each deep thud of his heart.

Maggie clung to him, her hands sliding to his shoulders as she backed up, pulling him into the room. Was this her answer? Or was this her way of saying goodbye? As her hands slid down his chest, stroking lower until she cupped his hard jack through his kilt, Kerr did not care. He only knew that he must be with Maggie. Forever. And forever would start with this night.

With a rise of his boot, Kerr kicked the door shut behind him.

CHAPTER EIGHTEEN

"O, thou art fairer than the evening air clad in the beauty of a thousand stars."

Christopher Marlowe – English Playwright

M AGGIE'S HEART BEAT like a hammer in a forge, the heat from it sending sparks to fly through her body. *My question stands.* He still wanted to marry her. Lord help her, she wanted to throw away all the tethers keeping her there. Her father and her family's honor. The wealth she could bring to the Darbys. The rank of countess and the trust of her queen. It all weighed heavily against falling in love with a Highlander, and yet here she was. Love? Was it love or merely lust? She must discover the answer. Everything inside her body screamed in agreement.

With her status, she did not need to wed. In fact, the queen liked her ladies to remain unmarried. Therefore, there was no reason to keep her maidenhood. And Maggie had decided during the dance as she looked into Kerr's stormy eyes, that she would give herself to him.

Had Kerr heard her prayers for his return? Had he known that fire was already smoldering inside her body? Did he know that she ached for his touch? She would tell him all of it, not with words, but with actions. She kissed him, tasting him and pulling up his tunic so she could slide her cool palms along his hot skin.

She wanted to steal his breath and his questions away. She had no answers except that she wanted him now, wanted this passion between them. So when he tried to speak, she kissed him fuller, opening her mouth and timidly touching his tongue with her own.

His arms grasped around her, pulling her in as his hands slid down to cup her backside through the layers of petticoats. The feel of the silk against her bareness, teased her. She gasped against his mouth when he rucked up the back, the cool air of the room slaking across her hot skin. His large hand massaged the globes of her, and she pressed forward against him.

Maggie's hands explored the chiseled muscles of Kerr's stomach and chest under the loosened tunic. Her skirts dropped as he withdrew to yank the tunic off over his head, throwing it in a heap. The light from the one lamp cast his skin in gold. The plateaus and ridges of his sculpted body, so different from her own, made her shiver, the heat battling with the chill in the room.

"I will rekindle your fire," Kerr said.

Lord, you already have. She almost laughed at the thought.

He walked to pass her but stopped, his hand rising to her unhooded hair. Despite his size and the intensity of his gaze, he was gentle as he stroked her cheek, his hand trailing down her curls. She met his gaze, neither of them saying anything. There were too many words to say, too many decisions to make that could sway them toward him leaving her there with her blood racing.

She turned as he stalked past, silent with a predator's grace, and watched him crouch before the hearth. Holy God, the muscles of his broad back were a thing of pure male beauty. Parts were red from the explosion. Did they pain him?

Maggie wrapped her arms around herself as she let her gaze explore. Could he feel her perusal? He turned toward her, still crouched as if he might leap forward.

The flames grew on the dry peat bricks, adding light to the room. She stepped closer, feeling the heat. But it was Kerr and the promise in his stare that lured her in. She held her breath as he straightened, standing tall.

His hand went to the front of his kilt that she noticed had tented out with his arousal. "Ye are sure?" he asked, his voice low. "I would not misunderstand and hurt you in any way, Maggie."

She swallowed, feeling the crux between her legs clench at the sight of his hand slowly moving along himself. "I want you, Kerr. Completely and without reserve."

"Ye have not answered my question."

"The morn is soon enough for important words," she said. "Tonight is…" She paused, untying the bow at the top of her smock so that it parted, revealing her collarbone and the swell of her breasts pushed high above her stays. "Tonight," her voice dropped to a whisper, "is about incoherent words and sighs." Maggie shifted her stays down, tugging the lacing open at the top until her breasts sprung free at the top. A thrill shot down her body as she watched Kerr's eyes lower, taking in the display of flesh, her nipples hard and her ample bosom pale.

"Sighs," Kerr said, "and your moans of pleasure, lass."

The rumble of his northern accent sent another wave of frantic heat through Maggie. She nodded. "Moans." The word came breathless from her parted lips. She raised her hands to touch her nipples, pinching them as he watched. He lifted his kilt higher until he could clasp his long, thick jack in his hand, moving up and down the shaft with an erotic rhythm.

"Oh God, Kerr," she whispered and took a step forward.

As if her one small step had cut through the shackles that had held him back, Kerr grabbed her to him, his mouth descending to hers. He caught her face in his hands, tilted her mouth to slide against his. She opened instantly under the pressure, both of them loving each other fiercely.

His skin was warm under her fingers, beckoning her like a moth to a flame. She stroked down the muscles of his back and stopped. "Do the burns hurt you?"

"Not when ye touch me," he said, and his fingers slid through her long curls. Her naked breasts pressed against this chest, the light curls of hair there teasing her nipples even more. He leaned over her. A trail of fire came from Kerr's lips as he kissed down Maggie's neck, his mouth finding one nipple.

"Oh yes," she said, feeling the suction and wet heat.

Once again his hands rucked up her petticoat as his mouth moved to her ear. "The room is still cold. I would keep ye clothed as much as possible," he whispered.

"Strangely," she whispered back, "I don't feel anything but heat right now."

He kissed her again as his strong fingers slid behind her between her thighs. She gasped against his lips as he found her heat, deftly sliding into her. Her knees felt weak, but she knew Kerr would hold her up if she fell. He kissed her that way, pleasuring her from behind, growing the fire in her as expertly as he'd started the flames in the hearth.

"Ye are perfectly wet, lass, sweet and hot."

His words thrilled her, emboldening her to reach down, grasping him under his kilt. He groaned as she stroked, exploring him until with a growl, he tore his mouth from hers. She almost cried out as his hand left her, but he lifted under her knees, carrying her the short distance to the bed, setting her down on the edge. Before she could scoot back, Kerr shoved up her petticoat and smock and bent his head between her legs.

"Oh," she gasped as he tasted her like he had the first time they had come together. His tongue and fingers worked together, building the fire into an inferno spreading through her. "Yes, Kerr," she said, her fingers curling into the coverlet on her bed as he loved her fiercely. "I want you," she cried as her body began to shake with release. The wall shattered, and the wave of pure bliss flooded through Maggie, over and over like pummeling waves of desire.

With a growl, Kerr drew back, turning her over so that she was half on the bed on her knees. Maggie gave herself completely over to the massive sensation. Every touch of Kerr added to it. She felt him seek her from behind and arched. He leaned over her back, one strong arm supporting under her breasts. Hot breath tickled her neck. "Take me, Maggie," he said. "All of me."

He thrust into her open body, and she gasped as he filled her, barely noticing the twinge of pain. He stopped, fully embedded, as he drew large inhales, not moving. Maggie pushed back against him and heard him groan. "It does not hurt," she said, and he pulled back farther only to fill her again. Maggie moaned. "It definitely doesn't hurt."

"Lord lass, hold on then."

Maggie curled her fingers into the coverlet and arched her back as Kerr rammed into her willing body. "Oh God, yes!"

Petticoats balled up, her breasts moving as they hung out the top of her smock, her hair a tangle of curls hanging about her head. She felt totally ravished, and she loved it. Every bit of it. "Yes, Kerr, yes," she said, meeting each one of his thrusts by pushing back into him. She cried out when his fingers pushed past her petticoat to find her in the front, rubbing against the nub that brought her more pleasure.

Moving inside and out, their bodies straining together, Maggie felt the storm build again within herself.

"I must come out," he said.

"No," she ordered as the waves began to crest. "Don't stop."

"Maggie, I wil—"

Her cry of pleasure overtook his words, her body clenching inside around him. Behind her, she heard Kerr roar as he too gave in to the primal release. His arms were wrapped around her, his mouth at her nape as he pumped into her, filling her with his heat.

As the waves slowed, they fell over to their sides in bunches of wrinkled silk. From behind, he pulled her tightly up against the curve of his body. Maggie listened to his breath slow like her own.

After long minutes, she heard Kerr exhale long. "Maggie," he whispered.

"Yes?"

"I am sorry I—"

She turned quickly in his arms, placing a finger over his lips. "No words like that tonight. Only moans." She gave him a small smile. "The only words said tonight must be wicked." Her smile faded. "Other words and consequences can wait for dawn."

Instead of finishing whatever apology he felt was needed, Kerr gave a small nod, his lips relaxing into a grin. "Wicked words are allowed?"

"Absolutely," she said, matching his grin.

"I have quite a few in my head right now." His gaze dipped to her breasts that were still perched high over the stays.

"I was hoping you did."

Kerr lowered his lips back to hers for a long leisurely kiss that she hoped would lead to a night of wicked words.

IN THE DIM light from the dying fire, Kerr watched the gentle rise and fall of Maggie's upper chest. The soft, fragrant skin lay exposed above the blanket draped over her naked body. Her hair lay tussled across the pillow in soft waves of golden red. Kerr breathed in their combined scent. It was intoxicating. Rather like a spell cast by some sorceress. It was the only explanation he had for the thoughts that had tumbled around in his mind before he'd fallen asleep, satiated and content with Maggie in his arms.

I could stay in England. She would be Countess Litchfield and he would be her Highland husband. And a knight after this afternoon's ceremony. If Elizabeth kept her word, they would have one-thousand pounds between them and the Litchfield estate. He'd turn into a foppish Englishman, and his father would skewer him if he ever saw him again. The feud would continue, and Rhona would never cease crying when Percy Hay was killed by one of her kin.

Kerr exhaled long, his gaze traveling along Maggie's long

lashes as they lay against the skin under her eyes. His stomach tightened. What words would be said today? Would Maggie be in his arms again this night or would he be riding back to Scotland alone? For those seemed like the only two futures available.

Dawn was breaking, the blackness outside the window lightening to a dark blue. He hated to leave her but knew she wouldn't want to be found once again locked away with a man. Her brother would no doubt call him out, and he and Maggie would have another wedge between them as he tried not to kill her brother in a duel for her honor.

Kerr ran a hand down his face. Her honor. *Daingead*. He had taken her maidenhead and innocence after the night of exploration and pleasure. Not once had she looked concerned about giving into their passions, the two of them teasing each other even more with wicked words whispered and cried between moans and gasps. The memory was rendering him hard again.

He pushed back the covers, hoping the chill in the room would help calm his need for her. It took all his discipline not to crawl back in and take Maggie up into his arms. He moved silently to the fire, adding peat to warm the room.

Clothes strewn about, Kerr quietly picked up her petticoats, stays, and smock, and laid them over a chair. He padded back to Maggie, leaning over to kiss and bid her farewell, when the sound of boots in the corridor stopped him. From the sound of it, a small army filed through the dark hall, passing.

Staring at the door, Kerr waited until the boots faded down the hall. Turning to quickly don his length of kilt, he smiled as he remembered how sometime during the night Maggie had made him teach her how to fold it and wrapped it around herself. The wool smelled faintly of flowers.

He went to the door, his boots and sword in hand. He'd wash and dress and find some delectable pastries in the kitchen to bring up with him after he was certain Lucy and Cordelia were in with her, so all was proper.

Kerr unlocked the door. With one last look at his sleeping

angel, he stepped out into the cold, dark hallway, locking the door from the outside. The gap under the door was wide enough for him to slide it back underneath with a good push. She would surely find it just inside.

Kerr rammed his feet into his boots and carried his sheathed sword in one hand as he traipsed back along the corridor, past doors that issued the deep resonance of snoring and a few whispered words as people began to rise. Down past William's room and then his father's with the laboratory Walsingham and Burghley were paying for, Kerr continued another few minutes toward his own room, which had been assigned at the other end of the palace.

As he neared, he slowed. The darkness could not hide the group gathered before his door, which was flung open. Kerr's hand moved to his sword, but he wouldn't draw it here before ten armed guards in the English royal palace where he was supposed to be honored and knighted later that day.

"What is this?" Kerr asked, causing the group to shuffle, turning toward him with an awkward flurry of swords.

Walsingham stepped out of his room, his black eyes looking even beadier in the light from the lamps. "Kerr Gordon."

"Aye."

"Upon orders from Queen Elizabeth, you are under arrest."

"Arrest? For what reason?"

"You are to be remanded to the Bloody Tower at the Tower of London."

CHAPTER NINETEEN

"The king has been very good to me. He promoted me from a simple maid to be a marchioness. Then he raised me to be a queen. Now he will raise me to be a martyr."

Anne Boleyn – Queen Elizabeth I's mother

"AND THEN LETTICE Knollys danced with Lord Robert, and I thought the queen would start throwing things," Cordelia said as she sat on the bed that Maggie had straightened quickly when the sisters had knocked.

When had Kerr left? Surely, he'd snuck away so as not to wake her, but she still frowned.

"Cordy," Lucy said, but her rebuke was lost as she giggled.

Brows arched over her wide eyes, Lucy nodded to Maggie. "But I saw the maid quietly snatch the crystal decanter away."

"That Robert plays with fire," Cordelia said, shaking her head. "Elizabeth will only stand so much before she banishes him from court."

Banishing from court. Was that an option? Maggie nibbled on the side of her fingernail. What could she do that would make Elizabeth send her from court but would not make her so angry as to banish her brother and father too or send Maggie to the Tower?

"You are solemn today," Cordelia said, studying Maggie. "Why?"

Lucy sat next to her sister. "We forgive you, Maggie, for what you had to do to protect the queen. You know that, don't you?"

Maggie flushed red, embarrassed that she was thinking of her own problems when her two dear friends had lost their mother. And that she had been the one to kill her.

Maggie walked closer, still in her hastily thrown-on smock. She took each of their hands. "I am truly sorry," she said, letting the truth of it in the tone of her voice.

Cordelia inhaled quickly, sitting up straight. She squeezed Maggie's hand back. "You had no choice. I saw the craze that had taken over Mother. She was not herself." She shook her head. "I am ashamed of it all."

"Her actions do not reflect upon you," Maggie said.

"Oh yes they do," Lucy said and looked to her sister. "We were questioned by Walsingham. Thankfully we were not tortured."

Cordelia met Maggie's gaze. "Thank you," she whispered, "for denying my involvement in any way, even when Norfolk said I was part of it."

Maggie gave her a sad smile. "You were coerced and threatened. I am happy that we found you and you told us about the plot before the queen or any of her ladies could be hurt."

"Let us never talk of it again," Lucy whispered, as if the walls could hear and report directly to Walsingham.

Heaven help Maggie, if that were true after last night. The things she'd said and did!

The three of them clasped hands in a three-way shake to seal their promise. "Agreed," Maggie said.

"What shall you wear today to the ceremony?" Cordelia stood, walking over to the racks of clothes where Kerr had hidden that first day. Maggie had made sure he wasn't there now. She'd found the key shoved under the door instead of on the hook next to it. He'd locked her safely in and left without a farewell.

"I thought you were done trying on the queen's gowns," Lucy said. "That you are too precious to her now."

Maggie watched Cordelia move the gowns one at a time,

their gems and pearls clicking together and the silk rustling. "I will still conduct the testing for poison and blades," Maggie said. "But then they will be handed off to another lady to wear for a day."

Her father and brother could certainly do the testing themselves. Without the responsibility for trying on the clothes, Maggie didn't have a true purpose at court. Maybe she could ask the queen if she could leave. As Countess Litchfield, wouldn't she have the ability to leave court?

"Of course, the queen wouldn't risk losing you," Cordelia said, lifting a simple, yet elegant blue gown with embroidered lace. "You are her champion."

The words that once would have made Maggie smile had the opposite effect. Elizabeth would not let Maggie leave her side, even after bestowing a title on her. Elizabeth dictated the movements of her favorites, banishing them from or demanding their presence at court. Maggie would be able to attend her when it would not be proper to have a man as a guard. There had even been talk on fitting Maggie with some light armor she could wear to help protect her queen.

Lucy dipped her face to meet Maggie's gaze. "What's wrong to make you pout so?" She glanced upward. "If there was a bird flying in here, it would likely shite on your lip."

Maggie snorted softly and rolled her eyes, making sure to suck in her lip. "I… I worry that Kerr Gordon will leave today." Which was completely true.

Cordelia laid the blue ensemble over a chair opposite the one that held Maggie's discarded gown from the night before. "But you haven't yet answered Kerr's proposal."

Maggie shook her head. "How can I when the queen has lifted me so high and is requiring me to attend her? How could I ever leave here?"

"Maybe he will stay," Lucy said, although her tone said what Maggie was thinking. Kerr Gordon would always return to Scotland.

"He is to be the next chief of his clan," Maggie said, letting the worry soak her words. "He needs to negotiate peace and support her sister in her bid to wed." She shook her head. "How could I ask him to stay?"

Cordelia frowned. "By opening your mouth and saying, 'Kerr Gordon, I want you to stay here in England with me.'" She flapped her hand. "'Figure out what to do to make that work, and I will be your wife.'"

"He does watch you all the time," Lucy said, smiling. "All the time," she emphasized each word. "Like a spell has been cast upon him. Maybe he will stay."

"Maybe," Maggie said with a weakness that echoed her hopelessness.

"You won't know unless you ask," Lucy said.

"Or demand," Cordelia said, lifting the gown again. "And in this blue ensemble, he will definitely say yes."

KERR PACED THE confines of the same cell he had been locked in before. The Bloody Tower was luxurious by the standards of dungeons and jailhouses, but it was still a prison. "Daingead," he murmured, running his hands through his hair. Had Maggie been informed? Or did she think he'd ridden away after he'd loved her all night? He banged his fist on the table as he passed.

He would demand that she be told of his whereabouts. But would that knowledge make her risk breaking into the Tower again? Would it hurt her less in the long run to think he'd vanished without so much as a farewell?

"Foking hell." Kerr kicked the basket of apples and bread the guard had left for him. The woven container couldn't withstand the force of his boot and broke apart. Apples flew out, several smashing into the stone wall behind it, while the bread thudded where it landed on the rug.

Kerr spun, sliding his sword from its sheath to swing it wildly in the ridiculously large space for a cell. Why hadn't Walsingham taken it from him? He didn't even know the charges against him. All his demands and questions had been met with stony silence from the ten guards Walsingham felt were needed to take him to the Tower without him escaping. He'd have tried anyway if he'd thought this wasn't some nightmare or farce.

"Why the bloody hell am I in here!" he yelled, but even the guards that had stood at first outside the locked door had departed. He threw his sword on the bed and strode to the door to yank on the bars over the small window. "Foking hell, Walsingham! A man must know why he is detained. What type of fool-laden government locks a man up without a reason?"

Kerr listened, but of course there was no response. "Damn you all," he said and turned back to his prison, striding over to yank open the glassed window to look out on a brown yard of trampled grass and mud, shrouded now in nightfall. The snow had melted, leaving a dead landscape that matched Kerr's desolate mood.

Mid-February was bleak and even bleaker locked in a Tower without having said farewell. "I am sorrowful for it, Maggie," he said and spun around to lean against the icy wall. He hadn't wanted to wake her, only to return with pastries from the well-stocked kitchen at Whitehall. "I should have woken ye," he murmured. "Ye deserve to know."

He pushed off the wall with his boot and strode to the small writing desk where parchment and an inkwell with a quill had been left. Another luxury of a prison for lords and princes.

My dear, Maggie Darby, Whitehall Palace

I have been detained by Walsingham under orders from your queen, even though I know not the charges set against me. I am heartily sorry that I was not allowed to return

Damn. Others would read this, and he certainly didn't want to reveal that they'd spent another night together, an amazing night he would never forget. He would not mind it, but Maggie probably would very much.

I am heartily sorry that I was not allowed to return after seeing you safely locked in your room. I have not abandoned you, and my question still stands.

He wiped a hand across his stubbled jaw.

But do not risk yourself or your family on my account.

Would telling her not to try to save him stop her from doing just that? Maggie was brave and clever, more so than any other person he had met before. Beautiful and unique in her freckled, tawny-haired, heart-shaped face way, but it was her mind that captivated him. It worked through details, putting them together to create a picture that most people would miss.

Telling her not to come would not stop her. "Mo chreach," he swore and continued writing, the quill scratching across the parchment.

I have been sent far away from London. I do not know where, so do not try to follow. But know that

That what? Kerr closed his eyes and exhaled. He had never been poetic and had hardly even written a letter except for battle strategies sent to his warriors along the perimeters of Gordon land. He inhaled and loosened his grip so as not to snap the quill.

Know that my thoughts are about you and

He paused long enough that the ink dripped from the quill. If he were to die at the block or the gallows or was left to waste away in the Tower, he wanted her to know.

And my heart is and will always be yours.
My everlasting love, Kerr Gordon

"HAVE YOU SEEN Kerr today, Father?" Maggie asked as he led her down the corridor toward the great hall where the ceremony would begin shortly.

"No. I have been working with William to set up our own laboratory next to my chambers. The queen is sparing no expense to make it as modern and complete as possible." He sounded almost childlike with excitement. "There are glass vials and beakers, a long polished worktable, candles and lamps, and Walsingham says he will obtain all the chemicals I have on a list I made for him."

"Truly wonderful," Maggie murmured softly. Kerr had left before she'd woken and hadn't returned. She'd even gone to the stables, her heart sinking when she saw that his horse, Caspian, was missing. Henry and Giles knew nothing about it even though they had softened toward him since he and William saved them from the explosion. Frustration churned with worry inside her.

Her father stopped her before they entered the hall. "What is wrong, child?"

"I… I think Kerr may have left court without… well without saying farewell."

Her father frowned. "I don't think he would do such a thing, not after all we have been through together."

And her father didn't know anything about last night. Cordelia and Lucy had helped her dress in the blue ensemble they said made her look royal and then had walked the halls with her trying to find Kerr. But even they did not know that Maggie had given her body, and likely her soul, to Kerr last night.

My question still stands.

Did it still? She'd meant to ask him to stay in England with her even though the very words made her stomach tighten in anticipation of his no. But after a day of worry that he had ridden away without her, the thought that he may actually do so made her distracted and ill.

Maggie shook her head and offered her father a smile, although it was mostly forced. "You are right. Kerr is honorable. He would not leave without telling me."

He patted her hand and turned to lead her forward, but Maggie stopped him. "Father."

"Aye?" He turned back to study her in the low light from the sconces lining the hall.

She opened and closed her mouth twice before the words would come. "I have given my life, so far, like the rest of the Darbys have, to the service of the house of Tudor and England."

"Aye, you have, my brave daughter." He smiled broadly. "And for that, William and I are grateful. As is the queen and her entire realm."

Lord. He was not helping. Maggie swallowed. "But I am... selfish," she said, lowering her voice. "I do not..." She took a large inhale, looking at a portrait of a judgmental royal ancestor hanging on the wall as she spoke. "I do not want to remain here at court to protect the queen. I want to be with Kerr. I want to say yes to his proposal of marriage, and that would mean I would return with him to Scotland." The words rushed out as if she were afraid that she might clamp her lips tight and they would never escape, and she'd be forced to swallow them down into her middle where they would eat away at her forever.

"And that, I fear, makes me very selfish," she said.

Reginald Darby took Maggie by the shoulders. "Margaret Isabella Darby," he said slowly. "Look at me."

Maggie inhaled fully, bracing herself for what she knew was true. She was selfish to even want to leave, even if she did not in the end. *If Kerr left me.*

She returned her gaze to her father's sharp eyes.

"Wanting a life away from court is not selfish," he said. "It is honoring yourself and what you dream for in life." He straightened. "My father wanted me to be a blacksmith." He scoffed and held out his hands. "Can you imagine me banging iron all day and burning myself?" He didn't wait for her to answer. "I would be dirty all the time." He shuddered dramatically. "Then where would our family be? Certainly not performing chemical analyses of poisons at Whitehall Palace and having a warm bath arranged for me every day."

"What if my leaving angers the queen and she makes you and William leave court?"

He clasped her hands in his large ones and looked closely into her eyes as if imparting a secret. "I want grandchildren more than I want a soft bed at Whitehall."

A small sob escaped her lips, and Maggie threw her arms around her father. "Thank you," she whispered and inhaled his familiar clean scent as they hugged.

"Perhaps tell the queen your plans *after* she gives you the five-hundred pounds," he said, and she laughed because they both knew Elizabeth could take it back if she was angry enough.

Reginald took Maggie's arm to lead her into the hall where others had already gathered. Small groups whispered together, all of them turning to inspect her as she walked in with dignity on her father's arm. But Maggie only looked for one person. Where was Kerr?

Now that she did not feel the need to ask him to stay in England, her stomach unknotted. But as her gaze moved from group to group, seeking, tension formed anew. He wasn't there.

William walked over. "Have you seen Kerr?" he asked. "We are about to start, and he is not in his chambers."

"I haven't seen him at all today," she said with all honesty, unless one counted the loving they had shared in the early hours of the morning. "William, I am worried something has happened to him. IIis horse is missing from the stables."

"Did he return to Scotland?" William asked. "Without his five-hundred pounds? What a fool."

"No," she said, glancing around for someone who would know. "I cannot believe it. I will not." But her heart beat faster as panic plucked at her resolve.

"Her Majesty, the queen of England and Ireland," the herald called out, and everyone turned toward the door next to the dais where Elizabeth, dressed in grand style of embroidered velvet, studded with hundreds of gems, walked with regal grace into the room. Maggie remembered how heavy the ensemble was when she'd worn it.

Everyone bowed or curtseyed, including Maggie. Elizabeth sat in her throne, and everyone straightened. Lord Walsingham and Lord Cecil joined her, one on each side. "William and Margaret Darby, come forward," the queen said, her voice stern.

William took Maggie's arm, leading her through the parted courtiers. Lord Burghley bent to speak in the queen's ear.

"Yes, yes, I know," Elizabeth said and shooed him. "I have unfortunate news." She looked directly at Maggie. "Kerr Gordon has been taken to the Tower to await my council's judgement."

Maggie's hand rose to cover her mouth. Relief battled with panic. He hadn't left her, but he was once again in the Tower.

"On what charges?" William asked.

Elizabeth glanced at Walsingham, and he cleared his voice. "For aiding Norfolk and Ridolfi in their plot against the queen."

"That is ridiculous," Maggie said, her voice louder than was prudent before Elizabeth, and the queen's eyes grew round. "I beg your pardon, Your Majesty," Maggie said, lowering her voice and bowing her head for a moment before meeting the queen's gaze. "Kerr Gordon was instrumental in stopping the assassination. He was not involved with Lord Norfolk or any of his accomplices."

She waved her beringed hand. "Even so," Elizabeth said, "there are other charges being formed against the Highlander. Some of which may not come to fruition. But for now, you need to know that he is back in the Bloody Tower."

Elizabeth studied Maggie's face. No doubt she was not used to seeing the mix of raw fear and stubborn anger in Maggie's countenance. She had always been docile around the queen until recently when she'd had to protect her with her body. "You care for the man?" Elizabeth asked, and the whole room seemed to hold its breath for an answer, as if they were starving beasts waiting for a bloodletting.

"Yes, Your Majesty."

Elizabeth kept her frown. "He has asked you to wed him. Is your father aware of this?"

Reginald Darby did not hesitate. "I have given my blessing of the union, Your Majesty." He stepped up next to Maggie. She glanced his way. Was he lying to the queen? 'Twas treason. Her father looked at her. "He asked me right after he asked you, the morning before you thwarted the assassination attempt."

"And you said yes, even back then?" she said, her voice soft.

"I said it was your decision, and I would support you either way."

Elizabeth snorted. "A decision such as marriage…" She shook her head. "Left to the heart instead of wisdom would be disastrous." She glanced at William Cecil, Lord Burghley. "I would have been wed years ago, and the kingdom would be in anarchy."

Maggie bowed her head briefly. "I am blessed that I do not have the weight of royalty upon my shoulders, Your Majesty."

"Yes," Elizabeth said and sighed. "'Tis tedious at its best and lethal at its worst." She allowed a slight grin as if amusing herself. "Although I do receive the most deliciously sweet treats to sample." She plucked off a comfit from the table next to her.

She swallowed the sweet and narrowed her eyes again at Maggie. "And what say you to Kerr Gordon's proposal?"

CHAPTER TWENTY

*"If I could be anything in the world I would want to be a
teardrop because I would be born in your eyes, live on your
cheeks, and die on your lips."*

Mary Stuart, Queen of Scots

MAGGIE'S MOUTH WENT dry. She felt the weight of the world,
her world of ladies and lords staring at her back, listening
to her words so they could replay them over cards and drinks.
Court life had been her whole life, even at home learning the
ways in order to fit in if called upon to serve.

She wet her lips. "I did not think I had a choice to say yes or
no," Maggie said. "Since Your Majesty has given me a position in
your household once more, along with my father and brother."

"Oh," Elizabeth said, leaning back. "My Lamb has been raised
to sacrifice her life, as my poison detector first and now as a
daughter and sister. Very honorable. But I have heard that if the
feeling is great enough, nothing will stop two lovers from joining
together." She frowned, her gaze raking the silent audience.
"Even when a queen forbids it," she snapped.

Elizabeth had imprisoned lovers before who had secretly wed
without her permission. But Maggie didn't care anything about
that right now. She only cared about getting Kerr free of the
Tower and whatever charges were being formed against him.

"Your Majesty," Maggie said. "If I could hear the charges
against Kerr Gordon, I will be able to prove them false. His heart

is not one for subterfuge. He only wishes to return to his clan in Scotland and end this feud between his clan and the neighboring clan so that his sister can wed her love."

"Such silly beings we are," Elizabeth intoned. "Allowing love to dictate so much in our lives." She sighed again but then stared hard at Maggie for a long moment. "But I fear that your Highlander will be executed quite shortly."

Maggie's heart jumped, hammering hard behind her breastbone so much that she pressed a hand against it, hoping she would not be sick before everyone.

"And your decision will have been made for you," Elizabeth finished, watching her closely. She waved a hand. "Your feelings for him are not strong enough. You will not suffer long, dear Lady Darby, and you will live your days in luxury here at Whitehall, using your cleverness to protect the realm." Elizabeth smiled again and took another sweetmeat to pop into her mouth.

Executed? Kerr was to be executed shortly. The sob that bubbled up in Maggie's middle fell from her mouth, and she placed her fist against it. Without another word, she turned, fleeing from the hall amidst gasps from the onlookers. *I do not care. I do not care about anything at all! Except for Kerr!*

Maggie tore down the corridor, her slippers slapping on the stone. She would never care about anything ever again if Kerr was executed. He was honorable and giving, strong and clever. If he died, it would be her fault for not convincing the queen that he was innocent.

She stopped in the shadows of the corridor and leaned against the wall. No one ran after her, not her father or William or Cordelia and Lucy. Had Elizabeth forbidden it? But Maggie wanted to be alone.

"What can I do?" she whispered. She took a deep breath, trying to clear her mind of the churning worry. This was a problem similar to dealing with a suspicious gown. The situation was full of poison, and Kerr would die if she did not figure out what to do, how to save him. And this time, Maggie did not care if she was poisoned herself. She caught another sob and tried to release it with a slow exhale. Because she realized then what she'd been too afraid to admit before the queen. "I love him," she whispered. More than herself. More than her family. More than her queen.

➤➤➤⟪⟪⟪

KERR STOOD AT the small, barred window of his cell. "Jailor," he called, but no one answered. He held the letter that he'd written. "Jailor!" Silence echoed back.

A surly-looking, lanky guard had brought his food but then left, leaving the key to the cell hooked on its post nearby. Near but quite out of reach. Such a risk, especially after Maggie and William had broken him out before. Did Walsingham know so little about keeping prisoners? They'd left him his sword and daggers, fed him well, and left him unguarded with a key six feet away.

A gust of an exhale came from him. But what good were his sword and daggers when he couldn't be free, couldn't bring pastries up to Maggie and tell her that he hadn't left her without a farewell. He must get word to her. Having her think that he'd abandoned her without a word after the night they'd shared pierced him more than any blade. "Magairlean," he said and turned back to the low-ceilinged room with arches set at odd angles to give it the appearance of several rooms. He paced to the window and looked out into the clear night. All was quiet.

How the bloody hell had he ended up back in the Bloody Tower? *Because I didn't leave London immediately, that's how.* He ran his hands down his face. *I couldn't.*

Kerr sucked in the cold air that found a way in around the panes of wavy glass. London's air was stale compared to the fresh flow of Highland wind. Here there was only stone and closely stacked buildings blocking any sun that made its way past the clouds. It was crowded with people and their carts, hawking their wares in desperate voices, their gazes searching for the crumbs of riches from those close to the aristocracy. Kerr supposed it was the same in Edinburgh, which he'd visited several times. Cities seemed to pull the life out of him. To feel alive, he needed wide open heaths and breezes raking through the abundant grasses.

But I also need Maggie.

He let the letter drop from his hand and crossed his arms over his chest. There must be a solution, even a convoluted one.

Footsteps sounded on the stairs outside his cell. He scooped up the letter and walked back to the door. He frowned at the light steps, his stomach tightening. The tapping did not sound like the heavy footfalls of a booted man. He'd heard the sound before, and he held his breath in hope and terror together.

The light from a lamp splashed golden across the rough stone wall at the top of the steps, and a figure emerged. A lad? But as the face turned toward the door, Kerr's breath caught, his heart slamming against his ribs. "Maggie?" he whispered.

She smiled broadly and released a big breath. "I have found you." She was dressed in the trousers of a working man with a tunic, cape, and a cap that bulged with the fullness of her hair.

"What are ye doing here?" he whispered. "The guards—"

"Seem to be away," she said, snatching the key from the hook. "There were none about." She hurried to his door, shoving the key in the lock and turning it. "You didn't think I would leave you in here, did you?"

"I had no hope that ye even knew where I was," he said as the door swung outward.

Maggie hurried inside, breathing hard. Her face was flushed, her eyes dark and wide as if taking in every possible threat, and her lush lips were parted. "Och, lass, ye are bonny," he said, pulling her into his arms, hugging her close.

She rested her cheek against his chest and wrapped her arms around his middle.

"I rather like the breeches," he said.

She pushed back to tip her head for a kiss, which he obliged her, despite the anxiousness growing inside him. Her lips were soft, the feel of her warm, but tension grew, and he broke the kiss.

"Maggie," he said, his voice rough. "Ye should not have risked coming here."

"I had to." She frowned up at him. "They locked you away without charges."

"But they could arrest ye, throw ye in the Tower, threaten ye with execution." He dropped his arms and turned to put some distance between them.

"Like they have to you," she said.

He looked back at her. "Execution?"

Her face pinched tighter in confusion. "They didn't tell you? Elizabeth has agreed to your execution, Kerr, without even telling us the charges."

He studied her. "She said this to ye?"

She nodded. "Before a room of witnesses and Walsingham and Lord Burghley."

"And yet they let me keep my weapons." He looked at the door. "And no guards." Something wasn't right. None of this was right. "The queen or Walsingham... one or both of them are playing at something."

"I don't care, as long as we can get you out of here and riding back to Scotland," she said.

Kerr gripped her shoulders with his two hands, bending to meet her face. "I am not leaving ye, Maggie." He watched her face for any signs at all. Sadness or apathy would be the worst. But her lips softened, her mouth turning up at the edges.

"I am not leaving you either, Kerr," she said.

It took a few seconds before he could pull breath. "My question still stands," he said, his voice low, trying not to hope.

"And my answer is yes," she said. "I will marry you, my wild Highlander."

His hope soared despite him trying to keep ahold on it. "Even if that means leaving Whitehall and your family?" he asked. "Because if we survive this night, I will not for long in England."

She wrapped her arms around his middle, speaking against his chest. "I have said my farewells. If Elizabeth doesn't mark me a traitor, I intend to visit William and my father. So yes to leaving England, and yes to your question."

Kerr's chest swelled with his inhale, and he held Maggie tightly. He knew they should already be racing down the steps, but the happiness that flowed through him couldn't be ignored or set aside for later. He lifted her, turning them in a circle as she laughed softly. Setting her down, he caught her face between his hands. "I love ye, Maggie Darby," he said.

Her smile grew to wipe away every shred of worry from her lovely face. "I love you too, Kerr Gordon."

His lips descended to capture hers in a kiss. Even with the brutal unfairness of Elizabeth and her minions and the uncertainty and danger around them, Kerr was happier than he'd ever been before in his life. No matter what happened next, he had Maggie's love, and he would do anything to protect her.

He broke the kiss, his forehead against hers. "We must go before they realize their mistake of leaving me unguarded with a betrothed who is brave enough to break me out of the Bloody Tower. Twice."

They made the bed look like he slept again and locked the cell door as they left, setting the key back on the hook. He had been ignored the entire time he'd been there. It was doubtful anyone would go in to rouse him until the next day.

Kerr went down the turning steps first, his dagger drawn. Maggie followed silently, and he kept his own steps light. At the bottom, Maggie blew out her lamp, leaving it on a table where two guards normally sat through the night.

"There was no one even for me to poison with my sweetmeats," Maggie whispered, patting a pouch she'd tied at her waist.

He cracked the door to look through. The night lay silent and cold. Even the wind quieted, and the moon hid in the clouds.

"Do you know where Caspian is?" Maggie said. "We are leaving by boat."

"Nay," he said, his chest clenching. "Was he not in his stall at Whitehall?"

"Not when I looked for you."

Bloody hell. Where would Walsingham keep him? How could he leave his faithful friend behind?

"Wait," Kerr said, her words breaking through. "Ye rowed over here by boat?" he asked, following along the wall. They paused in a shadow as two guards at the front of the tower gates exchanged positions. Maggie beckoned him to follow her through another archway that led to the Tower's dock along the Thames. In the muted moonlight, Kerr saw a small gondola sitting low along the dock with a figure in it.

Maggie hurried him down to it. "I've got him," Maggie said, motioning for Kerr to get in at the opposite end.

Kerr met William's gaze. "Ye take great risks William Darby."

"She would still be struggling against the current in the middle of the Thames if I hadn't gone with her," William said with a frown at Maggie before looking at Kerr again. "And she says she wants you alive." He shrugged as if he couldn't understand his sister.

Maggie snorted and climbed into the middle of the small, flat-bottomed boat. Kerr took up an oar at the other end, pushing them out into the inky dark waters. The Thames rose and fell with the tide, and it was high at the moment, so several ships were sailing out of London. Crowded, even on the waterways.

"Where are we letting out?" Kerr asked.

"The public dock closest to our house," Maggie said.

Kerr pulled on the oars. The changing tide had tamed the current, making it easier to row across. He kept an eye on the few hulking ships moving down river, trying to catch the wind to go out to sea.

"The two of ye are alone in this?" Kerr asked, hoping Maggie's father wasn't also involved.

"Lucy and Cordy know. They were thinking about coming with us, but decided not to," Maggie said.

"I will get them out of London if I catch the slightest hint of Walsingham arresting them," William said. "I still know things before anyone else." He frowned. "And my instincts are good." William met Kerr's gaze.

Kerr nodded. He felt the wrongness hanging in the night too. "Instincts that tell ye this escape was too easy?" Kerr asked.

"Aye," William said, his eyes turning back to the lit docks of The Tower.

"I barely had to sneak past anyone," Maggie said, her voice heavy with worry. "Could Elizabeth be setting a trap, knowing I would try to rescue you?"

No one answered. One answer would sound like a lie meant as comfort and the other would just add to the tension shrouding them like the mist coming up in patches off the water.

Kerr watched the shoreline that they kept close to along the Thames. There were small jutting public docks, each with a lantern tied to a pole at the end, although only half were lit. They rowed toward a dark one. Squinting, he could make out the shape of a horse waiting on the thoroughfare. He was all black and blended in with the shadows. "Caspian?"

"How…?" Maggie asked, her frown visible as she stared straight ahead at Caspian. She looked at William. "Perhaps Father found him?"

The winter breeze blew, but that wasn't what caused the hairs on the back of Kerr's neck to rise. He scanned the dock, but Reginald Darby didn't stand with his horse. As far as he could see, there was no one. Caspian stood alone, saddled and waiting.

The dock creaked as they drew closer, the current pushing against a thick chain that hit one of the posts underneath, issuing a *clunk* every so often. A few voices from several streets over mixed with a slight gust of wind around the eaves of a dark shop along the river. The water lapped at the boat, the sound of the oars dipping in and out slowing and stopping as they pulled up to the ladder leading to the dock above. The river was high, so it was only a few steps up. Maggie stepped out of the boat first, her breeches making the climb easy. Kerr followed right behind. He pulled his dagger, his warrior instincts screaming at him in the silent darkness.

"Maggie," he murmured. "Let me go first."

She stopped, and he walked before her toward Caspian. His horse threw his head up and down like he did before they rode together into battle. Kerr re-sheathed his dagger, stroking down Caspian's neck as he walked by. Kerr pulled out his sword, and the sound of steel against steel cut through the silence of the dark night. "Come out of your hiding hole," Kerr said, his voice stern and full of lethal promise.

Footsteps clicked on the pavement as a figure in a full skirt, draped with a cape, walked down toward the dock from a shadow. With her walked a man. Behind them walked a battalion.

"Put your sword away, Highlander, before Lord Walsingham orders the arrows trained upon you to be loosed."

"Good bloody lord," Maggie whispered beside him. "'Tis the queen."

CHAPTER TWENTY-ONE

"Though she be but little, she is fierce!"
William Shakespeare, *A Midsummer Night's Dream*

M AGGIE LEAPED BEFORE Kerr, spreading her arms wide in an attempt to cover his body with her own. It was instinct, and it was laughable considering how much of him there was to cover.

"He has done nothing wrong, Your Majesty. We have heard no charges against him."

The queen moved forward with Walsingham closely by her side. Lord Robert Dudley appeared on her other side, sword in hand. Even her father's faithful friend, Lord Burghley stood behind Elizabeth, all of them out here in the dark London night.

"Ah," the queen said, "but now there are charges against you, Lady Darby, Viscountess of Litchfield." It seemed that Elizabeth had still granted her a title, despite Maggie running out of the ceremony yesterday. It would probably be stripped from her today as she was thrown into a cold, stinking, rat-infested dungeon.

"The most notable being sneaking into the Tower of London and freeing a criminal. Twice." She held up two fingers. "There are also suspicions about you poisoning my guards the first time and your delay in revealing the blades sewn into my glove."

"I never would have let you touch that glove," Maggie murmured, feeling her face redden.

The guard, Henry, who still bore a bruise from where he'd been hit in the chapel, moved forward with a lantern and lit the lamp hanging above their heads. He glanced at her, his eyes sympathetic. Light cast a glow along the narrow dock. Hopefully William was paddling away in the shadows. Maggie glanced over one shoulder. *God's teeth.* Her brother was standing right behind them. With the brilliance the Darbys were afforded, one would think they would have better survival instincts.

Kerr stepped around Maggie, trying to block her. "My crimes are my own. Maggie has nothing to do with this."

Elizabeth laughed. "Oh, but she does have to do with all of this, Highlander, even without…" Her hands tumbled in the air, "the tangle of subterfuge." She looked to her side at Lord Robert. "See what love does. Makes one lose their senses."

"Exactly," Kerr said. "I ask pardon for Lady Darby, Your Majesty."

Elizabeth looked sternly at him. "And what will you grant me in return?"

"My life if that is the price," Kerr said.

Maggie's heart clenched, and her fingers curled into the sleeve of his arm. "No. No." She must think. "If we knew the charges, we could prove them false." Her gaze went to Lord Burghley. "Please."

The queen tipped her head, studying them, then cleared her throat. "Tell them the charge against him, Walsingham. 'Tis getting too cold out here, and I hunger for my warm hearth."

Walsingham stared at Kerr and sighed as if he hated this part of his job. "The queen has charged you, Kerr Gordon, for stealing the heart of Lady Margaret Darby, Viscountess Litchfield, her lady protector. And for taking her away from Her Majesty's court."

"Thank you, Lord Walsingham," the queen said, smiling. She tipped her head, studying them as Maggie recited Walsingham's words in her head. Stealing her heart? Could that be a real charge? The queen had locked up those who secretly wed before, but it was more for the political danger to her because of their union. And the offenders weren't sentenced to be executed.

"You would…" Maggie paused, her brows pinching together. "You would execute him for my loving him?"

"Do you then?" the queen asked. "Love the Highlander? He will not stay here. This wild, brawny man is made for the mountains, not a city."

Maggie held tightly to Kerr's arm. "I will go with him."

"Away from your family?" Elizabeth asked. "Away from your queen and country?"

This had been the question since Maggie realized how important Kerr had become to her. But when she learned he'd been arrested, the answer had become clear.

Suddenly Elizabeth's actions became clear. Maggie drew in a full breath. "You arrested Kerr to see if I would try to save him."

The smile on Elizabeth's face expanded. "Lord Walsingham will not count tonight as an escape. It hurts his self-worth as my Master of Security."

"There were no guards, and ye left me my weapons," Kerr said.

"Which is why there were no guards about," Elizabeth said with a small laugh. "Walsingham had them get out of the way of that blade of yours."

"You would not have escaped if this had not been a ruse," Walsingham said. "Constructed by the queen."

"Oh, Lord Robert helped too," Elizabeth said, clutching his arm. "As a queen, I know my love would die for me to save me from execution, or at least try." Her smile faded a bit as if the thought weighed on her. "But a common English lady and a Highlander. Without political loyalties or the confines of royal bloodlines…" She flipped her hand about. "Would they risk their lives for one another? 'Twas my own experiment."

She pointed at Kerr. "I was fairly sure that you would brave death for my lamb when you stayed in London despite having every opportunity to leave after she saved you the first time."

Elizabeth turned to Maggie. "But you." She tipped her head, looking thoughtful. "I needed to know your heart. And if Kerr Gordon caused you to forget your duties, then you must love him beyond sense."

Maggie inhaled slowly. "I do," Maggie said. She felt Kerr claim her hand, and they intertwined their fingers together. "With all my heart, I love him," she said, looking up at the strong features of Kerr. The glow of the lamp painted half his face gold, the other in shadow. He was complex and courageous, and she had so much love for him.

"And I love ye, Maggie lass," he said touching the side of her face. "When I couldn't find ye after the explosion, the thought of your life being snuffed out, your brilliance and smile disappearing from the world..." He shook his head. "I nearly ripped the cathedral door from its hinges. And then last night..." he stopped, capturing a tear that had escaped onto her cheek. "I will make ye my wife and love ye our whole lives." He leaned down to brush a kiss across her lips. Joy swelled inside Maggie, and she clung to him.

"Huzzah," came a small voice from the shadows, followed by a round of rapid applause from one pair of hands. Maggie looked out to see Lucy pressing high on her toes as if overtaken with joy. Cordelia handed her sister a handkerchief, and dabbed at her own eyes, a smile on her face too. Elizabeth had brought them to the dock along with Caspian.

Elizabeth smacked the back of her hand against Lord Robert. "You need to practice your courtly love, Dear Robin. You are lacking compared to this Highlander," she said, moving her hand up and down to indicate Kerr's build.

Lord Robert wore a cajoling grin, but it did little to hide his annoyance. However, the long-time favorite knew better than to argue his side with the queen. "I will endeavor to be more like the Highlander," Robert said to Elizabeth.

Out of the shadows walked Reginald Darby. "Father," Maggie whispered.

He bowed to the queen before coming up to Maggie. "My friend Cecil told me, so I came along." He looked to Kerr. "Love her and keep her well, son."

"I swear it," Kerr said.

Maggie let go of Kerr and threw herself into her father's arms, hugging him tight. "I love you."

"I love you too, Maggie," he said, hugging her back. "Your time serving is done. Time to find happiness for yourself." He pulled back to look in her eyes. "Your mother would be very joyful." She sniffed, smiling. Her father looked past her. "And William and I will visit if we can."

She smiled broadly. "And so will we."

"'Tis freezing out here," Elizabeth said. "Give them the letter and take me back to my hearth," she said and beckoned Lord Burghley. She turned to Kerr and Maggie. "Due to your impudence you both lose half your reward. But this letter should help your cause, Highlander. Do with it as you will."

Kerr took the sealed missive from Cecil, Lord Burghley. "Thank ye, Your Majesty," Kerr said, "but your words will not sway the Hays to form a peace with the Gordons. They are stubborn Scots and Catholics at that."

Elizabeth waved her hand. "The letter is not for your popish enemy."

Maggie looked where Kerr turned the folded parchment to see the name scrawled on the front. *Mary Stuart, Queen of the Scots.*

"Now say farewell to me, my dear lamb, and hurry to your old home where I have some more appropriate costumes for you to take on your journey," Elizabeth said, eyeing Maggie's trousers and cap.

Maggie curtsied deeply before the queen, which was awkward without the petticoats. Elizabeth seemed to find it amusing and chuckled, holding out her hand for Maggie to kiss. "Very good, Lady Darby. I expect letters describing your adventures north."

"Yes, Your Majesty," Maggie said, rising, her smile genuine. "I am certain there will be many adventures." Maggie felt Kerr right behind her, and Elizabeth held her hand out to him.

Maggie held tightly to her laughter as he awkwardly took the queen's hand. He bowed his head over it and kissed her knuckle before straightening. The queen looked sideways to Robert. "You, Dear Robin, certainly have more warmth in your kiss." She turned away. "Fare thee well," she said as she walked toward a waiting litter to be carried back to Whitehall.

William pulled Maggie into a hug and, stepping back, looked to Kerr. "I hope I don't have to help break you out of the Tower again," William said with a smile. "'Tis becoming rather tedious."

"I will return the favor if ye are ever imprisoned in Scotland," Kerr said, shaking his hand. Cordelia and Lucy hurried forward, past Lord Burghley who spoke with her father, the two men smiling. People living along the waterfront had opened their doors to peek out at the unfolding drama. Several talked together about seeing the queen as the guards moved out to follow Elizabeth's litter through the dark streets to a royal barge farther down.

"Write when you arrive," Lucy said.

"Let us know how fierce it is there," Cordelia said.

Kerr snorted. "We hang heads about the outer walls to deter attacks."

Cordelia's eyes grew round, but Lucy laughed. "'Tis like Tower Bridge." She patted Maggie's hand. "Hopefully the Gordons dip the heads in tar like they do in London, else the smell will turn your stomach."

"And the English call us savage," Kerr murmured.

Lucy shrugged. "Either way, you will feel right at home."

Home. Maggie hadn't had a home for seven years as she lived at Whitehall. Even though her stomach twisted with nerves as she faced a new life, excitement lit her. She took Kerr's hand, pulling strength from the warmth of it. She looked up into his face. He gazed back, love evident in his eyes. He did not merely look at her but saw her for who she was.

Kerr lifted her to mount Caspian astride in her breeches and rose behind her. He pulled her into the vee of his legs, his kilt raising up past his knees. Maggie waved as Caspian clopped down the cobblestone street into the dense shadows away from the dock toward her father's house.

Kerr's arm held her against his chest, and his mouth bent to her ear. "We will be alone for the night before starting out in the morn." The warmth of his breath and the heat in his tone sent a shiver of wanton heat through Maggie. She smiled and turned in her seat, loving the freedom of the trousers.

She lifted her leg over, turning so that she faced Kerr, straddling Caspian. Her thighs rested on his. "A night of wicked words."

His devilish smile made her heart race. "Aye, Maggie lass. All my wicked words are for ye." He reached up to pull her cap from her hair. With a gentle tug, the pins holding it gave way, letting the long twist fall around her shoulders. The horse continued to walk between the shops and tall houses lining the narrow road, his gait like a gentle roll of the sea.

Maggie and Kerr leaned into one another, their lips meeting. It was a kiss full of promise that, whatever the crown or their families or their enemies threw at them, together, she and Kerr would meet the challenges as one. Love made them stronger together than either one alone. She would sacrifice herself to save the man she loved, but she would never again be someone's sacrificial lamb.

28 February 1571

My dearest cousin, Mary Stuart.

Your loyal man and rumored betrothed, Thomas Howard, Fourth Duke of Norfolk, has been arrested and is being tried for treason after his assassination attempt against my person with

Roberto Ridolfi and Lord Johnathan Whitt. Lord Norfolk may also be responsible for altering your gift of gloves to me with lethal blades bent on slicing my veins open and spilling royal blood. In a futile attempt, he tried to cast blame on the Highlander, Kerr Gordon, who bravely brought your gift to the English court.

Kerr Gordon, along with my faithful lady, Margaret Darby, Viscountess of Litchfield, thwarted both attempts on my life. Lord Gordon has also proclaimed your innocence in all these matters. He has swayed me to believe that you would not have sent the tainted gloves if you had known such villains would molest them in hopes of murdering me and placing you, dear cousin, on the throne of England. I would his words be the utmost truth.

If you agree that his words ring true, then you will support his cause of uniting the Gordons and the Hays in Scotland. If you do not support his cause, I will believe you are irked by his interference in saving my life, twice. My counselors ask daily for your head, cousin. Do not give them evidence to use against you.

As the gloves were ruined, I do not have them to remember you by. Perhaps that is best.

Your cousin by blood and sister by mutual sovereignty.
HRH Elizabeth

Make sure to look for the next book in The Queen's Highlanders series. When the Christmastide's Lord of Misrule is found dead, Lucy Cranfield is asked to take on the role of Lady of Misrule at Queen Elizabeth's court. She can cajole a smile out of everyone except the brawny Highlander who has come to court to stop another assassin bent on putting Mary, Queen of Scots on the English throne.

Historical Note

In the 16th century, having fled her country of Scotland, Mary Stuart (Mary, Queen of Scots) was held in England under house arrest by her cousin, Queen Elizabeth I. There were many attempts to assassinate Queen Elizabeth to put the Catholic Queen Mary on the throne of England. Even the Pope encouraged Catholics to kill the protestant, Elizabeth.

Sir Francis Walsingham, Elizabeth Tudor's "spymaster," had an intricate network of spies to help him protect his queen. In 1571, Roberto Ridolfi, a Florentine banker, was a spy for Rome and acted as a go-between for Spain and Thomas Howard, Fourth Duke of Norfolk. Norfolk had plans to marry Mary Stuart after ridding England of Elizabeth. Together Norfolk and Mary would rule England, Ireland, and perhaps Scotland. The plot has been named the Ridolfi Plot by historians.

However, Walsingham discovered the treasonous plans and produced enough evidence to arrest Norfolk. Lord Norfolk was executed for treason in 1572 for his role, and Elizabeth never trusted her cousin, Mary again. Mary would be executed in 1587 after nineteen years of house arrest.

Acknowledgments

Thank you so much for reading Kerr and Maggie's story! You, readers and lovers of historical romance, make all the hours of research and writing worthwhile! If I could, I would have you all over for tea. And I do serve a lovely tea!

Thank you to Kathryn Le Veque for introducing me to Dragonblade Publishing and welcoming me to the Dragonblade Clan. Your dedication to historical romance and your authors is fabulous and so very appreciated.

A shout out goes to Heather Teysko, creator of the Renaissance English History Podcast and TudorCon in Lancaster, PA. Attending TudorCon allowed me to immerse myself in Tudor history, customs, and dress. With travel restrictions to the UK, I was still able to learn so much about the world of Elizabethan England, and I am forever grateful.

Also...

At the end of each of my books, I ask that you, my awesome readers, please remind yourselves of the whispered symptoms of ovarian cancer. I am now a ten-year survivor, one of the lucky ones. Please don't rely on luck. If you experience any of these symptoms consistently for three weeks or more, go see your GYN.

- Bloating
- Eating less and feeling full faster
- Abdominal pain
- Trouble with your bladder

Other symptoms may include: indigestion, back pain, pain with intercourse, constipation, fatigue, and menstrual irregularities.

About the Author

Heather McCollum is an award-winning, Scottish historical romance writer. With over twenty books published, she is an Amazon Best Selling author in Highlander Romance. Her favorite heroes are brawny and broody with golden hearts, and the feistier the heroine the better!

When she is not dreaming up adventures and conflict for rugged Highlanders and clever heroines, she spends her time educating women about the symptoms of Ovarian Cancer. She is a survivor and lists the subtle symptoms in the backs of all her books. She loves dragonflies, chai lattes, and baking things she sees on the Great British Baking Show. Heather resides with her very own Highland hero and three spirited children in the wilds of suburbia on the mid-Atlantic coast.

Twitter: @HMcCollumAuthor
FB: HeatherMcCollumAuthor
Pinterest: hmccollumauthor
Instagram: heathermccollumauthor
Goodreads:
goodreads.com/author/show/4185696.Heather_McCollum
BookBub: bookbub.com/authors/heather-mccollum
Amazon: amazon.com/Heather-McCollum/e/B004FREFHI

Printed in the USA
CPSIA information can be obtained
at www.ICGtesting.com
LVHW020554290424
778742LV00024B/527